THE LAST WITNESS

NATASHA BOYDELL

B

Boldwood

First published in Great Britain in 2026 by Boldwood Books Ltd.

Copyright © Natasha Boydell, 2026

Cover Design by Head Design Ltd.

Cover Images: Shutterstock

A CIP catalogue record for this book is available from the British Library.

Paperback ISBN 978-1-80557-114-8

Large Print ISBN 978-1-80557-113-1

Hardback ISBN 978-1-80557-112-4

Trade Paperback ISBN 978-1-80656-179-7

Ebook ISBN 978-1-80557-115-5

Kindle ISBN 978-1-80557-116-2

Audio CD ISBN 978-1-80557-107-0

MP3 CD ISBN 978-1-80557-108-7

Digital audio download ISBN 978-1-80557-110-0

This book is printed on certified sustainable paper. Boldwood Books is dedicated to putting sustainability at the heart of our business. For more information please visit https://www.boldwoodbooks.com/about-us/sustainability/

Boldwood Books Ltd, 23 Bowerdean Street, London, SW6 3TN

www.boldwoodbooks.com

PROLOGUE

He did not deserve to die. He was just a man driving home to his wife and children. One moment, he might have been thinking about what to have for dinner. The next, nothing.

I was in the car behind him, and I did not deserve that either. To have to see what I did, compelled to relive it endlessly, a horror movie playing on an eternal loop in my mind, the volume cranked up to full blast. Screech. Crash. Silence.

It haunts me day and night and I don't know how to get the graphic images out of my head. I fear that they will stay inside me forever, obscuring the happy thoughts, overshadowing positivity. Sometimes I can't help but wonder if, by dying, the man was dealt the better hand. That might sound appalling, but that's because you don't know what happened next. How the death of one person destroyed the lives of so many others, like a rock placed in front of a line of ants, forcing them all to change course. To march towards danger instead of safety. To follow each other blindly into darkness.

One man was killed, but there will be many more casualties in this tragedy. And I fear that I will be one of them. That my family will be next. It terrifies me that I can't keep them safe, and I hate that I'm being punished just for being in the wrong place at the wrong time. Now my testimony is critical to determining what happens next. Who is guilty of causing the accident. Who might go to prison. The responsibility I shoulder has become too heavy a burden to bear and it's smothering me, leaving me flailing in panic, gasping for what I hope will not be my last breath.

Everyone needs someone to blame. I am the only witness.

And that has put me in terrible danger.

PART I

1

I wake up choking on my own breath. My heart is thudding against my chest and my body is dripping with sweat. It was just a nightmare. *Just a nightmare.*

Beside me, my husband Tom stirs from the disturbance but continues snoring gently. I watch him sleep, listening to his rhythmical breathing and studying the lines on his face as my eyes adjust to the darkness. The room comes back into focus, my jagged breathing gradually slows down, and I am safe again.

It's the third flashback I've had this week. I push the memories away during the day so that I can focus on being normal. The wife, mother, colleague and friend that everyone expects me to be. But at night, I am punished for blocking it out, because the horror returns and I relive the accident repeatedly in my cruelly vivid dreams.

The accident. It's all I can think of, and I still struggle to comprehend that it happened, right in front of me. The day began as just an ordinary Tuesday, no different from any other. The sort of relentlessly grey January evening that welcomes melancholy. I was driving home, down a road I've travelled along a thousand times. I was tired and ratty after a challenging day, and the winter weather wasn't helping. I wanted to get home, peel off my itchy tights and pour a glass of wine.

My eyes saw it before my brain registered it. The car in front of me stopping at the T-junction. The lorry appearing from nowhere and ploughing straight into it. The car being railroaded into a tree and crumpling to half its natural size. I did not believe it, not at first, I was suspended in time. It didn't take long, however, for my stomach to lurch and my heart to start pounding. Nausea rose up as I gripped the steering wheel, staring through the windscreen, unable to accept what I had just witnessed.

When the memory returns to me in my nightmares, it's as high definition as the moment it happened. I can see the crushed car, steam rising from its bonnet. I can smell the thick, damp January air as I threw open the door and locked eyes with the lorry driver, staggering out of his cab, his face pale and his nose bloody. I can hear my strangled voice calling out to him to stay back as I rushed towards the car.

I knew immediately that the man inside was dead. Still, I raced towards him and checked his pulse, desperately hoping that I was wrong. In the seconds it took for me to confirm my worst fears, this man's life flashed before my own eyes. I saw his wedding ring and pictured a family at home, a partner waiting for him, children looking forward to seeing their dad. And then, as I heard the anguished scream of the lorry driver who had crept up behind me, I stepped back and yanked my phone out of my pocket to call 999. The emergency services arrived eleven minutes later.

This is exactly what happened. I *know* it. But my mind is playing tricks on me because in my dreams, the scenario plays out differently. In the dark depths of my subconscious, where my memories are free to shapeshift, the man is alive when I reach him and he looks straight at me, his eyes burning into my soul.

And he murmurs, 'Help.'

Sometimes, when I first wake up, I wonder if I was wrong about him dying on impact. If I could have somehow saved him. But I know deep down that he was already gone, no matter how much my mind is trying to manipulate me. Then I wonder why I'm dreaming of an alternative ending. Is it guilt that I couldn't save him or some sort of subliminal message? I did not cause this accident. I can't bring him back from the dead. I can't turn back the clock and change what happened. So, what am I expected to do?

Tom is still snoring. I rub my eyes, trying to shake off the last vestiges of sleep, and automatically reach for my phone, which is on the bedside table. When news of the accident hit the local media and word got out that I was the one who had witnessed it, friends and family flocked to me. They called and sent messages expressing sympathy, asking how I was and offering their emotional and practical support. But their lives have quickly moved on, and I am expected to do so too. After all, the poor man who died was not *my* loved one. It's not my life that has been destroyed. Not my family left to pick up the pieces.

Tom has said all the right things. There was nothing I could have done. I was just in the wrong place at the wrong time. Tragedies like this should make us appreciate what we have. We shouldn't take things for granted. And I know that he's right.

And yet I can't move forward because I'm trapped in that grey January day. The accident is etched in my mind, a mental tattoo that I can't erase. I'm traumatised. I'm angry. I'm *grieving*. And that's what no one understands. But how can they? They didn't see another human being die in the most horrifying way. They didn't grasp his limp wrist, praying for a pulse. His life didn't flash before their eyes.

And they don't bear the substantial burden of being the only witness.

I feel that burden now even more than I did when I first talked to the police, shivering in a scratchy blanket, my clothes damp, my bones cold. At the time, I wasn't thinking about what it meant to be a witness or what I was committing myself to by telling the police what I had seen. Even when I described how the car had been stationary and the lorry had ploughed straight into it, I didn't register the long-term implication of my words. When I shook my head at the suggestion that the car driver had perhaps already started to pull out of the junction, into the path of the oncoming lorry, I didn't appreciate how this could be used as evidence, a reason to blame someone for what happened, the deciding factor in whether the lorry driver goes to prison. Would I have done anything differently if I *had* realised? No, I wouldn't. I told the truth. The problem is that there's a miniscule margin for error. The physical difference between who was at fault is perhaps a metre. The implication is vast.

I know what I saw. And I stand by my statement, the one that led to the lorry driver being arrested on suspicion of causing death by dangerous driving. The responsibility weighs heavily on my shoulders, a constant reminder of my role to play.

I can feel it now, suffocating me. And I don't know how to make it go away. The trial, if it comes to that, will not be for months. A year even. What do I do until then? How do I go about my day-to-day life as if nothing has happened? How many times can I tell myself that I'm right about what I saw? How can I smile, knowing that a man is dead and his family are in pain? How do I cope with the guilt of being alive?

It could have been me. If it had been a few seconds later, it would have been my car at the junction. My family grieving. I should be relieved, but it doesn't seem fair.

'Help.' How? My mind is a tangle of thoughts, fears and emotions. I know it's probably PTSD, but I don't know how to unpick it, how to make it go away. I start to feel claustrophobic, so I climb out of bed, being careful not to disturb Tom. I need to get out of the bedroom, away from the scene of my nightmares. I'm both exhausted and wired and as I creep down the stairs and turn on the kitchen light, I'm already dreading the next day. I have back-to-back meetings followed by my daughter Frankie's parents' evening which, on its own, is enough to give me a sleep-less night. My once-joyful little girl is now a sassy thirteen-year-old with a swarm of bees in her bonnet. Everyone, it seems, is out to get her. Her teachers. Her younger brother. And, most of all, me.

I should be focusing on my own family. Lord knows we have enough to deal with. Frankie's a challenge right now and Tom and I haven't spent any quality time together in forever. I keep meaning to plan a date night, but life always seems to get in the way and I'm just so damn tired all the time that it's easier to slip into my pyjamas at the end of the day and have an early night. I should take Tom's advice and be grateful for what I have. I should appreciate the mundane and enjoy the small pleasures of having a healthy, complete family. I should organise that date night.

But I'm too caught up in the accident. It's changed me, and I'm not sure how to go back to the person I was before. And that makes me think of the lorry driver and what he must be going through. He is called Jason Turner and the fact that I know his name makes him more human – something which distresses me. I wonder if he is a good person, if he has a family, if he's going to admit guilt or deny culpability. If he deserves to go to prison and what right I have to be the person who gets him sent there.

I fill up the kettle and while I wait for it to boil, I open my laptop. As the screen lights up, my fingers hover over the keyboard. I know what I want to do, and I know that I shouldn't because it won't help. It's doomscrolling. But the urge is too strong and too overwhelming and so I open Google and type 'fatal accident on the A1081'.

The top hits are stories from local newspaper websites, and I scan the results, looking for anything new. I've done this every day since the accident. It has become a compulsion, a task I must complete, like checking my emails or brushing my teeth. I can't explain it and I know it's not good for me, but I can't stop.

I notice a new article and I click on it, ignoring the kettle as it boils. It's a follow-up story, with details of the man's funeral. His name was Graham Hunter. His widow, Samantha, has asked for donations to a local children's charity in lieu of flowers. The service will be held at a church in Harpenden next Tuesday. There is a photograph further down that I've seen before in previous articles. The official one provided by the family, I assume. It is of Graham and Samantha on holiday with their twin sons, who are identical. The boys are the spitting image of their father, their faces tanned, their dark-brown hair wet from the sea. Samantha is beautiful, her sun-kissed blonde hair loose around her shoulders, blue eyes sparkling as she beams at the camera, one slender hand resting on Graham's arm. They are a gorgeous family, I think. *Were* a gorgeous family. And then I slam the laptop lid down and clutch my stomach.

This googling must stop. It's a destructive behaviour pattern. I will no longer look up the accident, I vow. I will put it behind me as best I can and re-engage with my own life. Make more of an effort to be present and not take life for granted. Because Tom's right, life *is* short and I am so lucky to be here and to have what I have. A lovely family and a comfortable home. A job which I sometimes resent but which pays the bills and, along with Tom's wage, enables us to go on summer holidays by the sea. Holidays that Graham will never go on with his family again.

It can't make the thoughts go away so I run from them instead. I hurry out of the kitchen, desperate to put as much distance as possible between myself and the family photograph on my computer screen. I sit on the bottom step of the stairs in the cold dark hallway, trying to erase the image of Graham and his family.

Not my family. Not my life.

After a while, I begin to shiver in my thin cotton pyjamas, my bare feet numbed by the freezing hallway tiles. I get up and climb the stairs, gripping on to the banister. In our bedroom, Tom is still asleep and I slip into bed beside him and stare at his back. I consider waking him up just for some company, but I don't know what to say to him, how to explain how I feel. So instead, I close my eyes and wait for morning.

I must have drifted off eventually because the alarm wakes me from a deep sleep at six thirty. I reach for the snooze button and roll over, burying myself in the warm duvet. For a few blissful moments I forget what happened and then it all comes rushing back to me and I don't want to get up. Don't want to face the day. Tom rises immediately, rubbing his eyes before heading to the bathroom. He's always been an early riser, just like our son Max, who I can hear moving around in his bedroom already. His little face will appear around our door at any moment now, his eyes alert, impatient to start the day. Frankie, on the other hand, will need a bulldozer to get her out of bed.

I groan and bury myself deeper under the duvet. I'm bone-tired and I wonder how I will get through the day. Dread creeps over me, reminding me of the accident, of my statement, of the impending court hearing. Then I force myself to push those thoughts away and think about the day that lies ahead instead. The battle with Frankie to get her dressed and out of the door in time for school. Having to tidy up Max's endless trail of destruction. A meeting with a difficult colleague which I know is going to be challenging. Frankie's parents' evening. Juggling a demanding job with the children's timetables. It's the same every day, it never changes. Eat, sleep, survive then repeat. It's like I'm on a hamster wheel and I don't know how to get off. Then I remember that a man is dead, and I feel guilty, and ungrateful, and worried, and bloody *exhausted*.

Tom sticks his head around the door. 'Coffee, Ellie?'

'Yes please,' I reply, peeping out at him from under the duvet.

He nods and disappears again. This is our routine. Tom gets up first and makes coffee while I have a shower. By the time I emerge, Max will probably be in our bed. He'll chat incessantly to me as I get dressed and I'll try to keep up while my mind wanders elsewhere, planning my outfit and running through the day's itinerary. It won't be long, I think, before Max doesn't want to come in to see us in the mornings any more. He's ten years old and Frankie's withdrawal started at around eleven. That's when the doors began to slam and the eye rolls ramped up a notch. I need to enjoy this stage in my son's life before it's gone, and it is this thought that pulls me from the warm cocoon of my bed and drags me along the landing to the bathroom. The hot shower revitalises me and when I return to the bedroom, Max and Tom are sitting in bed, two peas in a pod. I give Max a cuddle, breathing in the warm, innocent child scent of him, and then I reach for my coffee, thanking Tom for the gesture.

'Did you sleep well, Max?' I ask.

'Yes, Mummy.'

'Any dreams?'

He scrunches up his nose. 'I don't remember.'

I kiss his cheek and then walk over to the wardrobe to choose my outfit.

'Are you going to drive to the station today?' Tom asks.

I still, my hands poised in mid-air. We live on the outskirts of St Albans and I have always driven to the train station because the two-mile walk is a stretch in the morning rush and a chore after a long day at work. But I haven't been in a car since the accident.

'I'm walking,' I reply.

Tom looks at me, his head cocked. 'It's freezing out there.'

'I'll be fine. I need the exercise.'

'What about tonight? The parents' evening?'

'I'll go straight from the station and meet you there.'

'I can pick you up, if you like?'

'No thanks.'

'Ellie, you have to get back in a car at some point.'

I turn away. 'I know. But not today.'

'This weekend, then?'

'Maybe.'

There was a time, long ago, when Tom would have come over to me then. Put his arms around me and given me a hug. Murmured in my ear that he loved me and was there for me. Perhaps I would have cried and released some of the anguish I'm feeling. But fifteen years of marriage and two children has changed us. We are a machine, Tom and I, efficiently running our family. Our days are filled with juggling our jobs, the children and life admin. Somewhere along the way, we've forgotten each other.

'Do you want me to tackle Frankie this morning?' Tom asks.

Our eyes meet and we share a sweet moment of camaraderie.

'It's okay, I'll go,' I say, putting on some tights and plucking a long, knitted dress from my wardrobe. After slipping it over my head and smoothing it down, I take a deep breath, walk across the landing and prepare to enter the lion's den.

Frankie's door is closed, as always. I knock gently and then open it tentatively. She's still fast asleep or at least pretending to be. I turn on her light and go over to her bed, gently shaking her awake. She tries to bat me away like an annoying fly.

'Go away.'

'Frankie, it's time to get up.'

'I said go away.'

'You'll be late for school.'

'I don't care.'

'Well, I do.' I grab the duvet and pull it off her. 'So get up.'

Frankie groans and looks at me in disgust through half-open eyes. But for once she doesn't kick off. She sits up, pivoting her long, pyjama-clad legs until they are dangling off the end of the bed. I'm preparing to back away in cautious victory when she takes me by surprise.

'Mum, you know that accident you saw?'

It floors me. I rarely get any words out of Frankie first thing in the morning, and these are the last ones I expected. I've given the children a very sanitised version of what happened, but I haven't divulged many details, and they haven't mentioned it since I first told them. I stare at my daughter in shocked silence.

'Err, hello, Mum? Anyone there?'

Even half asleep, Frankie is impertinent.

'Yes,' I finally say, my voice barely above a whisper.

'Did you know that the man's kids go to my school?'

I remember the two boys in the photograph. 'Do you know them?'

'Not really, they're two years older than me.'

My heart is racing but I try to stay calm. 'Are they back at school?'

'Yeah, I saw one of them yesterday.'

'Are your classmates talking about the accident?'

'Everyone is talking about it.'

Anger surges. 'Don't gossip, Frankie, not about something like this.'

'It's not gossip if it's true.'

'You know what I mean.'

Frankie stands up and stretches her arms. 'They've arrested someone.'

'I know.'

'Are you going to have to go to court?'

I nod, my heart plummeting. 'Possibly, yes.'

'Can I come and watch?'

'For God's sake, Frankie,' I snap. 'It's not a theatre show. A man is *dead*.'

I feel guilty as soon as the words spill out, but Frankie has pushed all the wrong buttons. My daughter's face quickly morphs from ashamed to aggrieved and then she stands up and barges past me. A few seconds later, I hear the bathroom door slam. I stare at the empty bed and wonder why I keep getting it so wrong with Frankie. It used to be so easy with her, but now every conversation is loaded with landmines that I could trip over at any second.

Then I think of the twin boys, having to go to school knowing that everyone is talking about them. The stares and the hushed conversations. My mind switches to the widow, Samantha, as I picture her trying to organise the funeral while fielding calls from old friends and distant relatives wanting to express their sympathies. I imagine her pretty face, the one I've studied in the photograph, contorted in grief.

I sway, nauseous and light-headed, and then a thought pushes through the darkness. I suddenly know what I need to do.

I need to pay my respects, to go to the funeral and tell Samantha that I'm sorry for her loss. Perhaps then I will find the peace that I crave. The thought solidifies in my mind at alarming speed, an anchor that I clutch on to. Until very quickly it feels like the only thing that will keep me from drowning.

'Help.' Maybe this is what I can do. Perhaps that's what my dreams are trying to tell me. I can't help Graham, but I can help his family. Provide comfort to Samantha by giving her what she needs to hear about her husband's final moments. *It happened very quickly, he wouldn't even have been aware of it, he didn't feel any pain.* I stand up and smooth out my dress, purpose giving me an energy I've lacked for days.

I am going to go to the funeral and meet this man's family.

And then maybe I can finally move on.

2

I can see my breath in the air as I hover outside the imposing stone church. I fold my arms over my woollen black coat and anxiously observe the other guests in the line in front of me. We are all waiting for an audience with Samantha, who is standing by the entrance. Fear grips my throat, and I question yet again what I'm doing here.

Samantha is only a couple of metres away from me now. She looks beautiful, even in grief. Her honey-blonde hair is drawn back from her face into a chignon. Her fitted black coat, black tights and low heels are understated and elegant. She is wearing a gold heart pendant necklace around her neck which she is fidgeting with. The expression on her perfectly made-up face is stoic, but I see the pain beneath it.

And I want to turn and run.

I didn't tell anyone that I was going to the funeral, not even Tom. I didn't think they would understand, even though I had convinced myself that it was the right thing to do. Now I'm here, I'm not so sure. I feel like an imposter, an unwelcome guest. And the closer I get to Samantha, the more I doubt my decision. What if she's angry that I've turned up without an invitation? But the details of the funeral were published in the local paper for all to see. And the number of people gathering outside the church would suggest that everyone is welcome. I had assumed, however, that I could hide among the crowds and approach Samantha if and when the time felt right, but now I'm in this official line. It's too much pressure. I wonder if I should lie about who I am, but I don't want to be dishonest. Perhaps I should just discreetly remove myself from the queue.

I'm in a storm of indecision when I see a man walk over to Samantha. From his age and the way he puts his arm protectively around her, I guess that he's her father. He catches my eye and I look away quickly, self-conscious and exposed. Clarity hits me like a ton of bricks, a brutal reality check. I do not belong here. I'm invading another family's private moment and it's self-centred and thoughtless of me. The accident has messed with my head and stopped me from thinking rationally. My decision made, I prepare to subtly make my escape without anyone noticing.

But before I have time, the large group in front of me steps into the church and Samantha turns to me, her elegant face searching mine. Her frown is subtle, but I see it. She is trying to place me, to work out who I am and whether she should know me. I take a deep breath and say the words I've rehearsed many times in my head.

'I'm so very sorry for your loss.'

'Thank you.'

There is so much more I want to say but I can't get the words out. I'm frozen to the spot, staring at this poor woman, my mouth opening and closing like a goldfish. The seconds feel like hours until, finally, I realise that Samantha is waiting for me to move on. I nod and walk into the church, searching for an empty pew at the back. I can't leave now, not without drawing more attention to myself. I'll stay for the service and then I'll go quietly. Return to my own life and leave Samantha and her boys to their grieving.

I look up then and see them. The two teenagers. They're sitting at the front of the church, dressed in suits that seem too mature for their age. They should not be having to wear them. My heart splinters at the thought of what they've lost and without warning tears spring to my eyes and spill down my cheeks. I hurriedly search in my bag for some tissues, embarrassed by my outburst.

A hand appears in front of me, holding out a tissue. I take it and look up at the woman offering it, nodding my thanks. I'm mortified and ashamed. And then, to my horror, the woman sits down next to me, watching as I dab my eyes.

'How did you know Graham?' she asks.

It's a reasonable question but for a moment I struggle to find the answer.

'I don't know him,' I say, and she looks at me in surprise. Oh God, she probably thinks I'm one of those oddballs who makes a hobby out of going to strangers' funerals. 'I... I saw the accident,' I continue quickly. 'I was in the car behind.'

Her eyes widen as she appraises me. She's around my age, tall with dark, curly hair and a steely expression which instantly intimidates me. Or perhaps it's just my own anxiety that's having this effect. I look down and fiddle with the tissue in my hand.

'You're the witness?' she asks.

'Yes.'

'What's your name?'

I pull off a shred of damp tissue. 'Ellie.'

'I'm Amelia. Samantha's friend.'

'Hi, Amelia.'

We sit in silence for a moment. I'm still looking at my hands, but I can sense Amelia's gaze on me. Eventually, she says, 'Why did you come today?'

My voice shakes as I respond. 'I wanted to pay my respects.'

Amelia nods, apparently satisfied. I wait for her to leave but she sits back in the pew, looking straight ahead, her eyes resting on the boys at the front. 'Those poor boys,' she says.

My heart feels like it's going to shatter into a million pieces. 'I know.'

'It's just so tragic.'

'Yes.'

'Of course Samantha is being incredible. She's in pieces but she's keeping it together, staying strong for the boys. If it was me, I would have completely fallen apart. I've never known a braver woman than Samantha. Or a more selfless one.' Amelia's eyes fill with tears and she plucks another tissue out of her bag. And then, to my immense relief, she abruptly stands up.

'I'm going to go and check on her,' she says.

I nod and glance over my shoulder, watching Amelia approach Samantha and put a hand on her elbow. She whispers something and they both turn to look at me. My face reddens as I realise what has happened. Amelia was sent to find out who I was. And now Samantha knows. My stomach churns at the unwanted attention. But then Samantha turns away again and I exhale. At least she hasn't asked me to leave.

A hush descends over the crowd as Samantha walks to the front of the church, followed by the pallbearers. And then the service begins and it is so devastating that I can't bear it. I try to stifle my tears because they are not mine to shed, and yet I can't stop them from escaping, especially when one of the boys stands up to give a short speech. He is so brave, that young man. And he doesn't deserve what has happened to him. None of them do and it crushes me. When he's finished, he goes over to sit with his mother and brother and I watch Samantha put an arm around him, pulling him in close. And then I can't look any longer. I spend the rest of the service with my head down.

As soon as it is over, I stand up to make a hasty exit. But the aisle is already clogging up with people, and I get stuck in the slow-moving crowd. I'm almost at the exit when I feel a hand on my arm, elegant fingers pressing gently into my flesh.

'Ellie,' Samantha says in a soft voice.

I turn to face her. Her eyes are red-rimmed. 'Hi, Samantha.'

'Amelia told me who you are. You're the witness.'

I nod. 'I'm so sorry for coming today, I shouldn't have—'

She interrupts me. 'How *are* you, Ellie?'

She's the one who has lost her husband and she's asking how *I* am?

'Oh goodness, don't worry about me,' I gush.

Samantha's face softens. 'What you saw, it must have been so traumatic for you. I'm sorry that you had to witness that.'

'I'm fine,' I reply quickly. 'Honestly, please don't give me a second thought. I really just came to pay my respects and tell you how sorry I was for your loss. I'll go now.'

'But you must come to the wake.'

'Oh no, I couldn't possibly.'

'Please. I'd like you to be there. I really appreciate you coming.'

'I don't know,' I say uncertainly.

Samantha's gaze is firm. Insistent. A hint, perhaps, of the woman she is. 'It's at the Black Sheep Inn, half a mile down the road. Graham's favourite pub. I'll see you there.'

Before I can answer, she turns and walks away, her heels clattering on the hard church floor. A wave of claustrophobia overcomes me, and I race outside, gratefully inhaling the biting winter air. My head is spinning as I try to decide what to do. I want to go home, to change out of my sombre clothes and put some distance between myself and this funeral. But would it be rude not to go to the wake after Samantha has extended a personal invitation? Uncertainty yanks me in different directions.

I pull out my phone and look up the pub. It's a ten-minute walk. I'm still not driving, but I couldn't reach the church by public transport, so I forced myself into a taxi. I'm already dreading the journey home, and the prospect of delaying it is tempting. More than that though, I now feel obliged to go to the wake.

More people are piling out of the church, some heading towards the car park, others walking down the path. I follow the pedestrians, keeping a respectable distance, and trying not to meet anyone's eye. I still feel like a fraud for being here but at least I now know that Samantha appreciates it. She has taken the gesture as it was intended, and my relief is palpable. I wrap my arms around myself, shivering, and the cold makes me involuntarily pick up my pace without realising what I'm doing until I'm right behind a group of people. They look back and nod, moving apart to let me in.

'How did you know Graham?' one of them, an older man, asks.

'An old friend,' I lie. But it's only a white lie because I can't keep explaining to strangers why I'm here. Samantha knows and that's all that matters.

The man explains that they are Graham's colleagues from work. They begin to share memories of Graham, half laughing, half crying, and thankfully don't ask me any probing questions. When we finally reach the pub, the car park is already filling up but there's no sign of Samantha. I order a glass of red wine from the bar and sit on a stool, self-conscious again. I decide to stay for as long as it takes me to finish this glass and then I'll go. The pub door opens and I hold my breath, expecting to see Samantha, but instead Amelia walks in. She catches my eye and frowns, her expression disapproving, and I look away quickly. Samantha may want me here but her friend doesn't seem to. Can I blame her, though? She's no doubt wondering what I'm doing here.

A commotion at the door makes me raise my eyes again and this time Samantha appears, her eyes covered by a pair of sunglasses, followed by her two sons. Everyone goes quiet as the family enter the room, and some people bow their heads. Then, to my surprise, Samantha heads straight for me and the chatter slowly resumes. I hold my breath, wondering why it's me, of all people, she has chosen to approach first.

She reaches me and points at my drink. 'I could do with one of those.'

I order her a glass and set it down on the bar in front of her.

'Thank you,' Samantha says, picking it up and taking a sip.

'It was a beautiful service,' I say.

'It was.'

'Again, I'm so sorry for your loss. And I want you to know that Graham didn't suffer. It happened very quickly, and he wouldn't have felt any pain.'

She takes her sunglasses off and her eyes are bloodshot. 'Thank you for telling me that, Ellie. It gives me a great deal of comfort.'

I relax a fraction, glad to finally have said the words I'd been meaning to say when I first met Samantha at the church. In all honesty, I'll never know if what I said was true but it's what I want to think, and what I want Samantha to believe too.

'I can't stop thinking about what you saw,' Samantha says, looking at me intently. 'How traumatic it must have been.'

'Please don't think about that,' I plead.

'But I do. It can't be easy for you.'

'I'm fine,' I say because this poor woman does not need to hear the truth.

'I know that you gave a statement to the police and I just want you to know that I appreciate what you're doing. Justice must be served for what happened.'

'Of course,' I say in a tiny voice.

'If there's anything I can do to help, just let me know.'

I'm appalled. 'I should be saying that to you, not the other way around.'

Samantha looks at me thoughtfully. 'I used to be a solicitor, although of course I can't be involved in this case. But I know that the next few months will be difficult for you. You'll be anxious about the trial, if it comes to that. You'll doubt yourself and your testimony. You'll be cross-examined by someone whose job it is to discredit you. Don't underestimate the impact this will have on you. But know that you're doing the right thing.'

Her words floor me. I have no idea what to say, how to respond. But I'm saved by Amelia, who appears at Samantha's side.

'Sam, the boys are asking after you.'

Samantha nods and gives me a small smile before following Amelia across the pub. I finish my drink and book a taxi, deciding to wait for it outside before I need to explain my presence to anyone else. I put my coat on and weave through the crowd to the exit, relieved when no one tries to talk to me. Outside, I hop from foot to foot and will the taxi to arrive. I'm more than ready to leave. Samantha's words are stuck in my head, adding to the pressure I already feel. *Don't underestimate the impact this will have on you.*

When the taxi pulls up, I yank the door open and step gratefully into the warm car. I've done it. It's over. I've said what I needed to say and now I'm ready to move on. I can go back to my life, the one I used to think was mundane and stressful but now realise how lucky I am to have. I can change out of these clothes, have a cup of tea, pause for a moment and be grateful for the small things.

I put my seat belt on and gaze out of the window as the car moves forward. My fists automatically clench and unclench. It's only my second time in a car since the accident and I'm acutely aware of every movement, every jerk and break. But my need to attend today was greater than my need to avoid being in a car. Now though, my fear comes rushing back to me. Screech. Crash. Silence. I concentrate on my breathing, trying to relax my tense muscles. I'm so consumed in stemming the rising panic that I almost miss her. But then I feel it. The sensation of being watched. Instinctively, I turn to look out of the rear window and see a lone figure standing outside the pub, right where I had been just moments earlier.

It's Samantha's friend, Amelia. She's looking right at me and for a brief second the intensity of her gaze makes me wither. It's like she hates me, which makes no sense as we've only just met and our interaction was brief. I quickly turn to face forward, my breathing shallow, but I can't resist looking back again. This time, Amelia is gone.

3

When I get home, Tom is sitting at the kitchen table. I start when I see him, feeling like a guilty child who has been caught stealing chocolate from the cupboard.

He looks up from his laptop. 'You're home early.'

'What are you doing here?' I splutter.

'The fire alarm went off at work and I couldn't be bothered to wait around in the cold for ages, so I decided to work from home for the rest of the afternoon.' Tom's gaze rests on my outfit. 'You look like you've just been to a funeral.'

I turn away and busy myself with filling up the kettle. I shouldn't be lying to him, I know that. He deserves better. But every time I try to get the words out to explain why I went and how I feel, they get stuck in my throat. So instead, I deflect. 'Everything okay? Why did the fire alarm go off?'

'False alarm. Probably the dodgy toaster in the kitchen.'

'I can pick Max up from football tonight if you want.'

'Aren't you working?' Tom looks at me again. 'Why are *you* back so early?'

'I took the afternoon off. I couldn't concentrate.'

Tom looks concerned. 'Everything okay?'

'Fine,' I lie.

'Why don't we pick him up together? Maybe we can go for dinner, the four of us?'

It feels wrong, doing something fun after the day I've had. But before I have a chance to respond, my phone rings. It's my witness care officer, Paula, updating me on the case. She tells me that Jason Turner will have a brief appearance at the magistrates' court in the morning, but the case will be escalated to the Crown court, which deals with the most serious offences. He is on bail and is unlikely to enter a plea tomorrow.

'What happens next?' I ask Paula.

'There'll be an initial hearing at the Crown court in a few weeks where he will enter a plea of guilty or not guilty. Then a date will be set for sentencing or trial. I'll let you know as soon as I hear.'

'Do you have any idea which way he'll go?'

'I think you need to prepare yourself for a not guilty plea. I'll be here to support you at every step of the way, Ellie.'

I thank her and hang up with shaking hands, relaying the conversation to Tom.

'How are you feeling?' he asks me.

'Terrified,' I say. At least I can be honest with him about that.

He closes his laptop lid and stands up to finish making the teas. 'I know this is hard for you. But remember, all you have to do is tell the truth.'

The truth. I did tell the truth. I'll tell the truth again in court. But that doesn't make it any easier, or the prospect of a trial any less daunting.

'Do you want to talk about it?' he asks me gently.

'No. But thank you.'

He shrugs. 'What about that dinner then? The four of us?'

'Not tonight.' I see the look of disappointment on his face and feel guilty again. 'How about Friday, though? It'll be a nice treat.'

Tom's face lights up. 'The kids love that Greek restaurant.'

I smile. 'It's a date.'

'Great. I'll make sure to leave work early.'

I look at the time. Frankie, who gets the bus from school, should be home any minute. But Max is not due to be picked up from football practice for another hour. I'm not sure what to do with myself. I'm too distracted to work and I need to keep busy.

'I'm going to go and change,' I tell Tom. 'Then I'll head to the shops. We need some bread. I'll pick Max up on the way back.'

I change into jeans and a jumper, and I'm shrugging myself into my winter coat when Frankie lets herself in and dumps her bag on the floor.

'Hi, sweetheart,' I say. 'Do you want to come to the shops? You can pick a treat.'

There was a time when Frankie would have jumped up and down with excitement at the prospect. But her look of disdain reminds me that she's not a little girl any more.

'I've got homework,' she says, jogging up the stairs without her school bag. Whatever Frankie is planning on doing, it's not homework. I remember her parents' evening the previous week. The feedback from her teachers. *She's a bright girl but easily distracted... she lacks focus... she could do so much better.* And then I take my handbag from the peg and let myself out of the front door. I'll tackle Frankie later.

I'm emotionally drained and I've got nothing left in the tank. I'll do better tomorrow, I tell myself, as I walk down the road towards the shop. I just need a good night's sleep and a reset. We'll go for dinner on Friday and then on Saturday I'll sit down with Frankie and have a word with her about her schoolwork.

She can't be the only thirteen-year-old lacking focus. It's normal. Natural.

I think back to my teenage years. What was I like as a thirteen-year-old? Consumed by my first crush probably. Worried about looking cool in front of my friends. Obsessed with wearing the right outfit. Rolling my eyes at my mother. Certainly not interested in my schoolwork. I relax a fraction. There's nothing to worry about with Frankie, she'll come out the other side soon enough. And Max is about as happy as it's possible to get. Yes, my family is fine. I'm the one who needs to sort my head out.

I reach the shop and pick up the essentials, but I still have half an hour before I have to pick up Max. It's cold but not wet so I decide to walk to the school and watch the end of his football practice. When I reach the field, he looks up and sees me, his face lighting up, which makes me grateful I still have one prepubescent child. I spot one of my good friends, Tamsin, at the sidelines and make my way over to her.

'Hey you,' she says with a grin. 'Don't often see you here.'

'I took the day off work,' I tell her.

'Lucky you. Do anything nice?'

I wince. 'No, just catching up on admin.'

She nods with understanding. 'Tell me about it. It's never-ending.'

We chat for a bit about this and that and then she asks me if there's been any update on the lorry driver, so I tell her he's been charged.

'How are you feeling about it?' she asks me, her face etched with concern.

'Terrible,' I admit. 'I just hope he pleads guilty. I don't want to give evidence.'

'It'll be okay. You're just telling the truth.'

The truth again. And I need to say it, to release my nagging fear.

'What if I'm wrong?' I whisper.

'About what happened?'

I look at Tamsin, my eyes pleading. 'Yes. What if I got it wrong, Tamsin?'

She shakes her head. 'You didn't.'

'It all happened so quickly. And the more time that passes, the more I worry.'

'That's natural. It's your mind playing tricks on you. But you gave your statement immediately after the accident when your memory was fresh, so don't doubt yourself.'

'What if they cross-examine me, though? They'll try to prove I made a mistake.'

'Stand your ground. Stick to your story. That's all you can do.'

I turn my gaze to Max. He's racing up the field without a care in the world. I wonder if the lorry driver has children. 'He could go to prison, Tamsin.'

She nods. 'I know. And it's awful. But he killed someone.'

I think of Samantha then. Of what she said to me. *'Justice must be served.'* Then I remember my nightmares. Graham looking straight at me. His words. *'Help.'*

I'm trying to help. I'm trying to do the right thing. I just hate that it's all on me.

I blink a few times to shake myself out of it. 'You're right, thank you. I'm just a bit nervous about it all. I've probably been watching too many courtroom dramas on TV. Although it's actually very different in real life.'

'How do you mean?'

'Well, everything happens so slowly. He'll appear at the magistrates' court tomorrow but won't enter a plea because he's facing such a serious charge and magistrates have limited sentencing powers. Instead, the case will be sent to the Crown court and then there'll be a hearing in a few weeks where he pleads guilty or not guilty. If he pleads not guilty, then a date will be set for a trial by jury, which could be months away, and I'll probably have to give evidence in person as I'm the key witness.'

She puts her arm around me. 'I'm not surprised you're nervous. But you'll be just fine, I'm sure of it. Anyway, you don't even know if it'll come to that yet. Hey, we should go for a drink and let off some steam. It'll make you feel better. How about Friday?'

'We're going for a family dinner on Friday.'

'Oh, lovely. Speaking of family, how's Frankie doing?'

I roll my eyes. 'Acting like the typical teenage girl she is.'

'Ah well, we've all been there.'

We move on to discussing our children and the normality of this conversation is just what I need. I'm already starting to feel a little better. I just need to block out the noise. Take things one step at a time. As if on cue, Max scores a goal and I cheer and clap, even though it's only a practice game. He looks at me and grins at my enthusiasm.

'He's really good,' Tamsin comments. 'I reckon he's got real potential.'

'His coach said the same thing.'

The whistle blows and the kids start gathering up their things. When Max is dismissed, he jogs over to me with Tamsin's son, Harry.

'Great goal,' I say, kissing the top of his head.

'Thanks. I'm starving.'

'Let's get you home for dinner.'

'Did you drive?'

'No, sweetheart, it's only a short walk.'

Max shrugs good-naturedly. We say goodbye to Tamsin and

Harry, who are going in the opposite direction, and then we start walking. 'How was your day?' I ask Max.

'Good. What's for dinner?'

'What do you fancy?'

We're deep in conversation about the merits of pasta over chicken nuggets when I hear a car slowing down beside us. I don't think anything of it at first but then I realise that it's crawling, even though the road ahead is empty. I glance at the car, a black SUV, but I don't recognise it. The sky is darkening and in my already agitated state, the presence of the car suddenly feels threatening. There have been reports of car thefts and burglaries in the area recently. What if someone jumps out and tries to rob us? What if they have a knife? There's no one else around to help us.

I swivel around to face the car, squinting at the darkened windscreen. But before I get a decent look at the driver, the car speeds off, racing down the road. My heart is beating at a million miles per hour as I read the registration number, trying to commit it to memory just in case it was someone dodgy. But Max is talking incessantly at me and the numbers and letters leave my mind as quickly as they arrived.

'Do you know that car?' I demand, pointing into the distance.

Max squints as he looks. 'No, why?'

'I just wondered if it belonged to any of your friends' parents.'

'Dunno.'

It's probably a mum or dad collecting their child from training. Maybe they slowed down to answer a phone call or check for a missing sports bag, before driving off again. I talk myself down, trying to shake off my apprehension.

'Come on, Max, chop-chop,' I say, picking up the pace, eager to get home.

I hurry along the pavement, as Max jogs to keep up. The quiet road does little to alleviate my anxiety, and I'm tense until we've turned on to our street. The bright lights from our front porch have never been more welcoming. I fumble for my keys and open the door, but before I step inside I glance over my shoulder and scan the road. There's nothing there. No black SUV. No one is watching us.

I release my breath and step into the warm house. Tom calls out a greeting from the kitchen, and as I slip off my shoes I finally relax. I think I'll have a glass of wine after I've made dinner. I'll take it up with me to the bath.

But I can't stave off the chill that evening. Not after warming up in our cosy house. Not after plunging myself into a hot bath. A sense of foreboding has taken over, leaving me cold to the bone. The funeral affected me more than I thought it had and, judging by my reaction to the black SUV, it's left me paranoid too. I can't stop thinking about Samantha and her boys, and about the way her friend Amelia looked at me. The possibility of there being a court trial, which will cause me months of anxiety, is at the forefront of my mind. I'd somehow convinced myself that going to the funeral would mark an end to this nightmare. But I was naive.

Because this isn't the end, I realise. It's just the beginning.

4

It's been six weeks since the funeral and life is tentatively returning to some semblance of normality. I've stopped obsessively googling the accident. I'm sleeping a little better. I'm busy preparing for a big presentation at work. I've sat down with Frankie and had a chat with her about her schoolwork. Max had a successful trial at a nearby football academy. I've got behind the wheel again and even though I drive like a ninety-year-old – my hands gripping the steering wheel as I crawl along, ignoring the frustrated beeps of motorists behind me – it's a huge step forward.

I'm telling myself that I've turned a corner. I haven't forgotten, far from it, but it's becoming easier to push it out of my mind and focus on the small things, rather than fixating on the overwhelmingly big picture. One step at a time. That's all I can do.

Today, though, it feels like one step forward and two steps back. The lorry driver is appearing at the Crown court and it's brought everything back again. I'll finally learn whether he intends to plead guilty or not and, consequently, my role in what happens next. I'm supposed to be working from home, but I can't concentrate, so I've popped into the town centre to clear my head and buy something for lunch. I'm browsing salad bowls when I hear someone call my name. I don't recognise the voice at first and I spin around with a polite smile, expecting to see a mum I half know from the one of the kids' schools. But instead, I find myself directly in front of Samantha.

'Samantha!' I'm so shocked that I almost drop the salad I'm holding.

'Ellie,' she says, looking equally surprised to see me. 'It's so strange that I've bumped into you today of all days. I've just come from the hearing.'

My heart plummets as I register Samantha's outfit. She's dressed smartly in a grey skirt suit and blouse. She's dressed, I realise, for court. It must have finished already.

'Do you know what happened?' Samantha asks and I notice that she's been crying.

I feel sick. 'No, not yet, my witness care officer hasn't called.'

'Jason Turner pleaded not guilty. It's going to trial.'

My legs threaten to give way beneath me as everything around me blurs. I'm going to court, whether I like it or not. I am the key witness for the prosecution and I hate it. I don't want this responsibility, I never asked for it. But then I remember that I'm talking to Graham's widow, and I'm being selfish for wallowing in my own angst.

'I'm so sorry,' I say.

Samantha wipes away a fresh tear. 'I hoped he'd plead guilty and save us all the distress of a trial. It seems that we have a battle ahead.'

We? Is she talking about *us*? Maybe she's referring to her legal team or her family.

'Do you fancy a coffee?' Samantha asks suddenly.

The invitation catches me off guard. In fact, this whole interaction has. Where are Samantha's family and friends? Why aren't they going for coffee with her? As if reading my mind, she says, 'Dad's in hospital. Amelia was here but she had to go back to work.'

'I'm sorry about your dad.'

'It's okay, it's a routine procedure. He offered to change the appointment so he could come with me, but I told him not to. With the long NHS waiting lists, I didn't want him to lose his slot. Anyway, it was a short hearing, it was over before it even started.'

I still haven't responded to Samantha's invitation. I glance around, like I'm expecting someone to come along and rescue me from this situation. But she is still waiting for my answer. Although I'd felt a strong urge to meet this woman after the accident happened, I've started to settle back into my own life and now this almost feels like an intrusion. How can I refuse her though? She's upset and I can hardly leave her alone, crying in the middle of a shop.

'A coffee sounds great,' I say.

She smiles, looking relieved. 'I know just the place.'

I put my salad bowl down and follow Samantha out of M&S. I've lost my appetite anyway. She leads us to a small café just down the high street and we order our drinks and sit down at a table by the window.

'How are you?' I ask, wondering if it's the right thing to say.

'Up and down,' she admits. 'Sometimes I wake up, you know, and I forget what happened for a minute. It's bliss. And then I remember.'

She looks away, her face etched with pain.

'I'm so sorry,' I say, helpless.

Samantha turns back to me. 'At least I've finally convinced the boys to see a counsellor. They didn't want to, but I persuaded them.'

'How are they coping?'

'As well as they can. They're back at school and the routine is good for them. But they have GCSEs coming up and they're struggling to concentrate. I don't know what will happen. They may not get the grades to stay on for sixth form.'

'The school will make allowances,' I reassure her. 'They're very good at Hillcrest.'

Her head tilts. 'You know the school?'

I flush. 'Yes, sorry, I should have said. My daughter, Frankie, goes there too.'

'She knows my boys?'

'Not personally, but she mentioned that they're a couple of years ahead of her.'

Now Samantha knows we've been talking about her. I want the ground to open up and swallow me. But thankfully she doesn't seem to mind.

'So, Frankie must be, what? Thirteen? Fourteen?'

'She's fourteen next month.'

Samantha smiles. 'A tricky age.'

'Oh yes. She hates me.'

'Boys are easier as teenagers. They just lock themselves in their rooms and we pretend that we don't know what they're doing.'

Samantha's face falls and I realise it's the mention of 'we'. This time, she means her and Graham. I want to reach out and comfort her, but it's inappropriate because I don't know her. We're strangers and I'm not even sure what I'm doing here. But in a way that I can't explain, it kind of feels right too. Natural. I can't work it out, this conflict of emotions. Maybe it's because we are somehow inextricably connected by this tragedy. It's brought us together, united us in a common cause.

'I've never seen you at the school,' she remarks, changing the subject.

'Frankie travels there on her own. And my son, Max, is still at primary school. I guess we probably have different events and parents' evenings with our children being in different years?'

'Yes. I must admit, I still sometimes pick the boys up. They hate it, of course, but they're all I have. Especially now.'

Samantha lets out a sob and this time I don't hesitate. I reach out a hand and rest it on her arm. She flinches slightly at the unexpected gesture but then I feel her muscles relax underneath me.

'I'm sorry,' I say again, acutely aware that I sound like a broken record.

She sniffs. 'Everyone is. But it doesn't make it any easier.'

'No,' I agree. 'But it will get easier. Until then, just take it one day at a time.'

Samantha blows her nose. 'You're right. Thank you.'

'I think you're doing brilliantly, I really do.'

'Some days I don't want to get up. I just can't face the day. I want to bury myself in the duvet and hide from everything and everyone. But then I remember the boys. They need me, and so I get dressed, I make breakfast. But everything is hard. It's so hard.'

My heart is breaking repeatedly for this woman and her children. I feel responsible, even though I didn't cause the accident. The lorry driver caused it. Didn't he? The crash, acutely vivid in my mind just a few weeks ago, is already beginning to fade. It's still there, it'll never go away, but it's blurring a little at the edges.

Our coffees arrive then and the interruption gives us both some much-needed time to reset. When the waitress leaves, Samantha is more composed.

'What do you do for a living, Ellie?' she asks as she stirs her drink.

'I work in marketing for a health insurance company.'

'Do you commute or work from home?'

'I go to London three days a week. How about you? You said you are a solicitor?'

'*Was* a solicitor,' Samantha admits. 'I haven't worked in years.'

'Do you miss it?'

'Sometimes. But I wanted to be around for Jamie and Marcus when they were growing up. Graham, he works...' She stops and corrects herself. 'He worked long hours. And we couldn't both have demanding jobs, so I decided to take a career break.'

'Will you ever go back to it?'

'Sometimes I think I should. But the more time that passes, the harder it is. And it's certainly not something to think about right now. I need to support the boys.'

'Of course.' I lean forward. 'I lost my mum when I was fourteen.'

Samantha's eyes widen. 'Oh, Ellie, I'm so sorry.'

'And it was hard, I'm not going to lie. It's still hard sometimes, even now. But I survived. I coped. It hasn't held me back and this won't define your boys, I promise. They will be happy again. They will have good lives.'

She puts her hand over mine and squeezes it. 'It's all I want. I really appreciate you sharing this with me. It means a lot. Sometimes it feels like life will never get better.'

'It will,' I tell her firmly. 'Trust me, it will.'

Samantha takes a sip of her coffee. 'I'm fixating on the court case, if I'm being honest. I suppose it's giving me a purpose. How are you now feeling about the trial?'

'Fine,' I say. But when Samantha gives me a shrewd look which tells me that she knows I'm lying, I decide to be honest. 'I'm really anxious.'

'That's to be expected.'

'I know what I saw. But I also know that – if I do get called up to the stand – the defence barrister will want to make me doubt myself, right? And I'm scared they'll tie me up in knots.'

'I can give you some tips if you like. I've spent enough time in courts.'

'Is that allowed?' I don't know what the rules are about witnesses talking to victims' widows, let alone getting advice from them.

'I'm not giving you legal advice,' Samantha says. 'Just a few coping mechanisms.' Before I can answer, she reaches for her phone. 'What's your number?'

I read it aloud and then she calls my phone, letting it ring once. 'There, now you have my number too,' she says. 'Just call me if you need anything. Anything at all.'

'Thank you.' I look down at the missed call and then put my phone back on the table. I'm not going to call Samantha, but it was a thoughtful gesture. Her phone beeps and she looks at it again, reading the message and typing out a quick reply.

'It's Amelia,' she says. 'Just checking in on me.'

I think of Amelia and the hostile way she looked at me at the funeral. The way she stood outside and watched me leave. And I can't stop myself from bringing it up. 'I don't think she approved of me being at the funeral.'

'What makes you say that?'

'I don't know. She just gave me a funny look.'

'Oh, don't worry about that. Amelia's always giving people funny looks. It's her resting face.'

I sag with relief. There we go then. I was just being paranoid.

'How do you know her?' I ask.

'We went to primary school together, can you believe? I've literally known her since I was four years old.'

'Wow. I don't know anyone from primary school any more.'

'Even on Facebook?'

I think about it. 'Maybe one or two on Facebook but I don't use it much.'

'Amelia and I have been pretty much joined at the hip since we were girls. We went to the same secondary school and we both studied law, albeit at different universities. But then we lived together in London while we were training. And then we both moved to Harpenden when we got married. It's a bit of a joke among our friends.'

I'm pleased for Samantha that she has such a close friend. Someone to look out for her. And I banish any lingering insecurities I had about Amelia. It's not like I'm ever going to meet her again anyway. I'm not in Samantha's life, this is just one coffee. Then I remember that I'll probably see Amelia in court, sitting next to Samantha when I give evidence. And the coffee curdles in my stomach and makes me nauseous.

'Are you okay?' Samantha is looking at me closely.

'Fine,' I say. 'Actually, I need to go. I have a work meeting.'

Samantha drains her coffee and stands up. 'Let's go.'

We put on our coats and walk towards the exit together. Outside, I'm preparing to say my goodbyes when Samantha unexpectedly leans in and hugs me.

'Thank you for the chat,' she says into my ear.

'Of course,' I say, embarrassed by this unexpected show of affection.

She pulls away. 'Call me any time. I mean it.'

I watch her leave, confused. I like Samantha. In any other situation, I'd be chuffed that I'd hit it off with a potential new friend. She seems like a really nice person and we got on well. But she's not *my* person, I remind myself. We don't know each other and the circumstances around how we met are just too difficult. I should keep my distance, and I'm sure she'll do the same. This was just a one-off, not to be repeated.

But as I walk home, I can't stop thinking about her. About how brave and stoic she's being when I can clearly see that she's suffering deeply. And the urge to support her returns to me, stronger than ever, as though it never went away. Maybe fate brought us together again because, for some reason, I am the one who can help Samantha.

She is not my person. But for a moment, I think that perhaps she should be.

5

A few days later, I'm in the pub having a drink with Tamsin when my phone beeps. I look at the screen and feel a flush of pleasure when I see a message from Samantha.

> Hi Ellie. Thank you again for the coffee. You're so easy to talk to. Are you free for lunch next week?
> S x

'Everything okay?' Tamsin asks.

Fuelled by a glass of wine and the company of a good friend, I decide to spill the beans.

'It's from Samantha. The widow of the man who died in the car accident.'

Tamsin pulls a face. 'Hold on, what? How did she get your number?'

I explain, a little guiltily, about how we met. Tamsin's eyebrows raise when I admit that I went to the funeral.

'Why on earth did you go there?'

'It just felt like the right thing to do.'

'How did you even know about it?'

'I read about it in the paper. Anyway, I got chatting to Samantha and then we bumped into each other on the day of the court hearing and ended up going for coffee. Then we swapped numbers.'

'What does she want?'

'She's invited me to lunch. She used to be a solicitor and she's offered to give me some tips for the court case because she knows I'm anxious about it.'

Tamsin scrunches up her nose. 'I'm not sure, El. I think there's a conflict of interest. Anyway, won't the prosecution team help you with that?'

'I have no idea.' I look down at my phone, my fingers itching to reply. The truth is that I have been thinking about Samantha a lot and, if I'm being honest, I'm pleased that I might have an opportunity to see her again.

'What does Tom say about it?' Tamsin asks.

I grimace. 'He doesn't know.'

'Why not?'

'I don't know. I just haven't found a way to tell him.'

Tamsin leans forward. 'Is everything okay between you two?'

It's a difficult question to answer. Everything is fine between us. We get on well. We rarely argue. We run our house and parent our children as a solid team, and it works. But for a while now I've been feeling like something is missing. Like we're living together but we're not *living* together. Not enjoying each other, physically or emotionally. In the evenings, he's so exhausted after a long, demanding day at work that we have dinner in front of the television and go to bed, sometimes without even having a proper conversation. When I try to ask him about his day, I usually get a monosyllabic response and it's clear he doesn't want to talk about it. And when I try to talk to him about my day, I feel like he's only half listening and his mind is elsewhere.

And even though Tom is a great dad, I still feel the mother-load. We both work, yet I do the lion's share of the family admin and sometimes I can't stem my rising resentment that he seems oblivious to how much I do. Whenever I've tried to talk to him about it, he's promised to help out more but after a week or so, we're back in our old habits again. I know this is a problem common to many married couples, because my mum friends have moaned about it often enough, but it's been festering inside me.

But ever since the accident I've been feeling so guilty about it. My problems seem mundane and trivial compared to what Samantha is going through and it's been a brutal wake-up call. I have a husband who loves me and I've taken it for granted.

Still, I try to explain it to Tamsin. 'When we were younger, we used to talk for hours. We'd go on long walks or leisurely lunches and put the world to rights. We were the centre of each other's worlds. Now it's like we've forgotten how to do it. Our conversations, when we have the energy for them, centre around the kids, or the dodgy sink tap, or what we should watch on TV.'

Tamsin laughs. 'That's normal. That's marriage.'

'And I'm fed up of shouldering the responsibility at home too, even though I have a busy and demanding job.'

'Tell me about it. Also marriage.'

'I know. But sometimes it just doesn't seem fair. Or enough. Is this it, for the rest of my life?'

My friend grins. 'Aha! You're having a midlife crisis.'

I frown. 'No.'

'Yes, you are. Don't worry, it happens to us all. We're in our forties, our hormones are all over the place. Our ovaries are spitting out eggs left, right and centre before they close up shop for good. Perimenopause is kicking in and causing havoc. We're stressed with juggling work and the kids. It can make us temporarily crazy, but it'll pass.'

I look at her hopefully. 'It will? When?'

'In about ten years.'

'Oh well, that's great. Thanks for the reassurance.'

'Look, men buy a sports car or shag their secretary. Women consider Botox and fantasise about snogging the twenty-five-year-old grocery delivery driver, and then feel shitty for even *thinking* it. But this unsettled feeling you have? This nagging worry that your marriage isn't as exciting as it should be? It's normal.'

'Well, I wish you'd told me all this before,' I say, and I'm only half joking, because the truth is that I'm fed up of wondering what's wrong with me. I've finally made an appointment to see a GP and get some help, whether that's medication or counselling.

'Just talk to Tom. Keep the lines of communication open. And tell him what you told me about going to the funeral and meeting the widow. I'm sure he'll tell you the same thing. It's not a good idea to spend time with this woman.'

That's what I'm afraid of. I don't want to be told that.

'But I like her,' I say meekly.

'It doesn't matter whether you like her. It's icky, Ellie. And I'm wondering why she's so keen to get in touch with you anyway, to be honest. What she wants from you.'

I frown. 'I don't think she wants anything from me.'

'But why reach out to you, of all people? It's a bit odd.'

'I think we just had a nice chat and she wants to do it again.'

Tamsin shakes her head. 'I don't buy it. I'm sure she's got plenty of people to talk to in her life, and you don't need to be one of them. Keep your distance, okay? You've got enough on your plate with the court case and seeing her will add even more pressure.'

I know she's right. I'm already feeling the pressure. A date has been set for the trial, in six months' time. I'm grateful that the wait's not any longer but it still feels like life is on hold until then. I'm trying to get on with things but it's constantly there, lingering at the back of my mind. At night, I lie awake, going over my statement again and again. Making sure I've got it right. Trying to work out if I've made any mistakes.

Tamsin's watching me with narrowed eyes. 'Put the phone away. I'm going to get us another drink.'

I do as I'm told and by the time Tamsin returns, my phone is safely in my bag. But I keep thinking about Samantha's message.

'How did Max's trial go at the academy?' Tamsin asks.

I welcome the distraction. 'Great. They've offered him a place.'

'That's amazing, congratulations! Hopefully he'll become a famous footballer and you can all live off his riches.'

I laugh. 'Here's hoping. I wouldn't mind a mansion. Complete with indoor and outdoor pool of course.'

'And a tennis court.'

'Maybe a riding stables? I've always wanted a pony.'

We laugh and I relax again. This is what I need. Inane conversation that takes my mind away from everything else. We talk a little more about the kids, and about our work and our husbands. By the time we've finished our drinks and decided to call it a night, I'm enveloped in a very welcome warm fuzziness.

I give Tamsin a hug. 'Thanks for this, I really needed it.'

She squeezes me tightly. 'Let's do it again soon.'

Outside, we go our separate ways. Tamsin lives close by and has a short stroll home. I contemplate calling a taxi but decide to walk instead. The weather is finally warming up and the spring-like feel in the air cheers me, even this late at night. I decide to put on a podcast and get my step count up. I plug in my earphones and settle on my favourite comedy show as I stride down the pavement, glad I chose to wear trainers. My mind drifts back to Samantha and her message but my night out with Tamsin and our conversation about it has served as a much-needed reminder that it would be unwise to forge a friendship with her. I'll send a polite but vague response in the morning, telling her I'm tied up with work but would love to meet up soon. And I'll talk to Tom, tell him how I'm feeling. I can't expect him to understand if I haven't explained it to him.

For the first time in weeks, I feel hopeful and it's a blessed relief. I stroll down the main road with a sense of purpose and I've just turned on to a quieter street when a creeping sensation comes over me. Am I being followed? I've always felt safe in St Albans but it's late and I'm a woman on my own. I remove my earphones and glance over my shoulder. A car is approaching slowly. As it gets closer, I realise that it's a dark SUV and my pulse quickens. Is it the same car I saw when I was with Max?

Instinct tells me not to speed up. I continue at the same pace, slipping my hand into my pocket and wrapping it around my phone so I'm ready to call for help. Fear is surging, adrenaline coursing through my body. I look around but the pavement is empty. There's no one around. I calculate my surroundings, trying to work out what to do if I'm approached, and I see a few houses dotted about. If I scream loudly enough, someone will hopefully hear me. But how have I even ended up in this situation?

The car slows down to a crawl as it approaches, and my fear accelerates. My heart is racing so fast I can feel it pulsating through my veins. Visions flash before my eyes of getting dragged into the car. Being held at knifepoint. Assaulted, or worse. I can't believe this is happening to me. I can't believe this is real.

I have to do something. I make a split-second decision and

pull my phone out, lifting it to my ear, like I'm making a call. At the same time, I spin around and stare directly into the car. It's too dark to make out who's inside but I want them to know that I've seen them. I want them to think I'm calling the police right now. That I'm not intimidated. After a couple of agonising seconds, the car speeds off down the road.

My first reaction is relief and it's palpable. I'm safe, thank God. My legs are trembling, but I force myself to keep going, desperate to get home as quickly as possible. I'm never walking home on my own again. Next time, I'll get a taxi and be done with it. My second thought, however, quickly follows, and it chills me to the bone. Cold, hard, undeniable realisation kicks me in the gut. I'm certain it was the same car as before and that means it's not a coincidence. Someone was following me. They're watching me.

And they want me to know it.

6

I'm still shaking when I get home. I let myself into the house with fumbling hands and head straight for the living room. Tom, who's watching TV, looks up at me and takes in my sweaty face and distraught expression.

'What's happened?' he demands.

'Where are the kids?'

'In bed.'

I look over my shoulder first to make sure neither of them have crept down the stairs after hearing me get home. 'I was followed,' I tell Tom.

Tom stands up, clenching his fists. 'Are they still out there?'

'No, they've gone.'

'Tell me exactly what happened.'

I'm too agitated to sit down, so I pace the room as I explain to Tom about the black SUV that followed me after Max's football practice and again tonight.

'Are you certain it was following you? Could it have just slowed down?'

'I thought the same the first time. But now it's happened twice, Tom.'

'And it's definitely the same car?'

'I'm almost positive.'

Tom rubs his head. 'Did you get a registration number?'

'No, it happened too quickly.'

'I don't think you should walk home on your own again.'

'I've already determined that for myself.'

I can tell from Tom's confused expression that he's trying to work it all out. Make sense of what I've just told him. 'Do you think they were going to rob you?' he asks.

'I have no idea what their intentions were. That's what scares me.'

'We should contact the police.'

'Yes,' I agree. 'But it's not urgent enough to call 999. They're long gone now. I'll file a report online.'

Tom nods. 'Good idea. It's probably criminals, looking for an opportunity.'

'But why me? Twice? It's really freaked me out, Tom.'

He comes over and puts his arm around me. 'It could be a coincidence.'

'It didn't feel like it. It felt targeted. Like they were out to get me.'

'But who on earth would be out to get you?'

'I don't know!'

Tom pulls me against him. 'It's okay. Calm down. You're safe now. I'm going to pour you a small whisky to settle your nerves.'

Tom disappears into the kitchen and emerges a couple of minutes later, holding a glass tumbler with whisky and ice. I take it from him and clutch it between my hands.

'At least you're driving again now,' he says. 'I don't like the idea of you walking on your own if there are criminals working the area.'

His comment makes me think of the accident, and dread starts to build up again.

'Could it be related to the crash?' I ask.

'How do you mean?'

'Well, I'm a witness. Do you think someone is trying to intimidate me?'

'Like the lorry driver? He wouldn't be so stupid.'

'What about his family or friends, though? Maybe they're desperate.'

I look at Tom, silently pleading with him to say the words I long to hear. To tell me that I'm being paranoid, I have nothing to worry about. To reassure me.

But instead, he seems to be mulling it over. 'It's possible, I suppose.'

I put my head in my hands. 'Oh God.'

Tom sits down next to me. 'Honestly, though, I don't think this has got anything to do with the court case. How would he know who you are or where you live? I think it was criminals looking for an easy target. That doesn't make me feel any better, but I'm sure it's not related to you being a witness.'

'Hopefully you're right,' I say, absorbing his words like a sponge. I need to hear them more than he knows. 'Actually, I'll get my laptop right now and report what happened.'

I retrieve my laptop, googling until I find what I'm looking for. I make my way through the online crime reporting form and when I'm done, I press send and exhale.

'Done,' I tell Tom. 'I wonder if anyone will follow it up.'

'I'm sure they will, but not tonight. So, let's go to bed.'

I take a few sips of the whisky, hoping it will help me nod off, and then follow Tom upstairs to get ready for bed. But I'm too on edge to sleep and even once we've turned the lights out and Tom is breathing deeply, I'm wide awake.

After about an hour of lying in silence, listening to my still rapid heartbeat, I decide to get up again and make my way wearily downstairs. In the living room, I pull the curtains closed and open my laptop. I haven't done any late-night googling for weeks but it doesn't take long for my fingers to remember the routine. Within seconds, I'm searching for the accident, and I quickly find an article about the court hearing.

A man has appeared in court charged with causing the death of a Harpenden motorist.

Graham Hunter, 45, died when his car collided with a lorry on the A1081 on 14 January this year. The father-of-two died at the scene.

Jason Turner, 53, of Welwyn Garden City, appeared at St Albans Crown Court today and pleaded not guilty to one charge of causing death by dangerous driving. He was released on bail. A date for the trial has been set for September.

I check to see if there are any more recent reports but there aren't. I return to the article and scroll until I see a photograph of Jason Turner. It looks like it was taken by a photographer with a long lens and I realise it's from the day of the court hearing. Jason is tall and broad, with greying hair. He's wearing a suit, and sunglasses cover his eyes. One hand is in his pocket and his head is lowered. I wonder if he knew he was being photographed. He looks like an ordinary, middle-aged man, not the type who would follow women around in an SUV. But how much do I really know about him?

I study the photograph, trying to work out how I feel about it.

About him. It's a mixture of emotions. Anger. Pity. Guilt. Fear. And I might be the one responsible for putting him in prison for a long time. I wonder again if he has children, grandchildren even. Does he deserve what he is going through? Could it have happened to anyone?

Does he know that I'm the witness?

I can't look any longer. I click off the article and distract myself by googling Samantha. It doesn't take long to find her Facebook profile, although it's set to private so I can only see one photograph. It looks like it was taken a few years ago and she's smiling at the camera, her fair hair blowing in the breeze. I click back and continue looking through the search results. A bit further down, her Instagram page comes up and this one is public. I scan her grid, which is full of photos of Samantha and the boys, or Samantha on nights out with friends. Amelia features in many of them, her severe face and dark hair a contrast against Samantha's open smile and honey complexion. Then I find one of Samantha and Graham. They look like they're at a party, perhaps New Year's Eve. Graham is wearing a headband with disco balls on it and Samantha is sporting a pink feather boa. They're grinning at the camera with their thumbs up. Behind them, I spot Amelia in the background and I frown. She's staring at Samantha and her face is anything but friendly. It's cold, just like it was when she looked at me.

'That's just her resting face.' That's what Samantha told me about her friend's funny looks at the funeral. And clearly Samantha didn't think anything of Amelia's expression in this photo otherwise she wouldn't have posted it. But I can't stop staring at it.

'What are you doing?'

I slam the laptop lid down guiltily and look up to see Frankie standing in the doorway in her pyjamas.

'Nothing. What are you doing up?'

'Couldn't sleep.'

'Do you want me to make you a hot chocolate?'

I brace myself for Frankie's eye roll or sneer. But instead, she says, 'Yes please.'

I get a saucepan out of the cupboard then fetch the milk from the fridge, pouring enough for two cups. Maybe it'll help me get to sleep too. Frankie sits on a stool and rests her elbows on the kitchen counter, watching me.

'What's on your mind?' I ask her.

'Nothing.'

'Sounds exhausting.'

Her lips turn upwards ever so slightly. 'What's on *your* mind?'

'I just had an odd evening, that's all.'

'Why? What happened?'

I have no intention of scaring the living daylights out of my teenage daughter. But she travels to school on her own and after what happened to me, it makes me nervous.

'I was thinking I might drive you to school for a bit. What do you think?'

Frankie looks like I've just told her she's grounded for a year. 'What? Why?'

'There's been a bit of crime in the area. Probably people just passing through and they'll be gone soon enough. But until then, I don't want you travelling on your own.'

'What kind of crime?'

'House burglaries and car theft mainly.'

'Well, I'm not a house and I don't own a car, so I think I'll be okay.'

'Still, it's important to be vigilant.'

I pour the hot milk into two mugs and stir in the chocolate powder. At the last minute, I add a few marshmallows to

Frankie's, just like she used to love as a child. This time she does roll her eyes, but she smiles as she takes it.

'I'll be fine, Mum. Honestly. I'm not a kid any more.'

We both look at the marshmallows and giggle. It feels like the first time we've laughed together in ages. 'Okay,' I say reluctantly, not wanting to ruin the moment. 'But just take extra care for a while, all right? Always travel with friends.'

'I will.' Frankie takes a sip of her drink. 'Speaking of friends, can I invite a couple more people to my party?'

Frankie's having a birthday party at the house in a couple of weeks. Negotiations have ensued and a resolution approved by all parties. Tom and I will be present, but we will stay in our bedroom unless required and we're only allowed downstairs in an emergency. The guest list is already over twenty.

'How many more people?' I ask.

'Like two or three.'

I nod. 'Of course, that's fine. Anyone I know?'

'No, just some new friends.'

'*Boy* friends?'

Frankie reddens. 'No.'

'*Girl* friends?'

'Stop it, Mum.'

I grin. 'Has this got anything to do with why you can't sleep?'

'No, that's because I'm worried about my history test tomorrow.'

Frankie has never worried about a test in her life and I know she's lying. But I don't push it. If she's got a crush on someone and she's inviting them to her party then good for her. I just hope they say yes. And that they're worthy of my Frankie.

We chat about the party for a bit, discussing how many pizzas we'll need to feed the masses and then Frankie stands up.

'Thanks for the hot chocolate. I'm going back to bed.'

'Sleep tight, darling.'

As soon as Frankie has gone, I drain my own drink and put the mugs in the dishwasher. Then I follow her up the stairs. I'm not sure I'll be able to sleep but I need some rest, and I need to stop myself from googling. I'm cross with myself that I've gone down that path again but it's just because of the evening I've had. Tomorrow, I'll feel better. I'll focus on Frankie's birthday and getting everything ready for the party. But I'm still thinking about the black SUV. About Graham and Samantha. About Amelia and the expression on her face in the Instagram photo.

And most of all, why I'm becoming so consumed by these people I essentially barely know.

* * *

Frankie has already showered when I get up to use the bathroom the following morning. It's so unlike her that I stick my head around the door to see if she's okay. She's blow-drying her hair and when she turns to me, I notice she's wearing lip gloss.

'You look lovely,' I call over the noise of the hairdryer. 'Going anywhere nice?'

She rolls her eyes again. 'Hardly,' she shouts back.

'I'm just wondering why you're getting so glammed up for school.'

She flicks her hair. 'I can't hear you!'

I know that she can but it's nice to see her up so early and enthusiastic about going to school. And if it's a love interest that has caused this new-found energy, then I'm not complaining, as long as it doesn't affect her schoolwork. I smile to myself as I go into the bathroom and see that Frankie's left her phone on the sink. I'm about to pick it up and give it to her when a message flashes up on the screen and I see it's from one of her friends who she's known since primary school.

> Can't wait for the party, Franks! Can I borrow
> your blue crop top? Pleeeeez!

I smile to myself, glad that everything is as it should be. Frankie and her friends are getting excited about an upcoming party. Max is bouncing off the walls about his new football club. I should make it a hat-trick and arrange a date night with Tom. I can finally talk to him properly, tell him how I'm feeling about the trial and what happened with Samantha. I still haven't done it and Tamsin's right, we need to keep the lines of communication open.

But the reminder of Samantha and the court case instantly brings my mood down. A toxic mixture of anxiety and guilt floods my body. Here I am, surrounded by my family, feeling happy, when Samantha's probably still in bed, struggling to get up. And Jason is facing years locked away in prison. It feels unfair. Wrong.

'*Help.*' Graham's haunting words return to me yet again, even though I know they're not real, he didn't really say them. But who do I help? How? What am I supposed to do?

Glancing at Frankie's phone, I slip out of the bathroom and find my iPhone on the bedside table. I hastily reply to Samantha's message.

> Hi Samantha, lovely to hear from you. Lunch
> would be great. I'm actually working from home
> and free today if you are? X

Two blue ticks tell me that she's already read the message. I imagine her, propped up in bed, trying to summon up the strength to face the day, and I'm certain that I'm doing the right thing. A couple of minutes later, her reply appears on my screen.

> Today is perfect. Shall we meet at the same café
> as last time? 1 p.m.? X

I give the message a thumbs up and then put my phone down, looking around furtively. But Tom is downstairs making coffee and I can hear Max chatting to him. I tell myself I've done nothing wrong. It's just lunch. No need to overthink it.

I rush back to the bathroom and jump in the shower, thinking about the day ahead. And I can't help it, I'm looking forward to seeing Samantha again. Perhaps I can tell her about the SUV and get her take on it. As a solicitor, she might have some good advice. And I can tell her a bit more about my life after Mum died and offer some tips on how to support the boys. Losing a parent is something no child should ever have to go through but maybe I can help a bit. Suggest something that Samantha hasn't thought of.

And so I let the hot water wash away my doubts and set my mind on the day ahead and my lunch with Samantha. I'm doing the right thing. I just know it.

7

Samantha is already there when I arrive. She stands up to greet me and this time it doesn't feel awkward when she gives me a hug.

'How are you?' I ask.

'Okay.' She shrugs. 'You know.'

'And the boys?'

'They're managing. They're seeing the counsellor every week and we're talking about things as a family. The school has been incredibly supportive too. You were right, they told me not to worry about the GCSE results. They've guaranteed their place at sixth form and they're giving them extra support.'

'Oh, that's wonderful news. I'm so happy to hear it.'

We peruse the menu and order, and then Samantha turns her gaze to me.

'Thanks for meeting me.'

'Of course.'

'I really appreciated our chat last time. I guess sometimes it's just easier to talk to someone you don't know so well, rather than close friends or family, who hover around wanting to help without knowing what to do.'

'I understand.'

'But if it's awkward, I totally get it,' Samantha says hurriedly. 'I don't want you to feel under pressure to meet up with me. I'd hate that.'

I smile reassuringly at her. 'I don't feel under any pressure. It's good to see you.'

Her face relaxes. 'I'm glad you feel the same way. So, how are you?'

'I'm fine. Busy preparing for Frankie's upcoming birthday party.'

'Oh yes, she's turning fourteen, isn't she?'

'That's right. She's having a house party. Tom's saying we should lock up the booze.' I laugh. 'But I don't think teenagers are interested in alcohol any more.'

'I know,' Samantha agrees. 'When I was a teenager, I used to steal my parents' vodka and fill the bottle up with water. And I would pinch my dad's cigarettes when he wasn't looking. Now the boys just want to go to the gym and drink protein shakes.'

'Frankie is glued to her phone. She sees her friends all day at school but as soon as she's home it's like she must message them all night otherwise she'll implode.'

'Oh, the boys disappear off to their rooms too, to spend hours online gaming with their friends. But at least they're not making TikTok videos.'

'Is this okay?' I ask suddenly. 'Talking about normal life?'

She nods. 'It's more than okay. It's what I need. A bit of normality. People not treading on eggshells around me all the time.'

'Is that what everyone else is doing?'

'Yes. My poor dad just keeps looking at me with the saddest eyes I've ever seen. And my mum, who lives in the US with her second husband, doesn't seem to know what to say to me. She just keeps crying down the phone. Even Amelia is being weirdly nice.'

'She's not normally nice?'

Samantha smiles. 'She's wonderful and I love her with all my heart, but let's just say she doesn't mince her words. I thought she'd be the first one to tell me to buck up and get on with it. But actually it's quite the opposite.'

'She's just worried about you.'

'I know she is.' Samantha looks up. 'Actually, she said she might join us for a quick coffee if she finishes a meeting in time. I hope you don't mind.'

My heart sinks, without me really knowing why. Is it that I just didn't take to Amelia or is it because I want Samantha to myself?

'Of course I don't mind,' I lie. 'It would be good to see her again. Do her children go to the same school as ours?'

'No, she has one child, a daughter, and she goes to private school.'

'Is she close with your boys?'

Samantha nods. 'Yes, they're like siblings really. They've known each other since they were babies. Charlotte's pretty much the same age as your Frankie.'

'They've never had crushes on each other?'

Samantha scrunches up her face. 'Absolutely not.'

'Do either of your boys have a love interest?'

'Not that I'm aware of. How about Frankie?'

I lean forward conspiratorially. 'I think she's got a crush. I don't know who it is though. I'm just hoping it's a pupil and not a teacher.'

Samantha grins. 'That Mr Applegate's quite hot though, isn't he? Do you know him? I think he teaches music.'

I laugh. 'Oh yes, he really is.'

We look at each other and smile. This feels so natural again. So *nice*. I'm drawn to Samantha, I can't help it, and it seems that she feels the same way about me.

No good can come of this. There's a small voice inside my head telling me to get out of this situation. Or maybe it's Tamsin's voice. But I ignore it.

I'm about to ask Samantha more about Jamie and Marcus when the bell above the door tinkles and I look up to see Amelia bustling in. I force myself to smile brightly.

'Amelia, hi!' Samantha stands up and hugs her friend. 'You remember Ellie?'

'Of course. Hi, Ellie.' Amelia smiles at me but it doesn't quite reach her eyes. She sits down and waves at the waitress so she can order a coffee. Then she turns back to me, coolly appraising me until I begin to feel uncomfortable.

'How are you?' she asks.

'Fine thanks. Samantha and I were just talking about a hot teacher at our children's school.'

I regret it as soon as I say it. Given that Samantha has just lost her husband it sounds callous. Thoughtless. Amelia raises her eyebrows in a way that makes me cringe inwardly and then she turns to Samantha, as though I've been dismissed.

'How did the boys' counselling sessions go?' she asks.

'Good, I think. You know what they're like; they don't tell me much.'

Amelia nods and an awkward silence ensues. It's not like this when it's just Samantha and me. It's Amelia's presence that's doing it. She's making the vibe uncomfortable. I rack my brains, trying to think of something to say.

'What do you do for work?' I ask Amelia. It's all I've got.

'I'm a lawyer,' she says.

Damn, I knew that already. 'What kind of law?'

'Property.'

It's like she's giving me the shortest answer possible. But if she doesn't like me, then why did she even come? I risk a glance at Samantha to see if she's noticed the tension but she's looking at her phone, reading a message.

'It's Laila,' she tells Amelia. 'She wants to arrange a dinner.'

'Are you ready to start going out? You don't have to,' Amelia urges.

'Well, I'm out now,' Samantha reminds her. 'I don't know, maybe it'll do me good.' She turns to me. 'Would you like to join us, Ellie?'

I can almost feel Amelia's disapproval. Why has this woman got it in for me so much? What have I done to her? I've barely said a dozen words to her.

'That's so kind, but you should spend some time with your close friends.'

Samantha looks like she's about to argue but then our food arrives, along with Amelia's coffee. I've ordered a salad and I pick at it, aware of Amelia's gaze on me. It's so uncomfortable that I consider making an excuse and leaving. Maybe Amelia's presence is the reminder I need that I'm getting in too deep. I shouldn't be having lunch with Samantha, she should be with her real friends. Like Amelia and Laila.

The lettuce tastes like cardboard as I chew it, my face reddening. I glance at Samantha and she's staring at Amelia with a look I can't quite interpret. It's almost like a warning. Her expression is hard, her eyes boring into her friend. I imagine it as her lawyer look, the one she uses to intimidate people in court. And it's so different to the one she's been wearing around me that for a moment I'm taken aback.

My gaze turns to Amelia and she's staring back at Samantha, a silent battle raging. But then her face softens, and when she turns to me she seems less hostile. 'What do you do, Ellie?'

I tell her a bit about my job, and then we move on to talking about our children. The conversation is not what I would call enjoyable but at least it's not as tense. But when I've finished my salad, I ask for the bill. I'm ready to leave. As soon as I've paid, I stand up and shrug my coat on.

'Thanks for lunch,' I say. 'It was lovely to see you.'

Samantha hugs me again. 'Thanks for coming.'

I hurry out and walk until I'm out of sight. Then I stop for a moment to gather my thoughts and make sure I didn't leave anything behind in the café in my haste to leave. And that's when I see it. The black SUV parked on the street, just up the road from where I had lunch. I stare at it in horror, my heart beginning to pound, as I consider whether to run away or confront whoever is inside. Indignant fury surges and I take a step forward and then another until I can see clearly into the car. But there's no one inside. I peer in through the window to look for any clues, but the interior of the car is pristine with nothing incriminating on show. I look around to see if anyone is watching me but no one is paying me any notice. With a final glance at the car, I move on.

My hands are trembling as I reach for my phone and message Tom.

> I've just seen the black SUV again. Parked on the high street.

He responds immediately.

> A black SUV or the black SUV? There's loads of
> them in St Albans.

He's right. I'm an idiot. There's every chance that it's not the same car as the one that followed me. This one could easily belong to someone who's just popped into St Albans to do a spot of shopping. But I still turn and check the car again, typing the registration number into my phone. There's no harm in being cautious.

I send Tom a quick reply, telling him that he's probably right, but as I walk home I'm unsettled. The awkward lunch, followed by seeing the black car again, has thrown me. And I can't reconcile with how I feel. The connection I have with Samantha against everything else. It's almost as though the universe is warning me to keep away.

I've pretty much convinced myself that I should cut off contact with Samantha when my phone vibrates and I see a new message.

> Thanks for a lovely lunch. I'm sorry about
> Amelia, she was having a rough day. She
> apologises if you thought she was rude. Let's
> chat again soon. S x

I put my phone back in my pocket without replying and continue my walk home. I want to forget about it all for the rest of the day. Concentrate on work and making the final preparations for Frankie's party.

But as soon as I get home, I sense immediately that I'm not alone. I can almost feel someone else's presence in the house. I go straight to the kitchen to see if Tom is there but it's empty. Then I return to the hallway, my hairs standing on end, until I see Frankie's coat hanging up on the peg. I relax again, but then frown. What is Frankie doing home so early? Is she ill? But the school would have called me if that was the case. Unless she forgot something and she's just popped home to pick it up?

I tiptoe up the stairs and across the landing to Frankie's room. Her door is closed and I know it was open when I left for lunch as I went in there to fetch her dirty laundry. I bet she's bunking off, the little madam. I creep towards the door, ready to throw it open and confront my daughter. I can't believe she's skipped school and just after she promised to pay more attention in class. Anger surges as I prepare myself for confrontation.

In fact, I realise, I'm too angry. I pause outside, giving myself a minute to calm down. Screaming blue murder at Frankie will not help. I need to keep my cool, tell her that this behaviour is not acceptable and march her straight back to school. But then I hear a noise. A giggle. And then another, deeper voice. Frankie is not alone.

I've opened the door in a split second, with such force that it swings hard and hits the wall. Two sets of eyes swivel towards me. I thought I'd braced myself but nothing could prepare me for what I see. The colour drains from my face.

It's not that Frankie is with a boy. Or that she clearly snuck out of school at lunchtime to be with him. No, it's neither of those things that bothers me the most. Because it's not what she's doing, it's who she's doing it with.

One of Samantha's twin boys.

* * *

'What's going on?' I demand, teetering on the edge of hysterical.

The boy stands up, his face flustered. 'We were just talking.'

'Mum.' Frankie's voice is loaded with warning. She's begging me not to kick off.

'You're supposed to be at school.' I stare at the boy. I don't know what his name is, which of the twins he is, but there's no denying that he's Samantha's son.

'We're going back now.' Frankie stands up. 'We just took a lunch break.'

'You're not allowed to leave school in Year 9,' I remind her. Then I remember that the boy is in Year 11. A whole two years older than Frankie. This is a nightmare.

'It was just one time, Mum. I haven't missed any classes. Come on, Jamie, let's go.'

At least I know his name now. 'Jamie, you go,' I say. 'Frankie, I'm driving you.'

'Mum!' Frankie is aghast.

But help comes from an unexpected quarter. 'It's fine,' Jamie says. 'You should go with your mum. I'll see you later.'

He walks out of the room, giving me a guilty look as he passes, and I hear him jog down the stairs and out of the front door. Then I turn my attention back to Frankie. 'What the hell, Frankie?'

She's just as furious as me. 'You embarrassed me.'

'I don't care. You're supposed to be at school, not kissing boys in your bedroom.'

'We weren't kissing, Mum. We were talking.'

'I don't care what you were doing.'

It's a lie because I do care. I care very deeply about my daughter skipping school to be alone with an older boy in her bedroom. But I'm most distressed about who the boy is. It's icky and it makes me uncomfortable. *Icky*. That's exactly what Tamsin said to me about my friendship with Samantha, which I conveniently ignored. Now, however, I understand. Our families' lives are becoming intertwined and it's not right.

'Come on, let's go,' I say. 'Straight into the car.'

The ride back to school is not pleasant. Fury radiates from both of us.

'The party's off,' I tell Frankie.

'What? No, Mum! You can't do that.'

'Yes, I can. You bunked off school.'

'It was just one time.'

'I don't care. One time is too many times.'

'I hate you.'

'I know you do right now. But this is your own doing.'

Frankie starts crying, hot, furious tears spilling out of her. 'We were just talking,' she shouts. 'He needed a friend.'

'I'm sure he has plenty of friends, in his *own year*.'

'He was upset about his dad.'

Shame is instant and it winds me. I grip the steering wheel, my tense knuckles turning white. 'How did you even get talking to him?'

'I went up to him one lunchtime. Told him I was sorry about his dad. He said I was the first person to say that to him. Everyone else was avoiding the subject.'

There's a small part of me that is extremely proud of Frankie. But the majority is still raging and I don't know where to direct it. What to do with it.

'Are you dating?'

'No.' But the way Frankie says it tells me she wishes they were.

'Is he one of the extra people you wanted to invite to your party?'

Frankie looks at me, eyes hopeful. 'Yes. Does that mean it's still on?'

'No.'

Her expression switches in an instant. 'I can't believe you're doing this.'

'You did it to yourself,' I remind her.

The rest of the journey passes in stony silence. I drop Frankie outside the gates and she gets out of the car without even saying goodbye. But I don't drive away immediately. I sit, with my head resting on the steering wheel, wondering where we go from here. What to do about this mess of a situation.

And the person I'm compelled to talk to about it is Samantha.

8

We meet a few days later at the park. It's Saturday afternoon and I'm glad to escape the house. Frankie is still not speaking to me and is barely communicating with her father, who backed me on the party being cancelled. When I told Tom about what had happened, he was as angry as I was. We were, thankfully, a united front.

But what I didn't tell Tom is who Frankie was with. And I know that I'm sinking deeper into a web of deceit. It ends tonight. Tamsin is babysitting because I don't trust Frankie to be left alone, and Tom and I are going out for dinner. I'm going to tell him everything. But first I need to speak to Samantha.

'I've talked to Jamie,' she says as we follow the path around the pond. I watch the ducks absent-mindedly. Frankie used to love coming to the park to feed the ducks and see the little ducklings swimming around in the spring. Now I can barely drag her out of the house, unless we're going shopping and I'm paying.

'How did it go?' I ask.

'He's very sorry. He realises that it was irresponsible of them to leave school. And he acknowledges that Frankie is two years younger than him. It won't happen again.'

'Thank you. And I'm sorry that I've dragged you into this.'

'You haven't dragged me into anything, Ellie. This involves Jamie. I'm very angry with him. But...' She hesitates and I wonder where she's going next. 'I'm also relieved that he has someone to talk to. He says Frankie's a good listener.'

If it was any other situation, I'd be glowing with pride. But I fail to muster any joy from Samantha's words. 'I'm glad she listens to someone,' I retort.

'It won't happen again,' Samantha repeats. 'I promise you that.'

'I'm not saying they can't talk,' I say hurriedly. 'It's just not okay for them to bunk off school. And there's the age gap.'

'I know. I've explained all of this to Jamie and he says there is nothing going on between them. I believe him, Ellie. I don't think Frankie is exactly his type.'

I'm not sure what she's implying and I'm too focused on Frankie to care. 'Hopefully we can draw a line under it all.'

'How is Frankie?'

'Oh, she's absolutely furious with me. I've cancelled her birthday party.'

Samantha is quiet. I wonder if she disapproves of my punishment, but I don't care. The crime warrants it, as far as I'm concerned, and Tom agrees.

'It was Jamie's fault,' she says. 'Not Frankie's.'

'He didn't drag her out of school.'

'No, but he persuaded her. She felt sorry for him.'

I turn to Samantha, but she won't meet my eye. 'Still, she agreed.'

'Look, do what you think best. You're her mother. But don't be too hard on her. She's a good person. Apparently, she's really been there for Jamie.'

'So, you think I should let the party go ahead?'

Samantha finally looks my way. 'That's your decision. But for what it's worth, I think she did a kind and thoughtful thing. Perhaps just in an irresponsible way.'

I look back at the pond. 'The world works in mysterious ways.'

'Are you talking about how it seems to have brought our families together?'

'Yes.'

'I know. It's strange, isn't it? You've been there for me and Frankie has been there for Jamie.'

'How are you doing?'

'Good days and bad days. Today's a good day.' Samantha turns her face towards the sun. 'Sometimes it's the small things, like the feeling that spring is coming. Other times it's bigger, like seeing one of the boys laugh. But it always gets me in the end. The sun peeks out of the clouds for a moment and then quickly goes behind them again.'

'One day at a time.'

'Exactly.'

We circle the pond, taking in the serenity of the park.

'How's Amelia?' I ask.

'She's good.'

'Feeling better after her rough day?'

Samantha's face temporarily clouds with confusion before quickly clearing again. 'Oh yes, that was just a work thing. She's fine now.'

I want to tell Samantha how I feel. Tell her that I don't think her friend likes me. But I'm not a teenage girl and there's no way of saying it without sounding immature and petulant. Anyway, she's got enough on her plate.

'I'm thinking of going back to work,' she says.

'Oh yes?'

'I need to do something, to keep busy, you know? All this sitting around isn't helping. But I don't want to work full-time because I still need to be there for the boys.'

'I think it's a good idea to get a part-time role,' I say. 'It'll give you a purpose.'

'Exactly. Stop me obsessing about this damn court case.'

She's not the only one obsessing about the case. Sometimes hours can go by without me thinking about it but then it hits me, hard and brutal. Other times it lingers on my mind all day, following me around like a shadow.

At least I haven't seen the black SUV again and I'm now certain that the one I saw near the café was a different vehicle. Tom has said as much, but I'm keen to get Samantha's view on it too.

'I thought I was being followed a couple of times,' I begin.

Samantha turns to me with a strange look on her face. 'Followed?'

'Yes, this black SUV was crawling along the road behind me. It happened twice and then I thought I saw it in town too, although now I'm not so sure.'

'Did you call the police?'

'I filed a report, but I got a standard email reply, and no one has been in contact.'

Samantha grabs me, her fingers digging into my arm. 'Be careful,' she hisses.

Her reaction frightens me. 'What do you mean?'

She glances around, as though checking that no one is listening. 'You're the key witness in a major case. A man could go to prison because of you and there will be people who are not happy about that. You need to watch your back.'

Suddenly the Frankie and Jamie drama feels like a pre-school spat. I have much bigger fish to fry, and Samantha's response feeds my insecurity.

'Could I be in danger?'

Her grip loosens and she continues walking. 'I don't know. I'm sure it's fine, but be vigilant, okay? He might try to intimidate you, but I don't think he'd hurt you.'

'You mean Jason? The lorry driver?'

She nods. 'Yes.'

'Have you ever known anything like this to happen before?'

'Yes, but the circumstances were different. They were domestic violence cases. Men trying to scare these poor, terrified women into not giving evidence against them.'

'You're freaking me out, Samantha.'

'Oh, I'm sorry, Ellie, I don't mean to. I just think you should be on your guard.'

'But how would he know who I am? Surely he doesn't have access to that kind of information?'

'There are always ways of finding things out, if you really want to. And he saw you at the scene of the accident. He knows what you look like, and what car you drive.'

'Oh my God. What if he approaches me?'

'He won't, I'm sure. And if he does, call the police and report him.'

'Okay.'

I've worked myself up into a state now and Samantha must sense it because she links an arm through mine and squeezes me. 'You're being very brave.'

'I don't feel very brave.'

'You are. I know how hard this must be for you. You unwittingly got involved in all of this. You were just in the wrong place at the wrong time.'

Tears threaten and I look away. How does she know what I'm thinking?

'But I want you to know how much I appreciate what you're doing,' Samantha continues. 'That lorry driver deserves to be punished for what he did to Graham. Because of his dangerous driving, the boys don't have a father. I don't have a husband.'

Now she's crying and that sets me off even more and the next thing I know, we're clinging on to each other, sobbing our hearts out, and people are sidestepping us on the path with looks of concern or horror. I don't know how long it goes on for but when our tears finally subside, I feel almost cleansed.

'Oh gosh, I needed that,' Samantha says, trying to wipe some mascara off her cheek.

'Here, let me.' I reach out and gently wipe the black smear away.

'Thank you.' She places a hand over mine.

And in that moment, any last shred of doubt leaves my mind. The world has brought us together for reasons that I can't explain. I hate how it happened more than anything, but I like having Samantha in my life, and she feels the same. Even our children have found each other and if Samantha believes that there's nothing going on between them, then so do I. I still don't like the idea of Frankie and Jamie growing close but who am I to judge when I'm standing here, clinging on to Samantha? Like mother, like daughter. Clearly we are both drawn to this beautiful, tragic family.

The next few months are going to be difficult for me, but they will be even harder for Samantha. And I am going be there for her, every step of the way.

'*Help.*' This is how I help. This is how I make the nightmares stop.

* * *

Several hours later, I'm struggling to put the clarity I felt earlier into words. Tom and I are at our favourite pub. We've ordered dinner and cracked open a lovely bottle of red wine and it's the perfect time to tell him everything that's going on. But I can't.

I don't want to lie. I don't want to keep this secret because that makes it feel dirty. But it's stuck inside me, refusing to budge. So instead I deflect, asking him about work. We talk about his parents and his younger brother who lives in Edinburgh. Then our food arrives and we tuck in with gusto. By the time we've finished our food and ordered a nightcap, I still haven't told him. And I know that it's now or never.

'Tom,' I begin hesitatingly.

He looks at me with an open smile and eyes slightly glassy from the wine. 'Yeah?'

'I need to tell you something.'

My tone makes him frown. 'What is it?'

'It's about the accident.'

'Go on.'

I take a deep breath. 'I've become friendly with the man's widow. Samantha.'

Tom is incredulous. And very confused. 'What? How did that happen?'

I tell him, with increasing shame, about attending the funeral and then meeting Samantha on a few occasions. Then I admit who Frankie was with the other day. Tom listens, his eyes getting increasingly wider until I think they might pop out of his head.

I'm relieved that it's finally out in the open but I'm worried about how he'll respond.

'But the funeral was weeks ago,' he says.

'Yes,' I admit.

'And you're only telling me this now?'

'I'm sorry.'

'Why didn't you tell me before?'

'I didn't know how to. I knew you wouldn't approve. And I was all over the place.'

'What's happened to us, Ellie?'

It's a question we should have asked each other a long time ago. I know that. But at least it's finally being asked.

'I don't know.'

'We used to talk about everything. We literally never ran out of things to say.'

'I know.'

'And now this hugely important thing has happened and you kept it from me for weeks. You continued meeting up with this woman and didn't tell me. You lied to me.'

He's angry. He's upset. And he has every right to be. 'I'm so sorry,' I whisper.

'What did I do to make you distance yourself from me?'

'You didn't do anything,' I insist. 'It was all me. My fault. I'm sorry.'

'Why?'

I play with my wine glass. 'I've been struggling for a while, a feeling that I'm drowning and I can't reach the surface. Tamsin reckons it's a midlife crisis but I don't know. Life felt like a game of survival. Running after the kids, meeting deadlines at work, keeping house, with no time to stop and think about what I want. What makes me happy. And then the accident happened and it totally obliterated me.'

He looks at me. He's a good man and he's trying to understand what I'm saying. 'So, instead of talking to me about this, you went and found this man's widow?'

'That's not what happened. I went to the funeral to pay my respects. At the time it felt like the right thing to do. And then Samantha and I got talking and we get along really well. She's the only one who understands what I'm going through.'

'But you're not going through the same thing. She's lost her husband. You're a witness in a court case.'

He doesn't mean to sound harsh, but his words hit hard. 'We're both anxious about the case.'

'Yes, but for very different reasons.' Tom shakes his head. 'Look, the midlife crisis stuff I get, okay? I'm not immune to it. I've been feeling weird about getting older too. At work, imposter syndrome is hitting me hard. I'm convinced some young whippersnapper is going to come along and steal my job any second and I'm constantly looking over my shoulder and feeling like I'm failing at the same time. And I just feel *old*.'

'You should have told me.'

'*You* should have told *me*.'

'I know.'

'But this stuff with, what's her name? Samantha? I don't get that. I'm sorry.'

I knew he wouldn't and that's why I didn't tell him. 'So where do we go from here?'

'I don't think you should see her. Not on any personal level. Keep it for court.'

My heart sinks. 'I don't see the harm in it,' I argue.

'It's messy, Ellie. And what with Frankie and her son becoming friends, it's even messier. It's almost incestuous.'

'That's not true,' I snap. I'm not sure why his words are getting to me so much.

'You have plenty of friends to talk to. You have all the support you need. Why do you have to pal up with this particular woman? She's a stranger.'

'She's not any more, not to me. We've become close.'

Tom looks at me in disbelief. 'You've only known her for a few weeks.'

'Yes, but we have a common cause. It's united us.'

'Your common cause is that her husband died and you witnessed the accident. Can't you see how inappropriate that is?'

'Friendships have been forged under stranger circumstances.'

Tom sighs heavily. 'Fine. Do what you want, Ellie.'

This is not how I wanted our night to go. I had hoped me opening up would bring us closer together but it's had the opposite effect. So, in a desperate attempt to get it back on track, I capitulate. 'No, you're right. I should stop seeing her.'

The relief on Tom's face is palpable. 'I think that's a good idea. And maybe we should keep an eye on Frankie too. There's no harm in her talking to this boy but I don't like the idea of them getting any closer. Anyway, isn't he a bit too old for her?'

'Jamie says there's nothing going on between them. Samantha made a comment that makes me wonder if he's gay, actually. I don't know, but she was quite adamant that Frankie isn't his type. She also thinks we should let the birthday party go ahead.'

Tom pulls a face. 'So now she's giving us parenting advice too?'

'She's not giving us advice. She said it was all Jamie's doing. He persuaded Frankie to bunk off school when she didn't want to. Maybe we're being too hard on her.'

'We can't go back on it now. She'll never respect us again.'

'I know, but maybe we can reach a compromise. Tell her she can have a couple of girlfriends round for a sleepover to mark the occasion, but still no party.'

Tom mulls it over. 'I suppose there's no harm in that.'

We move on to other, easier topics and by the time we've finished our drinks and are standing up to leave, I feel much better for having got it all off my chest. But I'm worried too because I've promised to stop seeing Samantha and, deep down, I know that I won't be able to do it. I'll work it out, I rationalise. Bring it up with Tom again in a few days and tell him that I'll just meet up with her occasionally. I won't lie to him again.

We step out into the cool evening and begin to make our way through the car park towards the exit. The pub is only a short stroll away from our house and I'm looking forward to walking off dinner. But then something catches my eye. It's a black SUV, parked up. And when my eyes scan the number plate, I know immediately that it's the same one that I saw parked in St Albans. Possibly the same one that followed me.

'Tom.' I stop and grab his arm. 'The black SUV is here.'

He follows my gaze. 'You sure it's the same one?'

'I'm positive. I remember the number plate.'

Tom frowns. 'Wait here,' he says.

I watch him head back inside but as soon as he disappears out of sight, I feel exposed. I can almost sense someone watching me. My eyes scan the empty car park and rest on the hedges beyond. Is someone there? I shiver, wrapping my arms around myself, as the feeling of being observed grows stronger, until it becomes unbearable. I turn and scurry back inside the pub, searching the bar area until I see Tom. He's walking around agitatedly, glancing at the other patrons. I do the same but I don't recognise anyone. I've committed the photo of Jason Turner to memory and I'm certain he's not here. No one is looking at me. After a couple of circuits, we both head back outside.

Tom rubs his head. 'I don't know. Could it just be someone who lives around here?'

'It could be,' I concede.

'It might be nothing to do with you.'

'You think I'm overreacting?'

'Maybe.'

I nod my agreement. 'Let's just go home.'

We both glance at the SUV as we pass, heading on to the pavement and strolling up the road. I look anxiously over my shoulder a couple of times, but the car doesn't move. It's not following us, at least not tonight. But the nagging feeling inside me is growing stronger every day, fuelled by Samantha's warning that I should watch my back. My gut tells me that I'm not being paranoid and that it's personal. I've now seen this vehicle four times, and I'm certain that someone was watching me earlier.

Something isn't right. And it's beginning to scare the hell out of me.

9

Frankie gets her sleepover party and although she's still mad with us for cancelling her big bash, she seems to have a good time with her two best friends. We also have a family celebration to mark her fourteenth birthday, and the grandparents spoil her with tech and gift vouchers that make her face light up. Harmony has, it seems, been restored to our household for now, except for one, tiny detail.

Samantha and I have been meeting up in secret every week. Sometimes we go for a walk, other times we have coffee or lunch. And we are growing even closer. She talks about Graham and how she's coping. She cries and, occasionally, she laughs. I feel like I'm witnessing her slow and painful healing, and I hope that I'm a part of that process.

She says that I am. She still finds it easier to talk to me than her close friends and family. She says I should train as a counsellor, as I'm so good at listening. I'm flattered but not tempted. I've got too much going on in my own head to be able to help anyone else and worrying that someone is following me certainly isn't helping. I'm constantly looking over my shoulder now, fretting that I'm going to see that imposing black car. But there's been no sight of it since we saw it in the pub car park and Tom's convinced that it's just a local resident whose car I keep seeing coincidentally. He says I'm on edge, looking for things that aren't there. Perhaps he's right because if it was something more sinister, wouldn't I know about it by now? It's a horrible thought, but in a strange way it gives me comfort because I haven't been approached by anyone and no one has threatened me. It's easier, and more reassuring, to dismiss it as a coincidence. Either way, I'm taking extra precautions just to be safe and I don't walk anywhere on my own after dark. At night, I close all the curtains, in case someone might be looking in. I scour the headlines for local reports of theft or burglary. And I keep an eye out for the SUV.

At least family life is distracting me. Our house is bustling and chaotic and I always feel safe and secure in our cosy cocoon. I'm still commuting into London a few days a week and the routine keeps me grounded, especially now that I'm driving again. I'm trying to forget about it and get on with life, but it's not easy.

I feel awful about not telling Tom that I'm still seeing Samantha. Truly wretched. But I don't want to rock the boat or cause an unnecessary row. There's no harm in what I'm doing, if anything it's the opposite. Being with Samantha is helping me to move past the accident, and if Tom can't understand that then there's no point in even trying to talk to him about it. I know I have to tell him eventually, but I keep putting it off.

I'm mulling this over one Sunday lunchtime as I push a trolley around the supermarket. We get our groceries delivered weekly, but I like to go at the weekend occasionally to browse the aisles for things I don't normally think to order. The kids are doing their homework and Tom is looking forward to watching the football on television later. It's a typical family Sunday and I'm feeling increasingly grateful for it, and more determined than ever to make the most of it.

I'm browsing the cereal aisle when I become aware of someone standing right behind me, too close for comfort. I spin around and see a man I don't recognise. He's a few years older than me with dark hair and a beard and he's holding a basket with one hand which is full of cider and crisps. His other is tucked into his jeans pocket.

And he's staring at me with a grin that's bordering on lewd.

'Can I help you?' I ask, sidestepping to put some distance between us.

He leans in and I can smell his breath. 'I know you,' he says quietly.

'Excuse me?' I look around, instinctively assessing my options. The supermarket is packed and all it would take is one call for help to get the attention of a dozen people. I have nothing to fear, and yet I am afraid of this man.

He gives me a wink and I step away again, nearly colliding with the cereal.

'Are you free now?' he asks.

'I think you're confusing me with someone else.' I try to move even further away from him, but he steps forward, bringing us closer together again.

'I never forget a pretty face,' he says. 'I know it's you.'

'I have no idea what you're talking about.' My voice is shrill and a couple of people look our way. The man notices too and instantly moves away from me.

'Is your husband here?' he whispers, glancing around.

'Yes,' I lie, because I can't think of what else to do.

He backs off, pulling his hand out of his pocket and holding it up in a peace gesture. 'Sorry, love. I'll message you.'

With a final wink, he turns and walks away, leaving me shocked and confused. What the hell just happened? Who *was* he? And why did he think he knew me? It must be a case of mistaken identity, is all I can think of. Still, I don't want to be in this supermarket knowing he's here too and that I could bump into him at any moment. I abandon my trolley and hurry out, getting into the car and locking it. I risk a glance at the exit to see if he's following me but there's no sign of him. I do a quick scan of the car park to see if the black SUV is there. Maybe he's the driver. Could he be a stalker?

I can't see the SUV, but the car park is huge. I consider driving around to look for it but I just want to get away, so I start the engine and reverse out. I drive faster than I have done since the accident and only slow down once I'm well away from the car park.

My hands are shaking and I breathe in and out deeply to calm myself. My mind is racing as I try to work out whether this stranger really knew me or if he just got confused. He backed away as soon as he thought Tom was there. Does he know Tom?

I can't work it out and by the time I've pulled into the driveway, I'm still none the wiser as to what just happened. I let myself into the house and walk into the living room to find Tom with his feet up, a cup of tea in hand.

'Want a hand with the shop?' he asks.

'I didn't get anything.'

Tom looks up at me in surprise. 'Why not?'

I hesitate. I should tell him but I'm oddly ashamed about what happened. 'I wasn't feeling well,' I say. 'I'm going to go and lie down.'

Tom's brow furrows. 'You must have caught Max's cold.'

'Yes, I think that's it.'

'Want me to bring you up a cup of tea?'

'No, it's okay, thanks. Enjoy the game.'

I go upstairs and check on the kids. They've finished their homework and are both in Frankie's room. Frankie is listening to music while Max plays with Lego on her bedroom floor. They're not screaming at each other for once, so I leave them be and go to my bedroom, lying down and propping my head on a pillow.

I can't get the supermarket incident out of my head. Perhaps if I wasn't already riled about the car following me it would have been easier to laugh it off. Now, after this bizarre encounter, I'm even more freaked out.

I hear the TV from downstairs and decide to call Tamsin so we can thrash it out, but it goes to voicemail. I put my phone back down on the bed, disappointed. I consider interrupting the football so I can talk to Tom about it. It's important so he won't mind, and it will give me the chance to broach the Samantha thing while I'm at it. I'm standing up to go downstairs when my phone rings. *Speak of the devil.*

'Hey, Samantha,' I answer.

'Hi, how are you?'

'A bit freaked out actually.'

I tell her what just happened, wondering what her reaction will be.

'He must have thought you were someone else,' She says immediately.

I close my eyes and exhale. This is exactly what I need to hear.

'Honestly, don't give it another thought,' Samantha continues.

'Thanks. I knew that really but it's good to hear someone else say it.'

'What are you up to?'

'Nothing really. The kids are chilling and Tom's watching the football.'

'Want to come over?'

I've never been to Samantha's house because we've always met out and about. And, as well as wanting to see her again, I'm curious about where she lives.

'Sure, that sounds lovely.'

'I'll text you the address.'

She hangs up and a minute later, her message comes through. I stand up, check my reflection in the mirror, pop on some lipstick for good measure, and head downstairs.

'I'm popping out,' I say to Tom.

'Where are you off to?'

I pause. I can't lie to him any more, it's not fair. 'I'm going to Samantha's.'

He's aghast. 'You're what?'

'I'm going to Samantha's,' I repeat.

Tom takes his feet off the coffee table and mutes the television. 'You said you wouldn't see her any more.'

'I know I did and I'm sorry. But we're friends and I really don't see the harm in it.'

'Are you even allowed to spend time with her with the court case coming up? Could it be seen as tampering with a witness or something?'

I've thought about this myself, but I don't think it's a problem. She's not directly involved in the case and I've already given my statement. Nothing she says will make me change it and she would never ask me to anyway. There's no danger to either of us.

'We're on the same side,' I tell Tom. 'There's nothing stopping us being friends.'

Tom shakes his head. 'I don't know what's got into you, Ellie.'

'Nothing's got into me. I'm going to have a coffee with a friend.'

'She's not your friend.'

'She is now.'

He holds his hands up and it reminds me of the creepy guy in the supermarket. I shiver involuntarily. 'Fine. Do whatever you want.'

He's annoyed and I can't blame him. But it's not going to stop me from going.

'I'll see you in a couple of hours.'

He nods and turns the television back up. Our conversation has left a bitter taste in my mouth, but I don't let it change my plans. I get into the car and type Samantha's address into Google Maps. I'll talk to Tom about it properly when I get home and try to make him understand why I feel the way I do.

Samantha lives about twenty minutes away and I gasp as I pull into her large driveway. Her house is *beautiful*. It's a period property which looks like it's been renovated to within an inch of its life. The sort of house you'd see on the pages of a glossy homes and gardens magazine. I pull up next to Samantha's car, a white BMW, and climb out, my trainers crunching on gravel as I make my way to the huge front door. As I ring the bell, I peer into the little camera above it, wondering if she's watching me.

The door opens and I smile in anticipation. But it vanishes again when I see Amelia, not Samantha, standing there and looking at me like I just stepped in dog poo.

'Oh, hi, Amelia.' I try not to sound as disappointed as I feel.

'Ellie.'

She opens the door wider to let me in and then marches down the hallway. I scurry along behind her, wondering why Samantha didn't mention that her friend would be here too. I follow Amelia out of some stunning black Crittall doors on to a pristine patio where Samantha is sitting on a cushioned chair, facing towards the sun. A cockerpoo rushes up to greet me, its tail wagging, and I bend down to stroke it.

'Who's this?' I ask.

'That's Cooper.'

I laugh as Cooper tries to lick my face. 'He's gorgeous.'

'The boys always wanted a dog. We finally gave in a few years ago.'

Samantha stands up and comes over to hug me. 'Drink?'

'Whatever you're having.'

'I'll make a fresh pot of tea.'

'Sounds lovely.'

She drifts inside, leaving me alone with Amelia. To distract myself from her cool, relentless gaze, I make a fuss of Cooper.

'He's so cute,' I say. Amelia doesn't respond, so I try again. 'Do you have a dog?'

'No.'

I look at her then and something snaps. I've had enough of her passive-aggressive behaviour. If she has a problem, then I want to hear what it is.

'What is it, Amelia? Why don't you like me?'

She gives me a look that could freeze hell over. 'What is it with *you*, Ellie?'

'Excuse me?'

'Why are you here? Why are you getting all pally with Samantha?'

'I just want to help.' It sounds meek, meeker than I am.

'Stay away from her.'

It sounds like a threat, and she has no right to do that. This time, when I answer, my voice is firm. 'Samantha wants me here. It's got nothing to do with you.'

'You have no idea what you're—'

We're interrupted by Samantha returning with a tray laden with cups, biscuits and a china teapot.

'Tea is served,' she says, placing it down on the table. Then she looks at us both.

'Everything okay?'

'Fine,' we both answer at the same time.

Samantha frowns and then busies herself pouring the tea and adding milk. I sit down next to her and Amelia does the same on the other side. We're flanking her, a silent battle of superiority between us.

And it's ridiculous. We both care about Samantha. We both want to help her. So why is Amelia so against me? Is she jealous that Samantha is confiding in me instead of her? It could easily be that. Once the thought has settled in my mind, I almost feel sorry for her. She's clearly possessive over her friend so maybe I'm going about this all wrong. I should try to be warmer to her, to show her I'm not a threat and we can all get along.

'How's your daughter? Charlotte, right?' I ask her, with what I hope is an encouraging smile.

'She's fine.'

'Is she enjoying school?'

'Yes.'

She's making it so difficult for me, but I'm determined not to give up.

'Samantha says she's beautiful. She must take after her mother.'

God, now I sound like a drivelling suck-up. What is wrong with me?

Fortunately, Samantha intercedes. 'Oh, Charlotte is simply stunning. She could be a model. In fact, she's been scouted but Amelia's not keen.'

'She's too young,' Amelia says. 'Anyway, it's a fickle industry. And very superficial.'

'Let her have some fun, Meli.' Samantha rolls her eyes. 'You're only young once.'

'Don't I know it.'

We're interrupted by one of Samantha's sons appearing in the doorway. I have no idea which one it is, but instinct tells me it might be Marcus. I've only met Jamie once but he seemed more at ease compared to the boy standing in front of us now, who wears a sombre expression and is dressed more formally.

'Marcus, darling!' Samantha gestures for him to come over. 'This is Ellie. Remember I told you about her?'

Marcus nods stiffly. 'Hi.'

I smile encouragingly at him. 'Hi, Marcus.'

He turns to Amelia. 'How's Charlotte?'

'She's good thank you, darling. She sends her love.'

He turns back to his mother. 'I'm going to the library to study.'

'Okay, darling, good luck.'

With a fleeting smile, he disappears back into the house. Once he's out of earshot, I lean towards Samantha and whisper, 'How are the boys getting on this week?'

'They're doing okay. Better I think.' Samantha's face falls. 'But it's still so hard.'

'Of course it is. But it sounds like they're coping really well.'

'On the outside yes, but I wonder what's going on inside. I hope they're talking to their friends about it because they've clammed up with me recently. Especially Marcus.'

'Well, that's just Marcus,' Amelia says, in a tone that suggests she's trying to prove she knows Samantha's children better than I do. Tediously, she's right.

'How do you mean?' I ask.

'Well, Marcus has always been the more introvert of the two,' Samantha explains. 'Jamie will rant and rave, cry and scream, and move on. Marcus broods. After Graham died, Jamie was in bits. But his tears helped him to heal. I haven't seen Marcus cry once.'

'Everyone heals in their own way,' Amelia reminds her.

'She's right,' I agree, half hoping that it will score me brownie points with Amelia.

'Marcus is refusing to see the counsellor now,' Samantha continues. 'He says he's had enough sessions and there's no need to go any more. I just don't know, in some ways I think he needs it more than Jamie, who's still going every week.'

We're silent for a while, mulling this over. I start thinking about Frankie, and whether she's still spending time with Jamie. She hasn't mentioned him and when I ask, she evades the question. But at least she hasn't been skipping school again.

'Any more signs of the black SUV?' Samantha asks, abruptly changing the subject.

'No,' I reply. 'Not since I saw it parked at the pub.'

'What black SUV?' Amelia asks.

'Ellie thought she was being followed by this car,' Samantha explains. 'She kept seeing it everywhere. We were worried that it was linked to the court case.'

'Really?' Amelia is looking at me in a way I can't interpret.

'Tom thinks I'm just being paranoid.'

'Well, I still think it's best to be vigilant,' Samantha says. 'But I don't think it has anything to do with what happened at the supermarket.'

'What happened in the supermarket?' Amelia's eyes are wide.

'Some pervert was leering over poor Ellie. It must have been terrifying.'

'Who was he?'

'I don't know,' I answer. 'I think he mistook me for someone else.'

Amelia's eyebrows rise but she doesn't say anything.

'Anyway, like I said on the phone, it's best to just forget it,' Samantha advises me.

'It's already forgotten,' I lie.

'You seem to attract trouble, Ellie,' Amelia comments.

'Oh Meli,' Samantha chastises.

'I'm just saying it like it is.'

Samantha puts a hand on my arm. 'She's only teasing.'

But I know she's not teasing, and Amelia knows it too. I take a sip of my tea, wondering how long I need to stay here before I can make my excuses. I've tried to play nice with Amelia but it's not working, and I'm exhausted from the effort and the bubbling tension between us. But then, to my surprise, she stands up.

'I'd best be off,' she says. 'I have to pick Charlotte up from a friend's house.'

'I'll see you out.' Samantha begins to stand up, but Amelia interrupts her.

'Don't worry, you stay here. I'll let myself out.'

She gives Samantha a quick kiss on the cheek but barely even nods at me, before heading back into the house. Samantha turns to me with an indulgent smile.

'I'm so glad you two got the chance to meet again,' she says.

My face must give my true feelings away because Samantha looks at me knowingly. 'Listen, don't take it personally. Amelia can be stand-offish until you get to know her. But she's honestly such a wonderful person. I know you two will become great friends.'

There is zero chance of that, as far as I'm concerned. But I care about Samantha and so I'll make the effort, even if Amelia won't. Lord knows Samantha needs her friends around her at a time like this and we all want to do what's best for her.

Samantha sighs. 'She's having a few issues with Charlotte at the moment. Her daughter is incredibly headstrong.'

'Sounds like my Frankie.'

Samantha leans in conspiratorially, even though we are now alone. 'Charlotte is what you might call high maintenance.'

I smile back in acknowledgement. 'Got it.'

'She's an only child and she's indulged. It took Amelia a long time, and a lot of heartbreak, before she conceived and I think it's affected how she parents. I adore her, don't get me wrong, but she panders to her daughter's every whim and you can tell. Charlotte is rather wild and Amelia struggles to keep her on track.'

'It sounds like your boys are very different.'

'They are. As I said before, Marcus is serious and studious. Jamie's more fun-loving and impulsive.' Samantha's smile vanishes. 'We used to say that Marcus took after me and Jamie took after Graham. But when it comes to appearance, it's no contest. They're the spitting image of their father.'

She looks away, taking a minute to compose herself and I can feel a lump in my throat. It must be so hard to look at her sons and see Graham every day. Even if their personalities are different, it's a constant reminder of their father.

'I'm so sorry, Samantha,' I whisper.

'I'm so angry,' she says quietly.

'Of course you are.'

'And I don't know how to release it. How to get rid of this feeling.'

'Are you still seeing your counsellor?'

'Yes. It's helping a bit. She keeps telling me to be patient. To allow myself to have these feelings and to know that they will pass.'

'It's good advice.'

'I don't know. I don't think it will ever pass. I think I'll always just be angry.'

'Maybe when the court case finishes, you'll have some closure,' I suggest.

She looks at me with hope in her eyes. 'That's what I'm banking on.'

The court case. It's fixed in our minds for very different reasons. But in a few months, it will be over and I hope we will both be able to find some peace.

'How's Frankie?' Samantha asks.

'She's good. We didn't let her have the party, but she had a sleepover with a couple of close friends, which went well. And she hasn't got into trouble at school again.'

We move on to other, easier topics and the time flies by. When the teapot is empty and the sun has dipped low in the sky, it feels like the right time to leave.

'Thanks for having me,' I say as I stand up. 'Mind if I nip to the loo?'

'Of course, I'll show you where it is.'

Samantha leads me through the huge, pristine kitchen, with its gleaming white marble worktops, and points at a door. I quickly use the toilet and when I emerge, the kitchen is empty. I see a bunch of photographs stuck to the large American-style fridge-freezer and wander over to take a look. I'm so lost in my thoughts that I don't realise someone has snuck up behind me until they grab my arm.

I gasp in shock and swivel my head to see Amelia glaring at me. What the hell? I thought she'd left ages ago. Has she been hiding in the house this entire time?

Was she waiting for me?

'Stay away from Samantha,' she hisses.

I wince in pain as Amelia's grip tightens. 'Why are you doing this?'

'Just stay away. I mean it.'

Tears pool in my eyes as I try to struggle free. 'Why do you hate me so much?'

'You don't belong here.'

I have no idea what's going on and I'm too upset to even begin to work it out.

'What on earth is going on?'

Amelia and I both turn to see Samantha, standing a few feet away, her eyes wide.

Amelia instantly releases my arm. 'Nothing,' she says.

'Meli, have you been here the whole time?'

'No, I forgot something and came back for it. I didn't want to disturb you, so I used the spare key you gave me.'

Samantha is glaring at Amelia, her hands on her hips. 'What did you forget?'

'My umbrella.'

It's a lie and we all know it. It's not even raining. But Samantha must decide to throw her friend a lifeline because she rolls her eyes and relaxes.

'Oh Meli, you're always forgetting things. Come on, I think I saw it in the hallway.'

They walk out together, leaving me alone in the kitchen again. I don't want to follow them because I don't want to be anywhere near Amelia. I'll wait for her to leave first, and then I'll go out of my way to never see her again. I've known from the start that she doesn't like me, but this was something else. Something more ominous.

Amelia's not just jealous of me, she wants me out of the picture.

10

It's been two weeks since I visited Samantha and Tom is still in a mood with me. I've tried talking to him about it but he's sulking, and I'm waiting for it to pass. But it's draining and it's getting me down, especially as I long to talk to him about Amelia.

In any case, I haven't seen Samantha again. I don't want to antagonise Tom any further and I'm still upset about what happened with Amelia. I've gone round in circles trying to figure out why she would act like that and the only conclusion I've come to is that she's threatened by me. She doesn't like my growing friendship with Samantha and she wants me to back off. I've even considered whether the black SUV belongs to her and she's trying to intimidate me, but that doesn't make any sense. Why would following me convince me to stop seeing Samantha?

Maybe Tom's right. I don't want Amelia to win this ridiculous battle she's started, but it would be sensible to keep my distance. So I ignore Samantha's message, asking if I want to go for a walk, and try to get on with my life. Instead, I get in touch with Tamsin to see if she fancies a drink, which we arrange for the following week, and I take Frankie shopping to spend her birthday vouchers. Even when she tries on a skirt so short that it makes my eyes water, I don't have a go. She twirls around in front of the mirror, reminding me that my little girl is not so little any more and I must let her make these choices.

'You look beautiful, Frankie,' I tell her.

She beams at me. 'Yeah?'

'Definitely. Trying to impress someone?'

Frankie immediately shuts down and she turns away. 'No.'

I frown. I want to push her on it, to find out if she's seeing anyone, but I don't want to ruin this mother–daughter bonding moment. So instead, I bite my tongue and suggest lunch. In the afternoon, I offer to take Max to his football match so that Tom can chill out and Frankie surprises me by saying she wants to come too.

'But you hate watching Max play football.'

She shrugs. 'It's a nice day and I need some fresh air.'

I smile at my daughter. 'It would be lovely to have the company.'

'Give me five minutes.'

We're perilously close to being late, and Max is hopping impatiently from foot to foot when Frankie finally emerges, fifteen minutes later. She's wearing her new skirt and she looks like she's put on a hundred coats of mascara.

'Frankie, we're going to a football match, not a nightclub,' I say sternly.

'I wanted to wear my new things.'

We're in so much of a hurry that there's no time to tell her to go and change. 'Put on a coat at least,' I tell her, before opening the front door and dashing to the car. Max jumps in and a moment later Frankie climbs into the front passenger seat. She's added a cropped jacket to her outfit, but it does little to hide her flesh.

As we drive to the football ground where the match is taking place, I can't stop stealing glances at Frankie's bare legs. She's going to be freezing.

'Why are you so dressed up to see your brother play football?'

'I told you, I just want to wear my new stuff.'

'Everyone else will be in sportswear and jeans.'

Frankie shrugs.

'Are you hoping to see someone there?'

Frankie's face reddens but she doesn't answer.

'Frankie?' I'm getting increasingly confused – and annoyed.

Max pipes up from the back. 'She's got a crush on the new coach.'

My temper evaporates as I stifle a grin. Poor Frankie, she's got no chance with whoever this new coach is. He's probably some hot stud in his twenties.

'Shut up, Max,' Frankie snaps.

'Frankie and Jamie sitting in a tree...'

My stomach lurches. 'Jamie?'

'Yeah, that's the new coach's name. He's helping out at weekends.'

I glance sideways and take in Frankie's expression, which is a mixture of fury and guilt. Now my stomach takes a deep plunge.

'Is this the same Jamie that you bunked off school with?'

Max leans forward, straining against his seat belt. 'You bunked off school?'

We both ignore him.

'Frankie?' I demand, my voice stern.

'It's nothing,' she says. 'Don't make a thing of it.'

'Are you two going out?'

'No.'

'But you fancy him.'

'Shut up, Mum!'

This is the last thing I need. I thought that Jamie was out of the picture but now I realise that I was being naive. If Frankie knows that he's helping out with the primary school football team, then it means they still talk to each other. And not only do I disapprove because of his age and the influence he has on Frankie, I don't like it because it's messy, especially now that I'm avoiding Samantha.

Maybe I'm overreacting. Samantha was pretty certain that Jamie isn't into Frankie, although I'm not sure if he's told her that. I hope she's not going to get her heart broken. But Samantha could be wrong. She didn't give me any evidence to back up her claim and I was in such a state at the time, I didn't push her on it. I decide to watch them carefully at the match and see if I can tell whether Jamie's interested romantically. And I'll talk to Tom when we get home and see what he thinks. Perhaps this will help to smooth over the cracks that have been growing since he found out I was still seeing Samantha.

When we pull up in the car park, Frankie opens the sun visor and checks her reflection in the tiny mirror. Then she climbs out, one gangly limb after the other, and I grimace. This is going to be a long match.

The first person I see is Tamsin, who waves at me and then raises her eyebrows when she sees Frankie, who is hovering, looking nervous. Max dashes off to his team and I walk over to Tamsin, leaning in to hug her.

'Why is Frankie dressed up to the nines for a kids' football match?' Tamsin asks.

'She fancies the new football coach.'

Tamsin laughs. 'Which one? Show me.'

I look around and spot Jamie, standing by the usual team coach. 'There.'

Tamsin follows my gaze. 'Oh, he's cute. Do they know each other?'

'They go to the same school. Jamie's a couple of years older.' I lean in. 'He's Samantha's son.'

'Samantha?'

'The widow of the man who died in the car accident.'

Tamsin stares at me with her mouth open. 'What the—?'

'I know, right? It's a mess.'

'How did that happen?'

'They got talking at school.'

We both watch as Frankie makes her way over to the sidelines. Jamie sees her and smiles. He seems genuinely pleased to see her, but not in a lewd way. Not in the way that horrible man looked at me in the supermarket. I suppress a shudder as the memory resurfaces and try to concentrate on Jamie and Frankie. Jamie lifts up a hand to wave, but he's quickly distracted by a child pulling on his shirt.

'Do you think love is in the air?' Tamsin asks.

'I bloody hope not.'

'Yeah, it's a bit weird, isn't it. Is he a good kid?'

'Well, my only interaction with him was when I found him in my daughter's bedroom after they bunked off school...'

Tamsin snorts. 'A bad boy, then. We've all been there.'

She's right. I certainly had crushes on a wrong 'un or two in my day. But it doesn't mean I like the idea of my daughter going through it too. We stare at Frankie as she lurks by the sidelines, looking awkward, and I feel a motherly urge to protect her.

'Let's go and stand with Frankie,' I say.

We both go over to her and Tamsin, who has always got on

well with Frankie, manages to draw her into conversation. Then I notice Max gesturing at me and it takes me a minute to work out he's telling me that he left his water bottle in the car. I nod in understanding and traipse back across the field to the car park. I've located the bottle and I'm locking the car when I see a man standing by the clubhouse, watching me. I look away and then back again and he's still staring. I start to walk back towards the pitch but I'm ruffled now and I can feel his gaze. *Not again. Why is this happening to me?*

I risk a glance at the man and see that he has moved away from the clubhouse and is heading towards me. My body immediately stands to attention, battling between fight or flight. I don't know whether to stand my ground, run or scream. But then I come to my senses again. It's the middle of the day at a children's football match. He's probably coming over to ask me to move the car or something. I have to stop with this constant suspicion. I turn to him with a polite smile and wait to see what he has to say.

He stops a couple of feet away from me and smiles. 'Ellie, right?'

'Yes, that's right.'

'I know you.'

It's so similar to what the man in the supermarket said that my pulse quickens. But I'm determined not to freak out unnecessarily. Perhaps he's a school dad I've met once before, or a parent who frequents the same regular football matches that I do.

'I'm so sorry, I'm being very rude, but have we met?'

He laughs. 'You don't recognise me?'

I tuck a strand of hair behind my ear nervously. 'I'm sorry, I don't.'

'I'm surprised, I've got to say. I mean you were *very* intimate, if you get my drift. How many other men do you share messages like that with, not to remember me?'

What the hell is going on? I glance over to the sidelines and see Tamsin and Frankie deep in conversation. Neither of them are paying me any attention.

I turn back to the man, trying to conceal my fear. 'I think you've got the wrong person,' I say, acutely aware that I've been here before.

He looks at me quizzically. 'There's no need to be ashamed, Ellie.'

'I'm not ashamed, I don't *know* you,' I plead, my voice rising.

'That's not what you were saying two nights ago, love.'

I'm spiralling now. 'I've never met you and I've never spoken to you. You've made a mistake. Now if you'll excuse me, I need to...'

The man reaches into his pocket and for one, crazy second I think he's going to pull a knife or a gun on me. My entire life flashes before my eyes. But he brings out a phone instead, taps a few times and turns it to me so I can see the screen.

'Like I said, Ellie, no need to be embarrassed.'

I look at the screen and recoil. It's some sort of private messaging app, one I haven't seen before, and the conversation is between two people. You can see their profile photos and I recognise myself instantly. It's a photo that Tom took on my thirty-fifth birthday if I recall, and it's been my Facebook profile photo for years. I snatch the phone and scroll, reading with increased horror, the messages on the screen. Oh my God, they're explicit. I'm talking about doing intimate things to myself and he's reciprocating. I feel sick to the bone and I have no idea what to do, what to say.

I hand the phone back to him with shaking hands.

'That's not me,' I say.

'It looks like you, Ellie.'

'I didn't send those messages. That's a fake profile. Where did you find it?'

The man pales, realisation dawning. I must look as distraught as I feel because his entire stance changes. 'You're sure it wasn't you?'

'I'm absolutely sure. Where did you find it?'

He looks around and then leans in. 'It's an app for people who want to meet for no-strings sex. We've been chatting for days.'

'*We* haven't been chatting.'

'Look, there's no shame in it. I'm sorry if I embarrassed you by approaching you here, but you were on your own and I—'

'Stop,' I interrupt him. 'That wasn't me, okay? What is the name of the app?'

The man gives me the name and I hurry away without even saying goodbye. I can still feel him staring but it's the least of my worries. Someone has put a fake profile of me on a dodgy app, and I have no idea who would do that. Or why.

I'm a mess by the time I reach the sidelines. Tamsin smiles at me and then her face falls as she sees the state I'm in.

'What's wrong?' she asks.

I don't want to say in front of Frankie, so I whisper, 'Tell you later.'

It's not until Max comes running over, asking what took me so long, that I realise I'm still holding his water bottle. I don't know how I get through the next hour. I try to concentrate on the football match, but my head is all over the place. Then it starts raining and Frankie asks for the car keys so she can go and wait in the car. At least I don't need to worry about her and Jamie if she's out of sight. But all I can see is that photo of me on the man's phone, and the dirty messages I was allegedly sending him.

With Frankie out of the way, it's my opportunity to tell

Tamsin what happened but I can't get the words out. I'm ashamed, just like I was when it happened at the supermarket, even though I've done nothing wrong. I still feel disgusting, and I wonder whether it will keep happening to me, if the whole of Hertfordshire thinks I'm looking to pick up random men on the internet to hook up with. My God, this is horrendous.

Who would do this to me? That's all I can think. Who hates me enough to mess with me like this? Only two possibilities spring to mind. Someone connected to Jason Turner, or Amelia. After all, all this strange stuff started happening just after the accident. I consider both options. If it's to do with Jason, it's an unconventional tactic. But then the same goes for Amelia. She's told me to stay away from Samantha and I have, so what would be the benefit of doing this to me? So, it must be Jason.

But what's he playing at? Is he trying to intimidate me without threatening me directly? It still seems too obscure. Unless this is just the start?

But no, it's not the start. Being followed by the SUV was the start and this is phase two, I realise with sinking horror. And I dread to think what phase three might be.

I can't think like this, it's not going to help. I'm getting myself worked up into a right state and perhaps it's for no good reason. Tom said I was being paranoid about being followed and he'll probably say the same about this fake profile. I need to get home as soon as possible so I can report it and hopefully have it removed. They may even be able to tell me who created it in the first place. And I'll call the police too and tell them everything. I still haven't heard from them since I first reported the SUV but things have moved on since then and I'm sure they'll take me seriously now, especially given that I'm a witness in an upcoming court case.

Having a plan makes me feel marginally better but I can't

stave off the fear that's gripped me and I look around, convinced someone is watching me. Tamsin knows something's up but after asking me several times what the matter is, she gives up and drifts away to talk to some other mums. Finally, when the match finishes, Max comes running over, his face the picture of victory.

'Five–nil, Mum! Five–nil! Did you see my two goals?'

I kiss the top of his sweaty head. 'I did, and you were incredible. Well done, darling.'

I'm desperate to go home but Max delays our departure, chatting to his friends, who are oblivious to the driving rain as they celebrate their win. Tamsin keeps shooting me glances, but I don't engage. I need to process this myself first, then I'll talk to her.

When we finally reach the car, I'm expecting to see Frankie inside, looking bored. But the passenger seat is empty. My anger flares. This is the last thing I need. I just want to go home so that I can report that damn profile.

'Where's Frankie?' I ask Max and receive a shrug in response.

I look around the now sodden pitch, my damp hair sticking to my forehead, despite the umbrella I'm clutching, but there's no sign of Frankie.

'I'll check the clubhouse,' I say, storming off in the direction of the building and Max scuttles along behind me. She's probably snuck off to see Jamie, and after everything that's happened at this cursed match the idea of my daughter flirting with a boy – especially this one – is even more off-putting.

It doesn't take long to locate Frankie. She's leaning up against a wall, chatting with Jamie who, thank goodness, is maintaining a respectable distance. She scowls when she sees me and sends a warning look my way but I'm too riled to care.

'We're going home now, Frankie,' I say, my voice sharp.

Jamie turns to me and I'm struck again by the likeness to his father. And it's all just too much. The accident, the SUV, Amelia, being propositioned by strange men, this thing with Frankie and Jamie who happens to be the son of the man I saw die.

'Now, Frankie!' I scream hysterically, and the entire clubhouse falls silent.

Frankie pushes herself off the wall and barges past me, pure fury on her face. I'm in a world of trouble with her now but I don't care. I take one last look at Jamie, who is gazing at me, more curious than alarmed, turn on my heel and march back out into the rain. Max trots along just behind me, silenced by my outburst.

It doesn't take long for the shame to hit me. I embarrassed my children in public. I embarrassed myself. What is happening to me?

We climb into the car and I start the engine and drive away. Neither of my children speak to me and the atmosphere is frostier than ever. I want to apologise to them, to explain why I reacted in the way that I did, but how can I? I can't tell the kids what's going on and I'm still too upset to think straight.

Finally, I can't bear the chill any longer. 'I'm sorry,' I say. 'I shouldn't have shouted.'

'I can't believe you did that,' Frankie replies, looking out of the window.

'I know. I'm sorry.' I have no defence, so I don't try to give any. She wasn't doing anything wrong, she was just talking to a boy. I shouldn't have screamed at her like that. 'I'm sorry if I scared you too, Max,' I say.

'It's okay, Mummy.'

'You did so well at the match today. I'm really proud of you.'

'Thanks.'

It's not a permanent ceasefire but it'll do. Frankie gets out of the car as soon as we pull into the driveway and lets herself in, going straight up the stairs to her bedroom. Tom, who has come to the door to greet us, looks at me quizzically.

'What's up with Frankie?'

'It's a long story,' I say. 'But guess who scored two goals?!'

We make a fuss of Max who is delighted, having already moved on from my earlier outburst. And then, when he's warm, dry and comfy in front of the television with a snack, I look for and download the app the man told me about. But I can't search for profiles without signing up, and that's the last thing I want to do. I'm trying to decide what my next move should be when Tom walks in and heads to the fridge.

'Tom, I really need your help.'

He turns to me, his face full of concern. No matter what issues are bubbling under the surface between us, there's never been any doubt in my mind that Tom would be there for me if I needed him. And I sure as hell need him now.

I explain what happened at the football match and then show him the app. He takes the phone and studies it, his face scrunched up.

'And you're certain the photo was of you?'

'Yes, absolutely, I recognised it immediately. It's my Facebook profile pic.'

He stands up. 'Jeez, I need a beer. Want one?'

'Yes please.'

He gets two bottles out of the fridge, opens them and hands me one. Then he sits back down. 'It must be fraud. A fake profile set up to romance and then con money out of people. It's got a name, hasn't it? Catfishing?'

Hope surges. It's a dire situation when the idea of someone stealing my identity to commit crime is better than the alternative. 'You really think it could be that?'

'What else would it be?'

'I don't know. Ever since the accident, strange things have been happening. First that black SUV and now this. It's really freaking me out.'

'But you haven't seen the SUV again recently, have you?'

'No,' I admit. 'But then this has happened instead. It's one thing after another.'

'Look, I get why you're upset, I really do. This is absolutely horrible. But don't take it personally, El. It happens all the time and you're this week's unfortunate victim. Here's what we'll do. We'll report this profile as fake and then you need to check all your social media profiles and make sure they're set to private.'

In that moment I love Tom more than ever.

'Thank you,' I tell him. 'I was in a right state and you've really calmed me down.'

He nods. 'Right, let's see how we can report this profile. I'll download it on my own phone and create an account.'

While Tom does some sleuthing, I open each social media app on my phone, one by one. I delete my X and Facebook profiles, reasoning that I rarely use them anyway, and I set my Instagram to private. I'm never letting anyone steal my identity again, it's horrible and violating. But I feel so much better now I know it wasn't targeted.

Tom pulls a face and looks at me, and I know what he's seen. He's found my fake profile. I snatch the phone off him and gasp as I see my photograph, along with my age, height, location and a description of why I'm on the app. Other than that particular description, most of the information is accurate, give or take a couple of inches. Sickened, I give the phone back to Tom.

'Don't read it,' I urge him. 'Please.'

'I won't,' he says, his eyes skimming the page.

'Just report it and let's forget this ever happened.'

'Doing it now.'

Tom takes a screenshot of my profile, then sends a message to the company, reporting it as fake. 'I'll keep my account on there for now, so we can check that they've deleted it,' he says.

'Good idea. How long do you think it'll take?'

'God knows. At least a few days, I'd imagine.'

'I feel sick at the thought of people recognising me.'

'It's only happened once, El.'

'It's happened twice.'

Tom's expression shifts. 'What? When was the first time?'

When I tell him about the supermarket incident, he's cross with me. 'Why didn't you tell me about it at the time?'

'I was really shaken up, and then we argued about Samantha, and after that it all went downhill. I'm so sorry, Tom. It will never happen again.'

'So, two strange men have propositioned you and you're only telling me now?'

'The first time I genuinely thought it was a mistake. It was only when it happened again today that I realised it couldn't be.'

Tom's face relaxes a fraction. 'That makes sense. But enough, Ellie. We're supposed to be a team, and we can't be that if you keep things from me.'

I reach out and take his hand. 'I know. I'm sorry. I love you.'

My phone beeps and when I pick it up, I can see a message from Samantha.

'It's Samantha,' I tell Tom immediately. 'I haven't seen her for a couple of weeks and I didn't respond to her last message.'

'What does she want now?'

I open the message and read it.

Ellie, are you okay? Jamie just got home and told me you seemed really upset. You haven't responded to my message either. I'm worried about you. S x

I show the screen to Tom, who reads it.

'Why was Jamie at Max's football match?' he asks.

'That's another long story.'

Tom takes a sip of his beer. 'I'm not in a rush.'

And so I tell him everything. About Frankie and Jamie and what happened at Samantha's house. And the more I talk, the more I realise what a fool I've been. I shouldn't be confiding in Samantha, or even Tamsin. I should be confiding in Tom. I'm so, so lucky to have him. And just because I feel bad for Samantha because she's lost her husband, it doesn't mean I should mess things up with mine.

Tom is incredulous. 'So let me get this straight, Samantha's best mate *threatened* you?'

'Pretty much, yes.'

'Why would she do that?'

'I have no idea. I think she's just really possessive over Samantha.'

'I'd stay well away from this Amelia.'

'I agree, which is why I haven't responded to Samantha's last message.' I look down at my phone. 'And I won't respond to this one either.'

'You have to respond.'

I look at Tom quizzically. 'You're the one who told me not to contact her.'

'I know, and I've been thinking about it a lot. I know you were messed up after the accident. And while I still don't understand why you would want to become friends with this man's widow, I can see that it's helping you.'

'You can?'

'Yes. Despite all this weird stuff that's been going on, you seem a bit lighter. Happier. So if this relationship is working for you, who am I to stand in the way? Especially as she might be our daughter's future mother-in-law.'

'Stop!' I hate the idea but then I see the look on Tom's face and I can't help but laugh. It feels good. This whole situation is getting out of hand, but the chink of light after what has been a dark day is a tonic. And I try to ignore my internal alarm warning me that it's not as straightforward as Tom is making it out to be. That I am not the unfortunate victim of a scam and it's personal. I don't want to hear it. I *can't* hear it.

'Thank you for understanding,' I tell Tom earnestly.

'It's okay. Her friend sounds like a psycho though.'

'She really is. You don't think this catfishing thing is actually her, do you?'

'No, surely not? Why would she do that?'

'I really don't know. I thought maybe it was her following me in the SUV too.'

'That's a bit far-fetched. And I thought we'd agreed that it wasn't following you in the end anyway. I'd just stay out of her way and hopefully she'll do the same.'

'I hope so. I mean I don't see Samantha that often. It's not like we're besties.'

Tom stands up. 'Another beer?'

'Let's have some wine. It is Saturday evening after all.'

We open the bottle and go to join Max in the living room. Soon after, Frankie comes down, complaining about being hungry and we decide to order pizza. As we all tuck in, the stress of the day starts to drain away from me. With the rain still hammering down outside, it feels cosy in the house. Safe and secure, surrounded by my family. It's like no one can get to me in here, in this cocoon I've wrapped myself in.

But later that night, just as I'm about to climb into bed, pleasantly tipsy and hoping for a good night's slumber, my phone beeps again. I reach for it, wondering if it's Samantha following up on her message which I still haven't replied to, but it's an unknown number. And when I see what's on the screen, I understand two things with horrific clarity. One, that my gut was right all along, and this is a personal attack.

And two, that I'm not even safe in my own home, and neither is my family.

11

I watch from the window as Paula, my witness care officer, climbs into her car and reverses off the driveway. I'm still looking at the street, even after she's gone.

Tom comes up behind me. 'We did the right thing.'

I turn to him, but I can't muster a smile. 'I know.'

I called Paula first thing on Monday morning. I hadn't slept all weekend because I was afraid to close my eyes. Afraid of letting my guard down for a second.

The message had no words. It was a fake photograph of me and a man, created using AI. I'm naked and so is he and I'm performing a crude sex act on him. And the worst thing is that it's taking place in our living room, which means that whoever has created this vile image has been to our property. They have stood outside our window and taken a photograph of the inside of our home. And I have no idea whether this photo is also doing the rounds on the internet. I can't help but think someone wants to destroy my reputation. To destroy me.

After I called Paula, she was at the house within an hour,

along with another police officer. I told them everything and they are looking into it. They've also promised to patrol our road regularly and keep an eye on things. But even as Paula reassured me, I could see something in her expression which made me think she wasn't completely convinced this was linked to the court case. If it was just the mysterious black SUV following me, she might be more inclined to think the lorry driver is to blame. But my fake profile on the dating app and this vile image has muddied the waters.

'It must be witness intimidation,' I had said, desperate for her to agree. 'They want to make me look untrustworthy or to scare me into silence.'

'It might be,' she had replied diplomatically.

The other officer, who was watching me closely, had interjected. 'Is there anyone else you can think of who might be responsible? An ex of yours perhaps?'

I had shaken my head. 'My husband and I have been together for nearly twenty years. I doubt any of my exes even remember me any more and I certainly didn't have any break-ups that were so unpleasant anyone would want to do this.'

'Have you ever been on a dating website or app?'

'No, absolutely not.'

'Is there anyone else you can think of who might want to cause trouble for you?'

Amelia. If Jason isn't behind this, then it can only be her. Would she really be so cruel and nasty just because I've befriended Samantha?

'I can't think of anyone,' I had replied because if I blamed Amelia and I was wrong, it would throw a cat among the pigeons and I don't want to cause any more trouble for Samantha, not after everything she's been through. And I don't want to give Amelia another reason to hate me either.

Now that the officers have left and it's just me and Tom, I can let my mask down. I slump on to the sofa, exhausted, and Tom sits beside me. 'I'm so sorry you're going through this,' he says, stroking my hand.

'*We're* going through it,' I correct. 'It affects us all.'

'It's disgusting what they're doing. I just don't understand why anyone would be so cruel. It must be connected to the lorry driver after all, just like you said. And it shows just what an unpleasant person he really is if he's letting this happen.'

'I think so too, and hopefully the police will prove it. I'm starting to wonder if it's all worth it though, Tom. If I just withdraw my statement, this will all go away.'

'That's exactly what he wants you to do, Ellie. Don't give in.'

'But I don't feel safe any more and I'm scared for the children too. I don't know what this person might do next, especially given they know where we live.'

'We'll pick the kids up from school every day until this is resolved. We won't let them out of our sight.'

'Frankie will hate that.'

'Frankie will get over it. Her safety is more important than her independence. But listen, let's leave the police to do their job, there's nothing more we can do right now. Why don't we go for a walk? We could both do with some fresh air.'

I don't want to go out. I'm scared and I'm also embarrassed. What if everyone has seen that fake photo? What if it's trending on the internet right now?

As if he can read my thoughts, Tom leans in. 'Don't spiral, Ellie. It'll be okay.'

'You don't know that.'

'Look, if it is the lorry driver or his cronies, and I'm convinced now that it must be, I don't think they would harm you. They just want to scare you into silence or to make you look untrustworthy when you give evidence. They're messing with you.'

'It's so unfair!'

'Yes, it is. But you must show that you are not intimidated and the only way you can do that is to go on living your life. You can't become a prisoner in your own home.'

I nod slightly but don't move from the sofa.

Tom stands up. 'Come on, El, it's a nice day. Let's go out.'

'I really don't want to.'

'I know, but the sooner you do it, the better you'll feel.'

He reaches out a hand and I reluctantly let him pull me up from the sofa. I slip on my shoes and coat and grip on to Tom's hand as we leave the house. The children are at school and we've both taken the day off work, so we have a rare few hours alone together. I should make the most of it, but it feels like anything but a treat.

'Let's stroll into town and have a mooch,' he suggests.

I walk with my head lowered, anxious about making eye contact with anyone. At the same time, I'm wondering if someone is watching us. I'm hoping Frankie and Max are okay, even though I knew they're safe at school. I think of the photo and feel sick.

And I wish to God that I had never witnessed that accident.

More than that, I wish that it had never happened at all.

The abrupt sound of my phone ringing almost gives me a heart attack and my heart rate only slows when I realise it's just Samantha calling. Guilt piles on top of my anguish. I still haven't replied to the worried message she sent me a couple of days ago.

'It's Samantha,' I tell Tom. He nods and I answer the phone. 'Hi.'

'Ellie. Are you okay? I've been really worried about you.'

'I'm not really okay,' I reply, my voice shaking.

'What is it? What's happened?'

I fill her in, glad at least that I can talk freely to Samantha in front of Tom now.

Samantha is horrified. 'Oh my God, Ellie, that's awful. Have you called the police?'

'Yes, they've been round this morning. They're looking into it.'

'That bastard.' Samantha is seething and I wonder if her rage is on my behalf or her own. 'It has to be Jason Turner. He's trying to scare you. And after all he's done.'

'Paula – that's my witness care officer – seemed a bit uncertain. I guess it's not the usual intimidation tactics.'

'Believe me, I've seen many tactics in my career, but they all have one thing in common when it comes to intimidating women. They want to belittle you, to defile you and to diminish you. It's disgusting but it works. It forces women to stay silent, because they are scared for themselves and their families.'

'What if it's not him though?'

'Who else would it be?'

There it is again. The million-dollar question. I don't want to tell her that Amelia is the only other person I can think of, but it's on the tip of my tongue and I can't bite it.

'What car does Amelia drive?'

'What? Why are you asking me that?'

'I'm just curious.'

'A Mini Cooper.'

I close my eyes. Not an SUV then.

'Ellie, surely you don't think Amelia has anything to do with this?'

'No of course not,' I lie. 'I just thought I saw her in town the other day.'

Samantha is quiet for a moment. 'Do you want to get a coffee?'

'I'm with Tom. Maybe later in the week?'

'Yes, of course. Call me if there's anything I can do.'

'Likewise.'

I hang up and look at Tom. 'She thinks it's to do with the court case too.'

'There we go then.'

'I hope we hear from the police soon. I just want all this to go away.'

'Me too. I'll work from home as much as possible so I can help pick up the kids.'

'I'll speak to my boss too, we'll work something out.'

Tom squeezes my hand. 'It's not forever, love. It's just temporary.'

We walk in silence, both lost in our thoughts. I'm thinking about court again now. There's four months to go and after feeling like life was on pause, time is now speeding up. Visions race though my mind of having to go into witness protection until then. Uprooting our family and moving to some remote cottage with twenty-four-hour security. But I push them away. I'm being melodramatic. I am not a key witness in an organised crime case and this is not a television drama. But it's starting to feel like it is.

We reach the town centre, and when Tom suggests lunch I reluctantly agree. We find a little café, tucked away on a side street and sit at the back. I can feel myself scanning the other diners, looking to see if anyone is staring. Trying to guess if they've seen the photo of me. And then I force myself to focus on the menu. I'm not in the slightest bit hungry but I know I need to eat.

We've just ordered when my phone rings, startling me again.

My nerves are frayed and I wonder if I'll ever stop being jumpy. When I see it's Frankie's school, my heart starts pounding, and I almost drop my phone in my haste to answer.

'Hello?'

'Mrs Appleby?'

'Speaking.'

'This is Linda from the school office. Frankie isn't at school today and we didn't get a call or email from you, so we're checking in to make sure everything is okay.'

My stomach sinks to the floor. 'Are you sure she's not at school?'

'Yes, she wasn't at registration and we haven't seen her all morning. We sent you a text message but you didn't respond, which is why I'm calling.'

How did I miss it? But I've been distracted all morning and I haven't checked my messages. The walls close in on me as worst-case scenarios flood my mind. This can't be happening. Please tell me this isn't happening. 'Oh my God.'

Tom looks at me in alarm and Linda hears my panic too. 'When did you last see Frankie?' she asks, her usually friendly tone now alarmingly professional and serious.

'This morning. My husband dropped her at the school gates. Oh my God.'

Tom is already reaching for his phone, having got the gist of the conversation. At first, I think he's calling 999 but then I realise he's opened the Find My app to look for Frankie's location. She has a GPS tracker on the watch she wears.

'We need to alert the police immediately,' Linda says.

'Hold on,' I reply, as Tom is mouthing something to me.

'I can see her location,' Tom says. 'She's at the park.'

'My husband has tracked her location,' I tell Linda. 'We're going there now. I'll call you back in a few minutes.'

I hang up and we rush out of the café without even cancelling our order. I have never known such raw fear. If something has happened to Frankie, I will not be able to cope. This is my worst nightmare. We run as fast as we can towards the park which, thankfully, is only a few minutes away. I can barely breathe by the time we get there and it is pure fear and adrenaline that keeps my legs moving.

Tom pauses to check his phone. 'I don't have an exact location but we're close.'

I look around, taking in the park, the lake, the wooded area.

'What if he's got her, Tom? What if he's hurt her?'

'Stop.' Tom sounds angry but I know it's really fear in his voice. 'Thinking like that isn't going to help. Let's focus our efforts on finding Frankie.'

'Should we call the police?'

'Let's give it a few minutes, and if we haven't found her we'll call.'

We start running around the park, shouting Frankie's name. Tom stops a couple of passers-by to show them a photograph of Frankie and asks if they've seen her, but they shake their heads apologetically. I'm about to call the emergency services when a woman walking her dog looks at the phone Tom is proffering and nods in recognition.

'I've just seen her,' she says. 'She was sitting on the steps to the bandstand with a couple of boys. They caught my eye as they were wearing school uniform.'

We thank the woman and race towards the bandstand. Relief is pouring over me. Frankie's okay. She's alive. The world is rushing back into focus again. But I can't truly believe it until I see her with my own eyes. Only then will I know Frankie is safe.

As we get closer to the bandstand, three figures come into view. I see Frankie and I almost crumple to the ground, my tired legs screaming in agony. But I keep going because I need to see her close up to really know she's okay.

It's only once we reach her that I notice who she's with. And then it all becomes clear exactly what's happened. Frankie hasn't been abducted, she's bunked off school again to be with Jamie and Marcus. And although I'm so thankful that she's okay, although I know that's what I should be focusing on, my pumping fear and adrenaline need an outlet and they morph into a hot and uncontrollable rage.

I've just been through the worst twenty minutes of my life, because Frankie decided to skip school to hang out with boys again. I'm going to kill her.

Frankie's face pales when she sees us. She glances quickly at her watch, realising that we've tracked her location. Then she stands up and, next to her, Jamie does the same. Only Marcus remains seated, his head bowed, refusing to meet my eye. He looks extremely uncomfortable and I remember Samantha saying that he's a studious boy. Not the type to bunk off, I suspect. I'm so upset and angry that I don't think I can speak.

Tom reaches them first and stops, with his hands on his hips, as breathless as I am. 'What are you doing, Frankie?' His voice is cold. His fear has also become fury.

Jamie speaks first. 'This is all my fault,' he says, holding his hands up in a conciliatory manner. 'I was really upset, and Frankie has been taking care of me.'

Tom's eyes pivot from Frankie to Jamie.

'Who are you?' he demands, and Jamie, to his credit, doesn't flinch.

'I'm Jamie. I'm Frankie's friend.' He places the emphasis on the word 'friend'. 'This is my brother Marcus. We were in a bad way this morning, it's our dad's birthday you see, and we...'

Realisation dawns on Tom's face at the same time as I understand what he's saying. It's Graham's birthday. Probably the first significant milestone since he died. My anger deflates like a balloon as a wave of sorrow overcomes me, and I can see Tom sag beside me too. Because how can we scream and shout, and rant and rave, when these poor boys have recently lost their father? I feel bad for being abrupt with Samantha on the phone now too. She had probably wanted to meet for coffee because she was upset and needed company.

My phone rings. It's the school calling again and I step away to answer, explaining to Linda that we've found Frankie, and I tell her who she's with.

'They're safe,' I tell her. 'That's the main thing.'

'Thank goodness. We were extremely worried and I'm so relieved that they are all okay. I didn't know that they were friends, with them being in different school years, so we didn't make the connection that they might be together. I will need to speak to the headteacher about this though.'

'Do your worst,' I say. 'Seriously, I mean it. I want Frankie to understand that this behaviour is not acceptable. That will be the message from us too, I can assure you.'

Linda's tone is soft, understanding. 'I'm just so glad she's okay. I can't imagine how worried you must have been.'

'Thank you. I'm bringing her straight back to school now. Jamie and Marcus too.'

I hang up and return to the bandstand.

'We're going back to school,' I say, looking at Frankie. 'We'll talk about this later.'

The teenagers don't argue. They pick up their bags and follow us, meekly, out of the park. Marcus maintains a slight distance, his eyes on the ground, refusing to engage. Tom hangs back a bit to talk with Jamie and I take the opportunity to speak to Frankie. I'm still shaking but I've calmed down enough to have a conversation with her.

'What are you doing, Frankie?' I say softly.

'They were really upset, Mum.'

'I know. But they had each other, and you know you can't just skip school. We were so worried about you, Frankie. We thought you'd been abducted.'

She glances sideways at me. 'Why would you think that?'

I don't want to tell her the truth because it will frighten her. 'Because we didn't know where you were. You're supposed to be at school. When the office called, I thought the worst. Please don't ever do this again.'

She must sense the desperation in my tone because she doesn't give me any sass. If anything, she looks shamefaced. 'I'm sorry, Mum. I won't.'

There is so much more to say but now is not the time. Tom and Jamie have caught up with us, with Marcus trailing behind, and we walk in silence for the rest of the journey to the school, depositing the children at the office and talking briefly to Linda. Jamie thanks us but Marcus just nods and disappears into the building.

'What will happen to them?' I ask Linda.

'I haven't had a chance to speak to the headteacher yet, but I'll explain the circumstances.'

'She won't be suspended, will she?'

'I very much doubt it. This is a unique situation and I think the headteacher will be sympathetic to that.' She leans in and whispers, 'My money's on a detention.'

We thank Linda and make our way home, all thoughts of lunch gone.

'Well, that was horrific,' I say.

'Tell me about it.'

'What do we do now?'

'We'll talk to Frankie when we get home. I think two weeks of being grounded will get the message across. And, to be honest, give us some peace of mind after you were sent that photograph. I have to say though, despite everything, Jamie is a nice boy.'

I look at him incredulously. 'The boy who's leading our daughter astray?'

'I know, I know. But he's going through a lot.'

The habitual guilt stabs me in the chest again. We may be dealing with a wayward teenager but at least we're able to do it together. At least Tom is here, with me. And after the day I've had, it takes all my strength to bite back my tears.

'His brother's a bit surly though, isn't he?' Tom continues. 'He didn't say a word.'

'Samantha says he's a serious, brooding type. I didn't even know Frankie was friends with him. Speaking of Samantha, should I call her?'

'I'd let the school speak to her first.'

'You're right. Shall we just go home?'

'Yes, I think so.'

We walk slowly, taking time to recover from our ordeal. When we get back Tom checks the dating app, and my profile is still live.

'Be patient,' he says. 'I doubt they deal with anything quickly.'

'I'm going to email my boss now and ask to work from home for a while.'

I open my own laptop and begin drafting the email. But I can't concentrate. Even writing a sentence is difficult. All I want to do is go to bed and hide from the world. It feels like everything is going wrong and it's just so overwhelming.

You can't become a prisoner in your own home.' That's what Tom said to me. But it's all I want now. To sleep until the trial is over.

And as I give up on writing the email, I consider calling Paula and telling her that I want to withdraw my statement, despite Tom telling me not to. I'll just say that I can't really remember what happened after all and I might have been wrong. If I do that, then all of this will stop.

Because it's now clear to me that whoever is doing this is ramping up their efforts. And I really don't want to find out what they've got in store for me next.

12

Three months to go. A clock is ticking incessantly in my consciousness, a countdown to the trial. And not a day has passed when I haven't considered simply running away.

We're muddling through though, Tom and I. We're juggling work with taking Max and Frankie to school and picking them up every day. It's not sustainable but my boss has been extremely sympathetic and so has Tom's. We're making it work for now.

Frankie escaped with a week's worth of detentions for skipping school and she's been on her best behaviour ever since. We grounded her and she accepted her punishment without a fuss. She thinks we're driving her to school because we don't trust her and we're happy to let her think that because the real reason is too horrible.

The police have found no link between any of the incidents and Jason. The SUV is not his, the phone that sent the photograph to me is unregistered, and he willingly gave up his electronic devices, which showed that he didn't set up my fake profile. But nothing else has happened since and so I reckon it was him, or his friends, after all, and the visit from the police scared him off. I'm so thankful that life is returning to normality but I'm on edge all the time. I'm waiting for the next thing to happen. The next threat or worse. And even an increased police presence doesn't make me feel safer.

My fake profile has been removed but the police don't seem to have made any progress in finding out who set it up in the first place. I guess there are hoops to jump through to get the information and I'm not top priority in the grand scheme of things. But that's difficult to stomach when it's having such a profound impact on my life. Sometimes, when I lie in bed at night, I can picture those men looking at me, and my imagination contorts their faces into evil, monstrous expressions, putting me into a cold sweat. I wonder if they've also seen the AI photo of me on some dodgy porn site and laughed to themselves at how I prudishly spurned their advances. I still haven't been back to the supermarket and every time I go into town, I'm convinced everyone has seen the photo and is looking at me.

Samantha called me the day after Frankie and the boys were caught bunking off school to apologise. She was mortified and I ended up reassuring her and telling her that I wasn't angry. We haven't seen much of each other since then because Marcus and Jamie are in the middle of their GCSE exams, so she's got her hands full. But we text all the time, checking in on each other, sharing snippets of our day. Last night we were on the phone for over an hour, talking about anything and everything. Tom raised his eyebrows when I returned to the living room, clutching my phone, but he didn't say anything. I'm thankful that at least our row about Samantha is well and truly over. And I think our heart to heart at the pub a couple of months back has reopened the door of communication between us. We finally shared our own, personal struggles and acknowledged that we've isolated ourselves from each other. I realise now that Tom didn't know how much I was struggling because I never told him, and so it's unfair of me to blame him for not being supportive. We are a proper team again and it's a ray of light in what is an otherwise bleak situation.

Every time I ask Frankie how Jamie is, she shrugs and says she doesn't know. I see the disappointment etched on her face and I wonder if Samantha has told Jamie not to contact her or if his silence is simply because he's knee-deep in studying for his exams. Either way I'm pleased, to be honest, but I feel bad for Frankie. I know how painful the first intense crush can be. I just wish she'd had it on someone else. I quizzed her about Marcus too but she said she didn't really know him and she wasn't friends with him. I wonder now if he was just tagging along on the day they played truant, perhaps wanting to be with his brother on what was a difficult day for them.

At least the sun is shining, lifting everyone's mood. We went away to the south of France for a few days in the May half-term and we all enjoyed a change of scene. It felt so good to be away from home, in a place where I didn't have to watch my back constantly. Where I could sit outside with a glass of wine and some delicious food and just be with my family. But the dread returned as soon as we touched down at the airport and it followed me all the way home again. It's like I've been covered with a heavy, impenetrable blanket. Ever since, I've been fantasising about selling up and relocating to France for a fresh start. I want, more than anything, to put all of this behind me.

There's something else, too. My mind is playing tricks on me again. It's rewriting history, spinning me around in circles until I no longer know how to ground myself. What if I'm wrong about what I saw? What if this wasn't Jason's fault? What if he's threatening me because he's angry that I've blamed him for something he didn't do? Is his revenge justified? And then I go off on other tangents. Surely his actions since the accident prove that he's vindictive. That he's so desperate to stop me telling the truth he'll go to deplorable lengths to shut me up. How far is he prepared to go?

Round and round I go, like a merry-go-round of terror.

Yet, life must go on. I can't show the children what a state I'm in. They need normality: homework and friends and clubs. And so I put on a brave face and go about my day. I paint over the cracks and wonder how long the patch-up will last before I break. I've been avoiding my friends, so when I see Tamsin standing at the sidelines when I go to pick up Max from football practice, I'm nervous about approaching her. I haven't responded to her last two messages. I force myself to go up to her and nudge her gently.

'Hey you.'

She looks at me, her face creased with concern and annoyance. 'Hello, stranger.'

'I'm so sorry I haven't been in touch.'

'What's going on? It's unlike you to go to ground.'

'I've had a lot on my plate. And it's all been a bit much.'

Tamsin's face softens and her sympathy tips me over the precarious edge I've been teetering on. My tears are instant, hot and urgent.

'Oh, love.' Tamsin puts her arm around me. 'Come on, let's go to the car. The boys have another twenty minutes of practice.'

She leads me to the car park and we climb into her Nissan. I inhale the familiar scent of upholstery and cheese-flavoured crisps and cry until my tears are finished.

'What is it?' Tamsin asks.

I tell her everything. About the photograph, talking to the police, Frankie going missing. And her eyes are as wide as saucers by the time I've finished.

'Oh my God, Ellie, why didn't you tell me sooner?'

'I don't know, I just didn't want to face it all, I guess.'

'You must have been terrified.'

'I was. I am.'

'But nothing has happened since, you say?'

'No, it's all gone quiet.'

'Then it must have been witness intimidation and the police have put a stop to it.'

'That's what Tom and I think too. But the police can't prove it was Jason.'

'It doesn't mean it wasn't.'

'I know.' I wipe my wet cheeks. 'But I'm scared, Tamsin. I almost rescinded my statement.'

'Maybe you should.'

I look at Tamsin in alarm. Up until now, she's been the one telling me to stick to my guns. 'Are you serious?'

'Look, you got mixed up in all of this through no fault of your own, and the safety of your family is the most important thing.'

'*Help.*' Graham's plea again. The words that aren't even real.

'I don't know what to do,' I cry.

'Oh, Ellie.' Tamsin puts her arm around me again. 'What a mess. Are the police at least keeping an eye on things?'

'Yes, they've been patrolling our road.'

'Good. And that car you kept seeing? Any sign of it?'

'Not for weeks. And the fake profile of me on the app has been removed.'

'Okay.' Tamsin nods with more certainty than I feel. 'So maybe it's all calmed down. Hey, do you want to stay at mine for a few weeks? All of you? It's no problem.'

'Thank you, but I want to keep things normal for the kids.'

'Sure, well the offer is there, any time. Just turn up if you need to.'

'Thanks, Tamsin.'

'It'll all be over soon, mate. And I reckon this man will be going to prison for a while.'

'If he's found guilty.'

'Of course he'll be found guilty. He did it. And hopefully he'll be charged for what he's doing to you too. It's just horrible.'

'They can't prove it, Tamsin.'

'Yet. They can't prove it yet.'

'You know, I sometimes think it could have happened to anyone.'

Tamsin looks at me, confused. 'What do you mean? The accident?'

'Well, with murder, that's intent, right? You've got to want to actually kill someone. But death by dangerous driving is different. A brief lapse of concentration and you could cause an accident that leads to someone dying. It could have been you, me, Tom.'

Tamsin frowns. 'But it wasn't any of us. It was the lorry driver.'

'Yes but my point is, what if he doesn't deserve this?'

'Surely his recent actions prove that he does. And anyway, even if it was a mistake, he killed a man. He ruined another family's life. He has to pay for that.'

'You're right,' I concede. 'I just hate that I'm the one making that decision.'

'You're not making the decision, mate. You're telling the court what you saw. The rest is down to the other evidence, the lawyers, the jury and the judge. Don't put this entire burden on yourself, it'll tie you in unnecessary knots.'

It already is. 'Aaaargh,' I scream in frustration.

'It'll be over soon. Just remember that.'

'I'm thinking about running away to France.'

Tamsin laughs. 'Well, that's one way to deal with it. Not sure you'll get the rest of your family on board though. Come on, the boys are nearly finished. Let's go.'

'Give me a minute.' I check my reflection in the visor mirror. I look awful but at least I don't have panda eyes. We get out of the car and head back to the field, just in time to see the boys running over, with beaming smiles and sweaty faces. At least Max is completely oblivious to what's been going on. He's living his best life, scoring goals and playing with his friends. He's growing up so fast and soon he'll be getting ready to leave primary school too. At least this time next year things will be very different. The trial will be well behind us and hopefully we'll be in a better place. I don't want to wish time away, but I'd do anything to fast-forward a few months.

'Hey, shall we go and get some dinner?' Tamsin suggests.

The boys cheer and I shrug. 'Why not. Tom's at home with Frankie.'

I send Tom a quick message to tell him the plan and then we leave the cars in the car park and walk to the high street, choosing a restaurant that's popular with the kids. Tamsin and I order some chips and garlic bread to share, while the boys tuck into their dinner. Slowly, I begin to unwind. Tamsin is great company and the children are having a blast. I shouldn't have shut myself off from the world like I did. Getting out and about is what I need to feel better, just like I felt when we went away to France. When I'm at home, with too much time to think, that's when I unravel. And I remind myself that there's nothing to be afraid of any more because all the incidents have stopped.

Maybe, I think tentatively, I'm over the worst of it.

I scan the busy restaurant to make sure no one is watching but it's full of other families and groups of friends enjoying themselves. Life is as it should be. Nothing to fear.

It's still light by the time we leave the restaurant and walk back to pick up our cars. The boys race on ahead and I stroll slowly with Tamsin, enjoying the warm evening.

'Thanks for this,' I say. 'And I'm sorry I've been a bit rubbish recently.'

'Don't be silly. Now I know what's been going on, I understand. I just wish you'd talked to me sooner.'

'I know, me too. I'm feeling a lot better already.'

'The offer to stay with us still stands, okay?'

'Thank you.'

'And don't suffer alone. You have a lot of people who care about you.'

We reach the cars, and I hug Tamsin goodbye and then Max and I jump in.

'Did you have a good time, darling?'

'The best!'

It's only a short drive to the house and the journey is filled with Max's chatter. I'm looking forward to getting home, putting on a tracksuit and relaxing. Maybe I'll go into the office tomorrow. Tom can pick up Frankie and I'm sure Tamsin wouldn't mind dropping Max home. I need to reconnect with life, see my colleagues again. But as I begin to pull into our driveway, my eyes are immediately drawn to our garage and the red paint that has been daubed across the white door. And as I process what I'm seeing, my foot slams down on the brakes, bringing us to a shuddering stop. A coldness seeps down my spine as I read what it says over and over again. And then I wrench open the car door, lurch to the bushes and throw up the food I've just eaten.

One solitary word has been smeared on our garage.

Liar

13

The police arrive within half an hour. They stand in our driveway, looking at the red paint, asking me questions. Did anyone see anything? Hear anything? Do we have any cameras? They knock on our neighbours' doors asking the same questions, looking for any smart doorbells or security cameras. Even when they've finished asking their questions, a patrol car remains in our street. It should reassure me but I'm beyond that.

Tom and Frankie were in the house when it happened. *In the house.* It horrifies me. They were in the kitchen, making dinner together and listening to the radio. They didn't hear a thing and they didn't even know it had happened until I staggered through the door, ashen-faced, and told them not to go out the front.

But Max saw it. And as we waited for the police, he had a lot of questions. *'What's the paint? Why does it say "liar"? Who's a liar? Who did it?'* And then it was impossible to hide it from Frankie either. So now everyone knows. Even our neighbours.

I'm a liar. That's what the message means. But I'm not, I know I'm not. Am I?

'What's going on, Mum?' Frankie demands.

'Nothing,' I say. 'It's vandals. I told you there's been a spate of crime in the area.'

'It doesn't look like random graffiti.'

'No, but that's what it is. Random graffiti.'

Frankie looks at me with shrewd eyes. She knows I'm fibbing, but she hasn't made the connection yet and I hope she doesn't. I don't want her to be upset too.

'Now that the police have been, I'm going to clean it up,' Tom says, standing up.

'I'll come and help.'

We leave the children inside, gather some things from the shed and go out to try to wash off the graffiti. At first it seems to make it worse, the red paint smearing and getting all over our hands and our clothes. But Tom puts some alcohol on a cloth and starts scrubbing and eventually it begins to come off. I'm conscious of curtain twitchers in the street, watching us, but I need this horrible message gone.

'This has gone too far,' Tom says, scrubbing furiously at the garage.

'I know. Do you think we should stay somewhere else?'

'Maybe, I'm not sure. Let's see what the police say first.'

'Tom, I think I should refuse to be a witness.'

Tom pauses, his hand poised mid-air. 'It's too late for that, Ellie.'

'It's not too late. They can't force me.'

'I don't know, maybe they can. And even if you refuse to take the stand, they still have your statement.'

'I'll say I've changed my mind, that I was wrong about what I saw.'

Tom puts the cloth down and turns to me. 'But you weren't wrong.'

'I just can't take it any more.'

'Look, I get it. I'm as upset as you are. But you're not a liar. And this intimidation is unacceptable. This man is a monster and this just proves it.'

'I'm so sorry, Tom. I'm just so sorry.'

'Stop that.' Tom puts his arms around me. 'This isn't your fault.'

'It is my fault. If it wasn't for me, we wouldn't be in this position.'

'You haven't done anything wrong, love. It's not your fault you witnessed an accident. No, this is all his fault. And he will pay for it.'

'Tamsin offered for us to all go and stay with her.'

'It's very generous of her, but it's still ages until the trial. That's too much of an imposition. Anyway, I don't want to be driven out of our home.' Tom glances behind his shoulder. 'The police car is still here.'

'I know and I'm pleased. But it's drawing even more attention to us. Goodness knows what the neighbours must think.'

'Who cares what the neighbours think?'

He's right, the neighbours are the least of our problems. But I'm overthinking everything now, each thought transforming into another uncontrollable worry.

Tom backs away and looks at the garage. 'That's most of it gone. Let's leave it for now and I'll repaint it tomorrow.'

'Don't you have to work?'

'I'll get up early and do it. We all need this gone.'

'Thank you, Tom.'

'Of course.'

Tom heads inside and I hurry after him, not wanting to be alone despite the presence of the patrol car. In the kitchen, he puts the kettle on.

'Tea?'

'Yes please.'

He makes the drinks and we sit down at the kitchen table. Max pokes his head around the door and looks at us.

'Am I a liar?'

My heart breaks for my little boy. 'No, Max,' I tell him, gesturing for him to come and sit on my lap. 'Of course you're not. This isn't about you, okay?'

'Who is it about?'

'No one. None of us. It was just bored teenagers being silly.'

Max mulls this over. 'I need some more football boots, Mum.'

I kiss the top of his head, immensely grateful that my son is not an overthinker. 'Have you outgrown your ones already?'

'Yeah, they're really ouchy. I've got a blister.'

'Okay, we'll go at the weekend and get some.'

'Can I have a snack?'

'There's some fruit in the fridge.'

Max scuttles off to the fridge, pulls out an apple and then disappears to watch television. I turn to Tom.

'Well, that was easy enough.'

'I reckon he's already forgotten about it.'

'I hate that he saw it, though.'

'Me too. But, as you can see, he's moved on.'

'I wish I could.'

A message comes through from Samantha, asking if I'm free for a chat.

'I'm just going to make a call,' I tell Tom, standing up and taking my tea with me. I go upstairs to our bedroom, settle myself down on the bed and call Samantha.

'Hey,' she says brightly.

'Hey.'

'Are you okay? You sound tired.'

'It's been a rough day.'

I tell Samantha about the message on the garage door.

'I hope you called the police,' she says.

'They've already been and gone. And there's a police car parked on the road.'

'I can't believe this is happening to you, Ellie. It's awful.'

I don't reply. I don't really know what to say. I'm all out of words.

'Ellie,' Samantha says, her tone worried. 'Are you there?'

'I'm here.'

'You're not thinking of changing your statement, are you?'

It's like she can hear my thoughts. 'It's crossed my mind,' I admit, forgetting for a moment who it is I'm talking to.

'Please don't.' Samantha's voice is tinged with desperation. 'Please don't let these people intimidate you. That's what they want.'

'I've had enough, Samantha.'

'I know. But your testimony is key to convicting this man. The man who killed my husband.'

Realisation is brutal. This is not an intimate chat with just any friend. This is a conversation with the widow of the man I saw die. A woman who is relying on me to give evidence in court so she can have justice for her husband.

I want justice too. But not at the expense of my own family.

'Listen, Amelia has a cousin who works in security.' I flinch at the mention of Amelia, as Samantha continues. 'Let me speak to her, see if he can help us.'

'In what way?'

'He may be able to assign someone to keep an eye on things.'

'Like a bodyguard?'

'Sort of.'

'Samantha, we can't afford that.'

'I'll pay. Let me do this.'

'No.' My voice comes out harsher than I meant. 'Thank you, it's an incredibly generous and thoughtful offer but I don't want you to do that. And anyway, the police are keeping a watchful eye.'

'They can't watch you twenty-four hours a day though. I want to make sure you're safe. You and your family.'

Does she really want to keep me safe, I wonder. Or does she just want to make sure that I don't back out of giving evidence? For the first time since I became friends with Samantha, I find myself questioning her intentions. But I quickly check myself. Even if the gesture is partly selfish, I can understand it. She needs me in that court. And this is the first time I've felt even the slightest bit of pressure from her. We've been spending time together for months and she's never once made me feel like anything but a friend. She's just upset because I've admitted I'm thinking of changing my statement.

I close my eyes and breathe in and out deeply. A thousand thoughts flash through my mind in those few short seconds. When I open my eyes again, my thoughts are clear.

'I'm going to take the stand,' I tell her. 'And tell everyone the truth.'

'That's not what this offer is about. I just want to help.'

'Thank you, but it's not necessary.'

'Will you at least install a couple of cameras around your property then? I'll text you the details of the company I used for my house. They were excellent.'

It's not a bad idea. 'That would be great, thank you.'

'And if you change your mind about Amelia's cousin...'

If Amelia's cousin is anything like Amelia, I don't want him anywhere near me. 'I won't but thank you again.'

'Not long to go now, Ellie.'

'So everyone keeps saying.' I check myself again. Remind

myself of who I'm talking to. 'Anyway, enough about that. How are the boys getting on? Studying hard?'

'Marcus is. He's really buckled down. Jamie is, well, being Jamie. I think he's convinced he'll pass on confidence alone. I just hope he does.'

'But the school has said they can both stay for sixth form, regardless?'

'Well yes, but I guess he'll have to retake a couple of exams, if he fails them.'

'They're bright boys, Samantha. They'll do fine.'

She sighs heavily. 'I hope so. Anyway, I'm desperate to get out. Do you want to go for dinner one evening?'

'Aren't you on revision duty?'

'Oh, what's done is done now. The boys will be fine for a couple of hours.'

I really don't feel like going out at all but I'm finding it increasingly difficult to say no to Samantha. And anyway, I need to keep busy otherwise I'll go mad.

'Sure, how about tomorrow?' I hear myself saying before I can change my mind.

'Fabulous! Harpenden okay? I'll book somewhere and send you the details.'

'Sounds great.'

I hang up and sit on the bed for a while. Somehow the dynamic is shifting between Samantha and me. I forged this friendship because I felt sorry for her and I wanted to support her after what happened. Now it feels like it's the other way around. It's a sign, perhaps, of the close friendship we've nurtured, but it doesn't sit well with me.

There's a gentle rap on the door and Tom peeks in. 'Everything okay up here?'

'Yes, thanks.'

He comes and sits down next to me on the bed. 'Good chat with your friend?'

'Yes, it was Samantha. She offered to pay for us to have a bodyguard.'

I wait, expecting Tom to laugh and scoff. But he's thoughtful. 'Maybe we should.'

I'm shocked. 'I said no. For one, it's really expensive. And anyway, it'll freak out the kids. But she did suggest we get some cameras installed and I think that is a good idea.'

'Me too.'

'She's going to text me the name of the company who installed hers.'

'Okay. Send me the details and I'll call them. You've got enough going on.'

'I'm sorry, Tom.'

'Stop saying sorry.'

'Sorry.' I smile weakly. 'I can't help myself.'

'Why don't I run you a bath?'

'That would be lovely, thank you.'

Tom stands up and a few moments later I hear the tap running. I lean back and close my eyes, listening to the rhythmical sound of the water in the background. Despite all my stress, I feel myself drifting off and I don't fight it. After weeks of chronic insomnia, sleep is pulling me down and I welcome it. I *need* it.

When I wake up it's dark. Tom is in bed and he's tucked my legs under the duvet. I'm still dressed and my mouth tastes sour. How long have I been asleep? I pat the bed until I find my phone and look at the screen. It's midnight. I've been out for hours.

I should go back to sleep but annoyingly I'm wide awake now. And I really want to change into my pyjamas. I sneak out of bed and tiptoe to the bathroom, taking off my clothes, washing my face and brushing my teeth. Then I slip back into the bedroom, put my pyjamas on and climb back into bed. I lie there, eyes wide open, in the dark.

I'm restless, agitated. With a glance at Tom, I stand up and peer through the crack in the curtains. The street is empty and the police car is no longer there. I wonder if Tom remembered to put the chain over the door when he went to bed. I'm about to go down and check when a movement catches my eye. Something, or someone, is in our driveway. My heart begins to pound and I hide behind the curtain, terrified. I turn to Tom, about to wake him up, but then I decide to take another look. It could be a cat, or a fox, and I don't want to disturb my husband unnecessarily. I force myself to open the curtain a crack and look down at the driveway again, squinting in the gloom.

The figure is too big to be an animal. It's a person, dressed in black. I can't see their face in the dark, but I know what they're doing. They're looking right at me.

'Tom!' I scream.

It takes him a few seconds to wake up but when he turns the light on and sees my expression, he's on his feet instantly.

'What is it?'

'There's someone on the driveway.'

Tom dashes out of the bedroom and I hear him pounding down the stairs, taking the chain off and pulling open the door. I look back out of the window and see him emerge. But while my head has been turned, the figure has disappeared. Now I only see the shadow of Tom, looking around the driveway, even getting on his hands and knees to check under the car. Then he stands and looks up at the window, shrugging.

By the time Tom is back upstairs, I'm sitting on our bed, shaking.

'There was no one there,' he says.

'But there was.'

Tom is pacing the room. 'Where the hell are the police?'

'I guess they can't keep watch day and night.'

'We should call them.'

'Let's do it in the morning.'

'I think we should do it now. What if he comes back?'

He. Was it a man down there? I didn't get a good look at the person and I didn't see their face. But something about their stature makes me wonder. I've seen photos of Jason and he's tall and stocky. This figure was slight. A young man perhaps.

Or a woman.

'It wasn't Jason,' I say quietly.

'How do you know?'

'It was someone smaller. Thinner.'

'It could easily have been someone he knows. I doubt he's doing all this himself.'

'Perhaps.' I look at Tom. 'I think we should stay with Tamsin for a bit.'

He shakes his head. 'Not yet. I don't want to be forced out of our own home. Let's get the cameras installed. And hopefully the police will give us an update tomorrow.'

'Fine,' I agree. 'But if one more thing happens, we're leaving.'

'Agreed.'

We climb into bed, side by side. At first, we're both too wired to sleep but after twenty minutes or so, Tom dozes off, leaving me alone with my thoughts. Thoughts so dark and distressing that I don't want to think them any more.

I go downstairs to make myself a hot chocolate. I'm heating up the milk when I hear footsteps behind me. The creak of a floorboard. Someone is walking across the hallway. The kitchen door begins to open slowly. In seconds, I've grabbed a knife from the block and I'm holding it out in front of me, ready to confront the intruder, fear pushing through every one of my pores, adrenaline keeping me upright.

Frankie stops and looks at me in horror.

'Mum!'

I drop the knife with a clatter.

'Mum, what the hell?'

I bend down to pick up the knife, taking the opportunity to gather my thoughts. 'I'm sorry, darling, I thought you were a burglar.'

'So you were going to stab me?'

'Of course I wasn't. I just grabbed it on instinct.'

Frankie is looking at me like *I'm* the intruder.

'I'm really sorry I scared you, Frankie.'

'What's going on, Mum?'

I consider the question. My initial reaction is to deny everything and tell Frankie there's nothing to worry about. But she already knows something is up. And she's older than Max; she can take the truth. Plus, I really don't want to lie to her.

'I saw someone outside, just now,' I tell her. 'In the driveway.'

'You think it was a burglar?'

'No,' I admit. 'I think it was the same person who did the graffiti.'

Frankie comes and sits on a bar stool, propping her elbows on the kitchen counter. The milk begins to bubble, and I get a second mug and pour it out evenly between them.

'Who do you think it is?' she asks.

I stir in the chocolate powder and hand her a mug. 'You know I'm giving evidence in this court case?'

'The one about Marcus and Jamie's dad?'

I wince at the reminder. 'Yes, that's right. It's possible someone doesn't want me to give evidence and they're trying to scare me.'

Frankie considers this. 'Who?'

'The man who is accused of causing the accident.'

'You really think he'd try to scare you into not going to court?'

'I don't know but it's the only thing I can think of.'

Frankie takes a sip of her hot chocolate. 'What are you going to do?'

I stand up straight as I answer Frankie. I have to be a positive role model for my daughter. 'I'm going to give evidence. I can't let these people frighten me.'

'Are we safe?'

Frankie's expression reminds me that she's still a child, underneath all that lip gloss and attitude. 'Yes, darling, of course we are.'

'Is that actually why you and Dad have been taking me to school every day?'

'Yes.'

She looks away. 'I won't skive again.'

'I'm glad to hear it.'

I perch on a stool next to her and we drink our hot chocolates in companionable silence. It feels harmonious, and I need to think of something else other than the graffiti and the figure in the driveway, so I broach the issue of Jamie again.

'Have you heard from Jamie?'

Frankie's lip wobbles. 'No.'

'Well, he's very busy, studying for his exams.'

'It's not that.'

I turn to her and notice her face is pale. 'What is it, darling?'

She's quiet for a moment, her adolescent instinct to keep schtum fighting with her need to get it off her chest. Finally, she says, 'Jamie isn't interested in me.'

I'm ashamed of the pleasure this news brings me. 'Ah, I see,' I say.

'And I found out the hard way.'

Oh no. I have a feeling I know what's coming next. 'You told him you liked him?'

Frankie buries her head in her hands. 'I tried to kiss him.'

I lean in and put my arm around her. My poor Frankie, she must be mortified. 'I'm so sorry, sweetheart. But honestly, we've all been there.'

'We have?'

I smile as I think back. 'I had a huge crush on this boy at school. One evening, at a house party, we were sitting together on the sofa and I thought it was the moment. I leaned in and puckered my lips. The poor boy leaped off the sofa like I was a bomb.'

Frankie laughs and I join in. 'What happened then?'

'He ignored me for weeks. It turned out he fancied my friend. I think they ended up going out for a while. I thought I'd never live it down, but I did, and so will you.'

'I'm too embarrassed to even look at him.'

I stroke her arm. 'Was he nice about it?'

'Yeah, really nice, but that almost made it worse.'

'Will you stay friends?'

'I dunno. I can't look at him right now.'

'I get that, I really do. But it will pass, and so will your feelings.'

It's the most intimate conversation Frankie and I have had in months and I'm so glad she's opened up to me. I wonder again if Jamie is gay. Samantha has not said anything more, since her cryptic comment about his 'type', and I don't want to probe. It's possible that Frankie's really just not his sort of girl, or he thinks she's too young for him. Anyway, it doesn't really matter. My priority is making sure that Frankie is okay and I hope our chat cheered her up.

Frankie drains her hot chocolate and gets up. 'Thanks for listening, Mum.'

'Any time.'

When Frankie's gone, I decide to sit in the kitchen for a while longer. But then I think of the figure I saw outside and I don't want to be alone downstairs. I put the two mugs in the sink and head back upstairs to the safety of my bed, and Tom.

But I still can't sleep and so I take my phone from the bedside table and open my browser. Without really thinking what I'm doing, I go to Samantha's Instagram page and scroll to the photo I saw of the New Year's party, when Amelia is in the background. And, sure enough, Samantha has tagged Amelia in it. I move on to Amelia's profile, scanning her photographs, which mainly consist of pictures of her cats and her daughter, Charlotte. Wow, Samantha was right, she's stunning. There's something about her striking features, though, that I can't put my finger on. I can see Amelia in her, but I can see something else too. There's a likeness to someone. Who is it? Is it an actor or actress?

And then it hits me and I almost drop my phone. She reminds me of someone whose photo I've studied a hundred times over the past few months. Whose face is etched in my mind. Who has begged me for help in my nightmares.

She reminds me of Graham.

14

'Cheers!'

Samantha raises her wine glass, and I clink it with my Diet Coke. I've driven to Harpenden because I feel safer having my car close by. We've met at a lovely Italian restaurant but as I peruse the menu, I realise that the thought of eating makes me nauseous. I'm nervous. Not just about my own safety but about being with Samantha.

I've been obsessing over the photo of Charlotte. Did I really see the likeness to Samantha's husband? And if I've seen it, why hasn't anyone else? Or am I just losing it, concocting outlandish theories in my head to distract me from my own problems. Still, now all I can think of is, did Amelia have an affair with her best friend's husband?

But it's so far-fetched. I'm being ridiculous. Aren't I?

Samantha is oblivious to my turmoil as she smiles at me. 'I can't wait for these exams to be over,' she tells me. 'The boys are exhausted and so am I.'

'Not long to go,' I reply. 'Do you have any plans for the summer?'

'No. I've considered booking a holiday so many times, but I haven't done it. I know I should because the boys deserve a break after all their studying. And we could all do with a change of scene. But it still feels wrong to go without Graham and to have fun.'

'You should go,' I urge her. 'It will do you all good.'

'But I feel guilty. And selfish.'

'You shouldn't. And I'm sure Graham would want you to go.'

'Perhaps.'

I can't help it, I have to find a way to bring Amelia into the conversation. 'Maybe you could go away with Amelia and her family? A group dynamic might make things feel a bit less intense.'

'Oh, she's already booked her holiday. They're off to California.'

'Wow, lucky them.'

'Her husband works for an American company and travels there a lot. He gets accommodation so they're making the most of it.'

'What's he like?'

Samantha looks at me in surprise. 'Amelia's husband?'

'Yes.'

She shrugs. 'Ed's a nice guy. He works too hard.'

'Are they happy?'

Now Samantha is looking distinctly suspicious. 'Yes, why are you asking?'

I backtrack. 'No reason, just making conversation.'

She considers this and seems to accept it. 'They've had their rough patches of course. Haven't we all? But they're solid.'

'What about Graham? Did Amelia and Graham get on?'

'Oh yes, they've always gotten on well, although they used to bicker and tease the hell out of each other. I think it was because they had known each other for so long. It was Amelia who introduced us, you see.'

'I didn't know that.'

'Yes, she met him at university. I actually socialised with him a few times when I went to visit her, but nothing happened between us. We got together years later.'

'Was Amelia happy about that?'

Samantha smiles. 'She was the one who set us up.'

'And was she excited when you got married?'

'Very. She was my maid of honour and she arranged the most spectacular hen do.'

'I didn't realise they were also old friends. She must have been devastated when Graham died.'

Samantha's face clouds over and I feel guilty. I've pushed her too far. I'm playing detective for no good reason other than my own implausible theory.

'She was,' Samantha says quietly. 'But she was there for me, despite her own grief.'

I decide to drop it. 'She's a good friend.'

Samantha smiles. 'She really is. Anyway, tell me what the police said.'

'Paula from witness services has been in touch to check in, and I've seen a police car in our road a few times. They're definitely keeping an eye on us.'

'Are you okay? It's a horrible thing to be going through.'

'I'm not really okay,' I admit. 'And we're considering going to stay somewhere else. Tom isn't keen but I've reached my limit. Every time I hear a noise, I think I'm going to have a heart attack. And it's tough, juggling work with chaperoning the kids everywhere just to keep them safe. I'm exhausted and overwhelmed, to be honest.'

'I'm so sorry, Ellie. I hate that you're going through this but I'm sure whoever is behind it wouldn't dare try to actually hurt you or your family. I hope the police manage to link all this back to Jason. Maybe they'll even put him in custody.'

'So far there's no evidence and I'm just worried about how far he'll go.'

'He wouldn't dare try anything dangerous,' Samantha says firmly. 'It's just scare tactics, I promise you. And at some point, he'll realise that it's not doing him any good. I mean, you're not backing down and it makes him look even more guilty.'

I don't tell Samantha about the figure I saw last night. How it's thrown me, because it clearly wasn't Jason. Anyway, he has alibis for all the times that the incidents happened, so the police can't pin anything on him. Apparently, he's cooperating fully. The obvious explanation is that Jason, or one of his family members, is paying someone to do the dirty work for them, but doubt is niggling at me.

'How's Tom?' Samantha says suddenly.

I'm startled out of my reverie. 'Sorry?'

'Tom. How is he?'

'Oh, he's fine. He's been my rock these past few months. I don't know what I would have done without him.'

'How did you two meet?'

I smile at the memory. 'I was on this awful blind date with a man I'd been set up with by a colleague. She clearly didn't know me that well because he wasn't my type and we had absolutely zero in common. After one drink I was more than ready to leave but then he insisted I owed him because he'd bought the first round. I chickened out of telling him to do one and went to the bar. And there was Tom.'

Samantha leans forward, intrigued. 'What happened then?'

'We made eye contact and started chatting. I told him about my terrible date and he said I should ditch the loser and have a drink with him instead. Well, I didn't need telling twice. I marched over to my date and told him it wasn't going to work out.'

'What did he do?'

'He told me I still owed him money for a drink!'

Samantha hoots with laughter. 'Did you give it to him?'

'I gave him a fiver. And then I went over to Tom and the rest is history.'

Samantha claps her hands together. 'I love this story.'

I grin. 'We've dined out on it many times.'

'And have you been happy, the two of you?'

I think back wistfully, suddenly overwhelmed with love for Tom. 'Yes,' I say. 'As with all marriages, there have been bumps in the road. Recently, though, I've really appreciated how fortunate I am. I really don't know what I would have done without him.'

Samantha's eyes fill with tears. 'You're lucky to have him.'

'Oh gosh, I'm sorry, Samantha, I shouldn't be going on about my husband.'

She shakes her head. 'Don't be silly, I asked.'

The arrival of our food is a welcome reset. My appetite has returned now that I've eased into the evening and I enjoy the delicious bowl of steaming pasta. I push all thoughts of what's been going on to the back of my mind and just enjoy Samantha's company. She's doing so well. Getting out, spending time with friends, supporting her boys. She's an inspiration. But I know that underneath it she's still suffering.

By the time we've finished, Samantha is a little tipsy and as I'm driving, I offer to give her a lift. I pull up outside her beautiful house and she gives me a hug.

'Thank you for a lovely evening,' she says.

'My pleasure.'

I make sure she gets inside okay then I begin to drive home. I don't drive in the dark much any more and I'm nervous, temporarily blinded by the glare of the oncoming cars' headlights. I'm concentrating so hard that I don't realise where I am until I stop at the junction and it hits me. I'm at the scene of the accident.

I idle there for a minute, staring at the junction. And just like that, I'm back in that Tuesday afternoon in January. I can almost see the car in front of me, the lorry ploughing into it. And I wonder again if I got the order of events right. I was so convinced at the time that I had but now I'm riddled with doubt.

The beep of a car horn startles me and I realise that someone is behind me. I put my foot on the accelerator and start to crawl up the road. But the car behind me is right up my backside. I slow down even further, giving it an opportunity to overtake me, but it remains on my rear, inching closer. It's intimidating. I can't make out the type of car it is, or who is inside. Could it be a young racer, getting impatient as I'm driving so slowly? Or is it something else? Is someone following me?

I speed up and the car behind me does the same. I'm beginning to sweat, afraid of what might happen next. And I don't like driving this fast. I want to call Tom but I also don't want to take my eyes off the road. I don't know what to do.

My hands are gripping the steering wheel, my palms clammy. I'm terrified that I'm going to crash but I just want to get away from this car. I wince as I see the roundabout approaching, realising that I have to slow down. As I look in my rear-view mirror I can still see the car right behind me. I force myself to concentrate on the road as I stop for the roundabout and then drive around it.

When I finally have the courage to look in the mirror, the car has disappeared. It must have turned off onto another road.

I exhale slowly, releasing the breath I've been holding on to. The car wasn't following me, it was just an aggressive driver who happened to be behind me. But it still seems like the world is out to get me. Everything feels personal now.

The rest of the journey home passes without incident, but I can't relax. Even when I pull into the driveway and see the freshly painted garage door, clear of any graffiti, I'm tense. The few short steps from the car to the front door feel daunting but so does staying in the car alone, so I get out and hurry towards the house, opening the door as quickly as I can and stepping inside. I close the door behind me and pull the chain over. I hear the comforting sound of the TV coming from the living room and I walk in to find Tom on the sofa, his feet propped up on the coffee table.

'Hey,' I say, sitting down and taking my shoes off.

'Good evening?'

'Yeah, it was nice. How are the kids?'

'Fine, Max is asleep and Frankie is in her room. How's Samantha?'

'She's okay.'

I put my shoes away and then cuddle up to Tom, enjoying the warmth of his body.

'I'm so lucky to have you,' I say.

He gives me a squeeze. 'We're lucky to have you.'

'Did you speak to the camera company?'

'Yes, they're coming round tomorrow to give us a quote. They can't do the installation for a few weeks though. They're booked up apparently.'

I wince. 'That's ages away. Should we try another company?'

'I'll make some calls tomorrow.'

'Thank you.'

We watch television for a while and then go to bed. It takes me ages to nod off but I eventually fall into a blissful and much needed sleep. And when I wake up the next morning, my head feels clear for the first time in weeks. The sun is peeking through the curtains and I actually feel ready to face the day for once.

I get into the shower and by the time I get back, my coffee is waiting for me. I sip it gratefully and then get dressed. It's only when I'm doing my make-up that I realise Max is missing and Tom hasn't returned to the bedroom. Where is everyone?

I check on Max first and find him in his room, reading a comic. Then I go downstairs and I'm immediately hit by a blast of fresh air because the front door is wide open. Sticking my head out, I see Tom crouching by the car, his hands black with dirt.

'What is it?' I ask.

He's examining one of the wheels. 'We've got a flat tyre.'

It's annoying, but I'm not going to let it ruin my day. 'Never mind, I can get the bus to school with Frankie and you can walk Max.'

He stands up and something in his expression sends a chill down my spine.

'They're all flat,' he says.

'What do you mean?' I look at the car and realise that Tom is right. Every single tyre is as flat as a pancake. And then I understand what this means.

'This isn't accidental,' I say.

Tom shakes his head. 'No. They've been slashed. And there's more.'

I step tentatively out of the house, dreading what Tom is about to show me.

'I popped out this morning just to make sure everything was

okay, and that's when I saw it,' he tells me. 'I'm sorry, Ellie. I'm really sorry this has happened again.'

He gestures for me to follow him to the back of the car and points at the rear windscreen. My skin prickles as I stare at the bright red paint emblazoned across it.

Liar, liar, Ellie on fire.

15

One month to go. The date I'm dreading but need to face to put behind me. I'm crawling towards it on my hands and knees, wondering if I'll make it.

We're still living at home because Tom has transformed into some sort of alpha male and is refusing to be driven out. It's like the more things that happen, the more indignant he becomes. He says he'll keep us safe, although I'm not sure how he plans to do that. But he did find a new CCTV company and although we paid over the odds for a quick installation, it's given us some peace of mind. Our tyres have been replaced and the red paint is gone, but I haven't driven the car again. I don't want to go anywhere.

I am a prisoner in my own home. I've been signed off sick from work with stress and although it's another thing to feel guilty about, I know it was the right thing to do because I can't concentrate. The children have broken up for the summer, but we haven't booked a holiday because no one is in the mood. Max is at football camp and Frankie is at drama, and the house is horribly quiet. But it's good that they're busy as I'm next to useless. I have to buck up, otherwise it's going to be a long summer.

I leave the house only to take the kids to their clubs and I avoid it if I can. But Tom has to show his face in the office sometimes and I fear those days. The days when I am forced to go out. When the house is empty and I dread who is watching me.

Jason Turner has not been charged with any additional offences. There is nothing that can prove he is responsible for what's happening, although an additional bail condition has been imposed on him, banning him from coming within a mile of our home. Apparently, he's now accusing the police of harassment.

I don't know what to think any more. What to feel. I've spoken to Paula about it and she's being supportive but she's also firm. I confessed that I didn't want to go to court any more and she sympathised before explaining that if I refuse to go, I will be issued with a summons and if I do not attend, I could be arrested.

Basically, I have no choice.

Paula says the amendment to Jason's bail means that he is unlikely to come to our home. And she's reminded me that there is no evidence pointing to the fact that it was him anyway. He has proof that he was at home when the incidents happened. But, like everyone else, she can offer no other explanation as to who could be behind it.

She's started preparing me for the trial, explaining how it will work, where everyone will be sitting and asking if I have any questions. She's offered to take me to the court so I can familiarise myself with the setting. I've said no because I don't think it will help and, if anything, it will make me even more nervous.

I haven't seen much of Samantha. She's been a little distant lately and I'm not sure why. Perhaps she's worried about the trial or maybe she doesn't want to put me under any more pressure than I already feel. But I haven't reached out to her either, as I'm not up for socialising. We've both got plenty on our minds.

'Liar, liar, Ellie on fire.'

It was a juvenile threat, but it had the desired effect. I'm living in abject terror. Sometimes I wish I'd just driven away from the accident. I imagine how different my life would be right now. How easy. But it would have been a terrible thing to do and I don't think I could have ever forgiven myself. I did the right thing, I told the truth, and I'm being punished for it. It's so damn cruel and unfair.

I'm sitting on the sofa, trying to summon up the energy to sort out the mountain of washing that needs doing. I have three hours before I need to pick up the kids and I've got no work to keep my brain occupied. I consider having a drink but it's the middle of the day and I don't want to go down that slippery slope. I'm feeling lethargic and claustrophobic, cooped up in this house. I need to get out. I need *air*.

Screw it, I'm leaving. Before I can change my mind, I put my shoes on and grab my keys. I look like crap and I'm not wearing a scrap of make-up, but I don't care. Glancing up at the camera in the porch, I double lock the front door and triple check that all the windows are closed. Then I head tentatively for the town centre.

As I walk, I keep looking over my shoulder at the passing cars. But none of them slow down and none of them are a black SUV. They are full of regular people, going about their regular lives. The bright summer sun makes the world seem safer, a little less intimidating. I feel a surge of energy, accompanied by a touch of defiance. Tom is right, we can't give in to intimidation. We have to live our lives.

The town centre is bustling when I arrive, full of families enjoying the holidays. Mums taking their children shopping, teenagers hanging out outside Starbucks. I make a promise to myself that I will spend some quality time with Frankie and Max next week. I'll bring them shopping, maybe take them into London for a day out. We'll make the most of this summer and then we'll book an amazing trip in October when the trial is behind us.

I'll go back to work in September too. My company has been extremely supportive, but I can't hide forever. And being back in the routine will be good for me. Yes, I think. Leaving the house was a good idea. It's given me a vigour that I've been lacking for weeks. I decide to pop into M&S and have a look at some clothes. Maybe I'll buy some bits and bobs for our October holiday, even though we haven't booked it yet. We have some air miles to use up and I'd like to go somewhere hot, the Canary Islands perhaps.

I'm looking at the racks in the holiday section when I see Amelia, walking towards me. Our eyes meet and she looks as appalled as I am. I see her hesitate, her indecision clear on her face. She is wondering if she should turn around or come over. I'm hoping she'll do the former and my heart sinks when I see her continue towards me. This is the last thing I need on my first, tentative venture out of the house.

'Hi,' she says, coming to stand opposite me, her eyes on the swimming costumes.

'Hi,' I reply. 'Are you holiday shopping?'

'Yes, we're going to California on Sunday.'

'Samantha told me you were going there. It sounds wonderful.'

'Yes.'

I don't need a reminder of how taciturn Amelia is, but she's obviously happy to give me one anyway.

'Will you be back for the trial?' I ask.

'Of course.'

Then I remember Amelia's daughter. I'd almost forgotten about Charlotte while I've been wallowing in my own angst. And then I see her, a few feet away, on her phone.

'Is that Charlotte?' I ask.

Amelia glances behind her shoulder. 'Yes. On her phone as usual.'

She picks out a bikini that I would never dare to wear, but which would look stunning on her lithe figure. While Amelia is distracted, I take a moment to appraise Charlotte. She is tall, taller than her mother already. Her hair is dark and shiny, her cheekbones high. Does she look like Graham in the flesh? Not particularly. The more I think about it, the more silly the whole idea is.

I visibly shake my head to rid myself of the thought and then I see Amelia looking at me curiously.

'How are you feeling about the trial?' she asks.

I'm so surprised that she's asking me a question that I struggle to answer for a moment. Eventually, I say, 'Fine.' If Amelia can be monosyllabic, so can I.

'I hear you've been having some more trouble.'

Trouble is an understatement. Clearly Samantha has filled her friend in on what's been going on. I'm not surprised, but I still feel uncomfortable about them discussing me.

'Yes, but it seems to have stopped now.'

Charlotte drifts over, looking at the bikini in her mother's hands.

'Is that for me?' she asks.

'No, it's for me.'

'You can't get away with that, Mum.'

I stifle a laugh. Clearly Frankie is not the only sassy teenager around here.

Amelia frowns. 'I work hard for my body, I'm allowed to show it off.'

Charlotte takes it from her mother's hands, ignoring me completely. Private school certainly hasn't taught her any manners. Now she's close up, I can't resist having another look at her. Whatever I saw in that photo is gone and I can't see any resemblance to Graham. But then she looks at me and I see it again. A brief flash that almost makes me stagger backwards.

'Come on, Charlotte, let's go,' Amelia says, giving me a curt nod. Charlotte puts the bikini back and follows her mother, leaving me standing there, gormless.

I blink a few times, trying to centre myself. But I'm agitated, this time for a different reason. And although I know I shouldn't do it, although I'm fully aware that I have far bigger fish to fry, I instinctively reach for my phone and call Samantha.

* * *

She has made a salad by the time I arrive at her house in a taxi. She's laid the outside table and I see a jug of what looks like freshly made lemonade.

'Would you like a glass?' she asks, gesturing at the jug.

'Lovely,' I say.

'It's wonderful to see you.'

'Yes, it was time I dragged myself out of the house.'

'Are you back at work yet?'

'No, I've been signed off until September.'

Samantha looks at me with concern before pouring me a glass of lemonade and handing it to me. Then she sits down and takes a sip of her own. She looks tired too and she's lost weight. The stress of the upcoming trial must be getting to her.

'Where are the boys?' I remark, looking through the doors into the empty house.

'They've gone surfing in Cornwall with their friends. The family of one of the boys in the gang has a house down there and his parents offered to chaperone.'

'How long are they there for?'

'Two weeks. They'll be back next Tuesday.'

I take a deep drink, wishing it was wine and wondering if I really have the gall to do this, and then I blurt out, 'I just bumped into Amelia and Charlotte in M&S.'

'Oh yes? Were they holiday shopping?'

'They were.' I try to ignore the butterflies fluttering in my stomach and grip onto my glass. 'You're right, Charlotte really is beautiful.'

'She is,' Samantha agrees.

'And that glossy, dark, straight hair...' I add.

'It's gorgeous, isn't it.'

'Does she get that from her dad?'

I risk a glance at Samantha and she's looking at me curiously. 'Yes,' she says.

I nod and take another sip, wondering what to say next. Desperate to ask but too afraid to verbalise what sounds completely ridiculous. How do you ask someone if their husband is the father of their best friend's daughter?

No, this is stupid. I've got it all wrong. I'm seeing things that aren't there.

I'm about to change the subject when Samantha speaks suddenly. 'I suppose you might as well know...'

I swear my heart stops for a second. 'Know what?'

Samantha sighs heavily. 'Amelia and Ed have been together for a long time. They met at university when they were eighteen. They decided to have children in their mid-twenties and they tried to conceive for years but it wasn't happening. So, they had some tests done and it turns out that he has a low sperm count. *Very* low.'

My eyes are wide as I consider what she is going to say next. What secret I'm going to hear and what the implications of it are.

'They tried two rounds of IVF but it was unsuccessful. By then Amelia was a mess and she couldn't take a third. She wanted a child so much and they were looking into adoption, and then she came to me with an idea.'

I'm about to fall off my chair with anticipation. 'What was her idea?'

'She was going to get a sperm donor. She even had some profiles with her for me to look at. And as we perused them over a bottle of wine, we became increasingly drunk and silly. I kept thinking about my boys and the wine had made me nostalgic and forgetful of how damn hard the past year had been. I only remembered the good times and I couldn't bear the thought of Amelia not experiencing the joy of becoming a mother like I had. The next thing I knew, I was offering Graham's sperm.'

Of all the things I was expecting to hear when I came to Samantha's, this was not it. 'You offered her Graham's *sperm*?'

'Yes. And at first Amelia said no way. Then we laughed about it and passed out on the sofa. The next morning, Amelia asked me if I'd been serious. She said she'd been thinking about it since dawn and had warmed to the idea because at least with Graham, she knew what she was getting. She knew his medical history, his personality, etc.'

'How did you feel about that?'

Samantha pulls a face. 'Hungover and mortified. In the cold light of day, it seemed like the worst idea in the world. But then I saw the look of hope on Amelia's face, the desperate anticipation, and I knew I couldn't say no.'

'What did Graham say?'

'He was apoplectic. And he absolutely refused to do it. But then he talked to Amelia. Don't forget that they had been friends for years. And he knew as much as I did about the struggles she'd had and how much she wanted to conceive.'

'So, he agreed?'

'He did, and so did Ed, because he knew how much it meant to Amelia to become a mother. He worships Amelia and would do anything for her. After that, things moved incredibly quickly and none of us really had time to back out.'

I've nearly finished my lemonade and Samantha pours me another. I thank her and wait for the next instalment of a story that has blown my mind.

'You suspected, didn't you?' she asks.

'When I saw Charlotte, I noticed a resemblance, because I've seen Graham's photo. But I wondered if I was being ridiculous because no one else seemed to have seen it.'

'You aren't being ridiculous.'

I lean forward, breathless. 'Did they, you know?'

'Of course not,' Samantha says abruptly. 'It was all very clinical. No sex.'

I lean back again. 'I see.'

'And it was successful the first time, would you believe? And so Amelia got her much-longed-for baby and life went on.'

'But isn't it strange, knowing that Charlotte is Graham's daughter?'

'Funnily enough, the strangest time was when Amelia was pregnant. We didn't know how to act around each other and I kept looking at her bump and thinking about how Graham's baby was growing inside her. But she had a difficult pregnancy and when she was induced early, I was so worried, and all I could think was, *please let that baby be okay. Please let Amelia be okay.* Nothing else mattered.'

'I'm guessing they were.'

'Yes, they were both fine. And when Charlotte was born, when I saw her in Amelia's arms, I knew. Charlotte was Amelia and Ed's daughter. She always would be.'

'Do the kids know?'

Samantha shakes her head. 'No. Absolutely not.'

'They've never suspected?'

'You know what children are like. Too wrapped up in their own worlds to even notice what you clearly did. And it's not like it's an uncanny resemblance. There's just a little something in her features, but she's inherited plenty of Amelia too.'

'Do you think they'll work it out eventually?'

'I doubt it. But if they do, we'll tell them, if that's what Amelia wants.'

'What about your other friends? Did they suspect?'

'A couple of very close friends know. No one else has mentioned it, until you.'

I'm speechless. And a little weirded out. And most of all, floored by Samantha's selfless gesture towards her best friend, despite the turmoil it would cause her.

'Did it cause any problems between you and Graham?'

'It did during Amelia's pregnancy. Graham wasn't very sympathetic when I was struggling and kept saying that it was my idea, not his. But I realised that he was finding it difficult too and we were dealing with it in different ways. Almost blaming each other, and that wasn't fair. After Charlotte was born, we talked it over and made a pact to always think of her as Amelia and Ed's baby and that was that.'

'What about Amelia? Did it cause a rift between you?'

Samantha shakes her head. 'Nothing we couldn't move past.'

'I can't believe you did that.'

'Well, Graham did it, really. But like I said, it was all clinical. Charlotte is not our daughter. Amelia and Ed have raised her, they've loved her.'

'Thank God nothing has ever happened between her and one of your boys.'

'Don't,' Samantha says sharply, and I can tell I've touched a nerve. 'I'll admit it's given me sleepless nights. But thankfully they see each other as siblings, and I don't think that will ever change. Anyway, I don't need to worry about Jamie.'

'Why is that?' I ask curiously, although I already suspect the answer.

'He's gay.'

'Ah, I see. And Marcus?'

'More interested in his books than girls. Anyway, Charlotte would never be interested in him. She prefers trendy, popular boys.'

'You told me once that Charlotte was high maintenance. Has it ever been difficult for you to keep your opinions to yourself, given the circumstances?'

Samantha answers immediately. 'No. She is *not* my daughter. Amelia and Ed were always free to raise her as they wished, and Graham felt the same. Anyway, she's a lovely girl really. She'll calm down when she gets older. Would you like some salad?'

I can't believe we've gone from this insane story to discussing salad. But Samantha has had years to get used to it and I'm touched that she trusts me enough to share this personal story. I bet Amelia would be furious if she knew and I can't help enjoying the small pang of pleasure that gives me. But while Samantha might be okay with it all, I wonder if Amelia is. This kind of thing has to mess with your head, surely?

And what about Graham? How did he really feel about it?

'Please don't tell Amelia I told you,' Samantha says suddenly, reaching out and gripping my arm tightly. 'I really shouldn't have. I don't know what came over me.'

'I won't, I promise.'

'She would *kill* me if she found out you knew.'

'I honestly won't say a word to anyone.'

'And don't tell Frankie.'

Samantha's grip is beginning to hurt. She looks terrified. I cover her hand with mine and try to gently prise it off me but she's still clinging on.

'Samantha, you have my word that no one will ever know about this.'

She exhales. 'Thank you. Christ, I really shouldn't have told you.'

'I'm glad you did. But it goes no further.'

'Promise me, Ellie. Whatever happens, please promise me.'

'I promise.'

We change the subject, but I can't stop thinking about it. And I'll admit, the scandal has been a welcome distraction. For a few minutes, I almost forgot about the vandalism and the threats. I lost myself in someone else's crazy story and it was a blessed relief.

But when Samantha drops me home, I remember again. I inspect all the tyres to make sure they're inflated. I check the rear windscreen and then look up and down the street to see if there's a black SUV. And then I decided to bite the bullet and take the car to pick up the kids, emboldened by spending a few hours out of the house.

For a split second, as I turn the ignition on, I wonder if the car is going to blow up with me inside. '*Liar, liar, Ellie on fire.*'

But of course it doesn't. The engine rumbles gently and I reverse out of the driveway, my mind returning to what

Samantha told me. And the panic on her face when she realised she'd said too much. She regretted sharing her story with me as soon as she'd done it. She was genuinely afraid. And maybe it was because she knew Amelia would be angry and upset, and she was worried I'd tell Frankie who would, in turn, tell Jamie. After all, it's a huge thing, and it would have a catastrophic effect on both families' lives if it got out. It's no wonder Samantha wants to make sure I don't say anything to anyone. I'm honoured she's trusted me with this.

But then I realise what's bothering me. '*Whatever happens, please promise me,*' Samantha had said. What did she mean?

What does she think is going to happen?

16

I've been thinking non-stop about what Samantha told me. It's like I can't get it out of my head, no matter how hard I try. I told Tom because he's my husband and I trust him implicitly to keep this secret, and he was as shocked as I was. It's like a story you'd read in a women's real-life magazine, and I just can't believe Samantha would be involved in something like that. It does explain why Amelia is so protective over her though, so fiercely loyal. She owes her everything. And I'm wondering if that's why she was so hostile with me, because she was worried Samantha was getting too friendly with me. Perhaps she was trying to protect her own secret, rather than her best friend.

It's a strange thing to be obsessing over, but I probably just need something to fill my mind with other than my own anxiety about the court case. There's just one week to go and I'm on tenterhooks from the moment I wake up. Not that I'm getting much sleep. I know I look terrible and I just can't seem to stomach food. It churns my stomach, making me queasy and I'm constantly agitated, checking the chain is over the door and that the windows are closed. Even when I'm sitting down, my leg is twitching.

I check the cameras constantly but there's been no sign of anyone other than the four of us and the odd passing cat. Tom keeps saying how pleased he is that we didn't move out and reassuring me that the police and cameras have scared off the culprit. He thinks that now the trial is so close, whoever it is has given up their efforts.

I'm not so sure.

I've told Samantha that, after I've given my evidence, I'll be by her side for the rest of the trial. Although she's been distant with me lately, I know it's because she's stressed and I won't let her push me away. I'm proud that I've helped her through her darkest times and that I've been a source of emotional support when she needed it. And, against all the odds, I've made a close friend at the same time. Because I know that Samantha and I will be friends for life now, whatever happens.

'*Whatever happens.*'

I still don't know what that means. Perhaps Samantha was referring to the court case. The lorry driver might be found guilty or not guilty and she wants me to keep my promise either way. Or maybe she's worried that we might drift apart after the trial and she wants to make sure I don't tell Frankie in case she informs Jamie.

But her secret is safe with me.

In any case, Frankie seems to have moved on from Jamie. There's a boy in her year at school who's caught her eye. He asked her to the cinema last week and she was grinning from ear to ear. She didn't even complain when I told her that I would be dropping her off and picking her up, although she made me park a little way down the street so she could walk the last twenty metres on her own. I watched her like a hawk but all I saw was two teenagers grinning at each other on the pavement, looking happy and a little awkward, as they walked into the cinema together. Just as life should be.

At some point Frankie is going to crave her independence again. I know that we're cramping her style by watching her every move and the older she gets, the more she'll resist it, especially when her friends are getting the bus on their own. But hopefully in a couple of weeks, Jason Turner will be behind bars and we can all rest easy again.

I don't want to think about what will happen if he isn't found guilty.

But, to be honest, I also don't want to think about what might happen if he *is*. If I have sent someone to prison for a long time and ruined another family's life in the process. There is no happy ending to this story, no matter how much I yearn for it and no holiday to Tenerife is going to plaster over the cracks that have ripped my life apart this year. A man may lose his freedom, Samantha will never get her husband back, and my life will never be the same again, after everything that has happened.

Last week I suggested to Tom that we sell up and move to the other side of London. A fresh start in a place that's still commutable to the city for when we need to be in the office. He was shocked at first and I was only half serious when I brought it up myself, but now I think we're both starting to come around to the idea. Tom's parents live on the south coast so it would be easier for us to visit them and vice versa. And although the kids would be upset to leave their friends and their schools, they'll come around eventually. The timing is perfect because if we move now, we can do it before Max starts secondary school and Frankie starts her GCSEs.

The real reason is unspoken but understood between us. I'm not sure I'll ever feel safe in St Albans again. I'll constantly be thinking that someone is watching me, or is out to get me. And I'll miss Tamsin and the other school mums, and Samantha too, of course, but we'll keep in touch and I must do what's right for my family. For me.

I've even started looking at properties for sale and I scroll through a few now, adding one or two to my favourites. It's a beautiful day, Tom is at work and the rest of us are chilling at home. Max is playing football in the garden, Frankie is waiting for a friend to come over and I'm sitting on a bench on the patio with a cup of coffee, facing the sun. It's peaceful, the calm before the storm perhaps. I'm immersed in looking at properties, swiping through some photographs of a house on a new development in Surrey and being seduced by brand-new appliances and spotless bathrooms. I haven't got it in me for a house refurb and the idea of moving into a brand-new home, which doesn't need any work, is tempting after the year I've had. I'm researching school catchment areas when the sound of the doorbell makes me jump.

'I'll get it,' Frankie calls from inside the house and I relax again. It'll be her friend and no doubt they'll head straight upstairs to Frankie's room without even saying hello. I glance at Max, who is practising penalties, and then return to my phone.

'Mum?'

I look up and see Frankie, proffering a parcel at me.

'Oh, thanks, darling.'

I take the parcel and pop it on the bench next to me.

'What is it?'

'Don't know, probably something boring I ordered from Amazon.'

Frankie hovers, bored and impatient for her friend to arrive. 'It was on the doorstep when I opened it. No delivery driver.'

'You know what they're like these days, they chuck parcels and run.'

Frankie shrugs and heads back inside, having already lost interest in the conversation and the parcel. But I glance at it again. There's no branding on it, which suggests that it's not Amazon after all. What have I ordered?

My curiosity is piqued and so I put my phone down and open the parcel. It's about the size of a shoebox and it's been sealed with brown parcel tape. Too lazy to go inside and find scissors, I rip it open and prise open the parcel, peering inside.

And then I scream.

'Run!'

The world is frozen in time, as Max looks at me, confused. I run towards him, pick him up and race to the end of the garden, throwing us both on the ground. I don't even feel any pain as we crash down on the hard, scorched grass.

'Liar, liar, Ellie on fire.' I scrunch my eyes closed and wait for the explosion as Max wriggles underneath me, confused and distressed.

Five, four, three, two, one. *Boom.*

But it wasn't loud enough. It was just a pop. I open my eyes and turn my head to face the package. It's still intact and there are no flames. I can't smell burning. But I remain where I am. My arms are trembling from the force of holding Max.

'Mum, you're hurting me!'

I look down at Max. Tears are spilling down his face. Still I don't move. There was a grenade in that box, I saw it with my own eyes. It didn't have a pin in it. What if it hasn't gone off yet? What if it's just a matter of seconds?

'What's going on, Mum?'

Frankie has appeared in the patio doors and is looking at me.

'Get back!' I scream.

But she ignores me, walking towards the box and peering in.

'Frankie, no!'

She picks up the grenade and studies it. 'What on earth have you been ordering?'

I'm hysterical. 'Frankie, put it down and get back in the house.'

'It's not real, Mum.'

'How do you know?'

She proffers it to me. 'Well for one, it's made of plastic.'

Slowly, I push up off the ground and help Max up. He's still sobbing. Tentatively, I walk over to Frankie and realise she's right. It's a toy. On closer inspection it has a battery inside it and the pop I heard was a sound effect.

'What's this?' Frankie lifts out a piece of paper from the box and reads it. '"Liar, liar, Ellie on fire. Boom."'

I snatch it from her and angrily rip it to shreds. Even now I know we're safe, I'm trembling. Max is still crying and I fling my arm around him, trying to reassure him but it's hard to do that when I'm a mess myself. Even Frankie's face has finally paled.

'Someone was trying to scare you,' she says, realisation dawning. 'They wanted you to think it was real.'

'Yes,' I whisper.

'It's not real, Mum, I promise.'

How has my fourteen-year-old ended up being the grown-up here? I finally shake myself out of my frozen terror and march inside the house.

'Pack a bag each, kids. We're leaving.'

* * *

I call Tom as I'm throwing some clothes into a bag.

'Where are you going?' he asks.

'To Tamsin's house.'

'I'll leave work now and meet you there.'

For once, the children do as they are asked. Within fifteen minutes we're loading the car and I'm reversing off the driveway. We drive to Tamsin's in almost silence. We're all shaken and I can't think of anything to say that will make any of us feel better.

It's only as I pull up outside Tamsin's house that I realise I haven't even called ahead. I just hope that she's home. My prayers are answered when she opens the door.

She takes one look at us, surrounded by bags, and ushers us in. She calls to Harry that Max has come over, fixes everyone a snack and ensconces them in front of the television with a film. And then she closes the door and looks at me with concern.

'What's happened?'

I tell her about the grenade and the fear on her face proves that I haven't overreacted.

'You did the right thing coming here,' she says.

'I'm sorry to intrude on you like this.'

'Don't be silly. We're happy to have you.'

I put my head in my hands. 'I can't believe this is happening again.'

'It'll all be over soon, mate.'

'I don't know what to do, Tamsin.'

Tamsin sits down next to me. 'We should call the police, of course.'

'I destroyed the evidence. I ripped the note up because I was in such a state.'

'They might still be able to find fingerprints on it, or the grenade or package.'

'You're right, I'll call. I just need a minute.' I take a few deep breaths and look at Tamsin. 'I'm going to change my statement.'

'You're what?'

'I'm going to tell the police that I can no longer be sure of what I saw. That I was distracted. It's the only way to make this stop.'

'You can't now, it's too late. For one, it could get you into a whole lot of trouble. And, anyway, it might mean that this Jason Turner bloke gets away with it.'

'I don't care any more,' I cry. 'I just want to keep my family safe. I'm scared, Tamsin. I'm scared they're really going to hurt one of us.'

'They?'

I throw my hands up in the air. 'I don't know! That's the problem.'

'Look, mate, calm down. It's going to be okay. The grenade was just a hoax. Yes, they meant to scare you but not to do you any physical harm. Nothing they have done has actually hurt anyone. It's just intimidation. Remember that, okay?'

'There's still a week to go. Anything could happen between now and then.'

'Look, you'll stay with us until the trial. No one knows you're here. And then you'll go and give your evidence and it'll be done. No point in trying to scare you then.'

'But he might want revenge.'

'He'll be behind bars.'

'You don't know that. Anyway, there's his family and friends.'

'Stop it. You're spiralling. Let's just take this one step at a time.'

'We're thinking of moving away,' I admit.

Tamsin's face falls. 'Moving where?'

'Surrey.'

'But that's not fair, to drive you away from your home, your friends.'

'Maybe it's what we all need. A fresh start.'

'Look, see how you feel after the case. When the dust has settled, you might have a different perspective on it. This is where your life is, Ellie, you and the kids. Have you told them you might be moving?'

'No, not yet.'

'Well don't say anything for now, I'm certain you'll change your mind.'

'I don't think so, I really don't. Not after this. In fact, the sooner the better.'

Tamsin looks crestfallen. 'I'm coming to court too,' she declares. 'I want to look this bastard in the eye.'

'It'll be a full house in the courtroom at this rate.'

'What the hell are the police playing at? Why haven't they been able to link any of this to the lorry driver or his family?'

I shrug. 'I don't know. For a while I even thought it might not be him.'

'Who else would it be?'

'I considered Samantha's friend, Amelia.'

'What, she doesn't like that you're pally with her best mate, so she sends you a grenade in the post?'

I look at Tamsin and, unexpectedly, a giggle escapes. A tiny chink of comedy in the depths of hell. It's a small mercy but I'll take it. I'll take any light relief at the moment.

Tamsin squeezes my arm gently. 'It's not Amelia, it's *him*. Jason Turner. Or his buddies. I'll be by your side from now on. And so will Tom. You don't need to be afraid.'

'But I am.'

We're interrupted by the doorbell ringing and fear jolts through me until I remember that we're at Tamsin's house and we're safe. Unless he's found us here?

But Tamsin returns with Tom, who is flustered.

'I got here as quickly as I could,' he says, coming over to hug me.

'Thank you,' I murmur into his ear.

'I'll go and check on the kids,' Tamsin says, disappearing and giving us some privacy.

Tom pulls away and looks at me. 'You okay?'

'No.'

'Me neither. I checked the camera footage on my phone but all you can see is a figure dressed in black from head to toe, dumping the parcel, ringing the doorbell and going. They must have known the camera was there because they didn't look up once. I don't think the police will be able to identify them.'

'I don't even think we should tell them.'

'Come on, Ellie, we have to.'

'No,' I insist. 'They've been next to useless about the previous incidents. This won't be any different. I just want to forget all about it, okay? We're safe at Tamsin's.'

'But how long can we stay here? We can't move in forever.'

'We'll stay until the trial. And after that, I think we should move straight to Surrey. We can rent until we find somewhere to buy. I can start applying for schools and we might even get the children in straight away if they have spaces.'

'Are you serious?'

I look at my husband. 'Yes.'

'But it's so sudden.'

'We've already been talking about it. We need this, Tom. I need this. I will never feel safe again in St Albans. Even after the trial.'

Tom gazes at me for a few minutes and I see nothing but love and worry in his eyes. He doesn't want to do it, but he will because he loves me.

'Okay,' he says.

I hug him. 'Thank you,' I whisper.

Something resembling optimism courses through me, the prospect of an end being in sight, and I decide to strike while the iron is hot. I pull out my phone to look at properties available to rent in the Surrey towns that I've already shortlisted. Tom, bless him, looks over my shoulder, pointing at one he likes the look of. It's a three-bed house, within walking distance to a train station with a direct line into London. And it's close to the schools I've been looking at for the kids. It'll do, for now, and it'll give us time to sell our house in St Albans and find a property to buy in Surrey.

'I'll phone the agent to arrange a viewing,' I say, about to press dial.

But I never get to make the call because just then I hear a crash, followed by Tamsin's frantic screaming.

17

I gaze at my reflection in the mirror. Smooth down my already crumpling white shirt and wipe the sweat pooling above my lips. Then I turn to face Tom.

'You ready?' he asks.

'No.'

He takes my hand. 'Come on. It'll be okay.'

We have been staying in a hotel for the past week. It's far from ideal and the kids are climbing the walls but at least we're safe. After Tamsin's window got smashed by a brick, with a flaming piece of cloth wrapped around it, we had no choice.

'Liar, liar, Ellie on fire.'

Luckily, Tamsin acted quickly and put out the fire before it could spread, preventing any major damage. But shards of glass from the window left cuts on Harry's bare arms. They weren't deep but Tamsin rushed him straight to hospital to be safe. I still feel so guilty about it because I'm the reason why it happened. The poor children were shaking with fear and Tamsin tried to put on a brave face, but it was obvious that she was deeply upset and afraid too. I should never have gone to her house, because I put her family in danger, and although she has repeatedly reassured me that it wasn't my fault, I could see her relief when I said we were leaving that day.

Of course, Jason Turner has an alibi. He was at the pub all afternoon for his birthday, conveniently with all his friends and family, and camera footage proves it. The police went door to door but there were no witnesses to the incident. Whoever is doing this got away with it again. But it proves that I was followed from my house to Tamsin's. And that was enough for the police to move us into temporary accommodation.

And the most ridiculous thing? Jason Turner has issued a formal complaint against the police for harassment and the negative impact on his mental health. He insists he's not behind any of these attacks on my family and it's a witch hunt.

Well, we're both getting our day in court. As I take one last look at myself in the mirror, scrutinising my sunken eyes and dark circles, my stomach plummets. This is not how I wanted to feel when I finally gave evidence. I wanted to be ready, to be energised and strong. Instead, I'm a quivering mess, exhausted from stress and lack of sleep.

I've thought about it constantly over the past week and I know what I have to do now. I haven't told anyone my plan and I wouldn't say I've made peace with it either but it's the only option I have left. Now I just have to summon the strength to carry it out.

I let Tom lead me out of the hotel room and down the corridor to the lift. We descend in silence with our hands intertwined and walk to his car. I notice that there is a police car pulled up next to it and it follows us all the way to court. When we arrive, Tom finds a place to park and we enter the imposing building, side by side. I feel like there's a target on my back and every noise or toot of a car horn makes me jump. Tom squeezes my hand as he pushes open the door. The room is full of smartly dressed people waiting to go through security. As I sway, nauseous, I marvel at how this is just a normal day for some of them. The lawyers and the staff who work here are on the payroll, nothing more and nothing less. But there are other people too, just like me, who look bewildered, and I wonder if they're also here to give evidence or to watch their loved ones in the dock. I wonder if any of them are family or friends of Jason, if one of the people standing just a few feet away from me is responsible for threatening us. A young man catches my eye and I quickly look away, fearful that he might confront me.

Paula is waiting for us on the other side of security.

'Hi, Ellie,' she says with a warm smile. 'How are you feeling?'

'Fine,' I lie.

'Would you like a tea or a coffee?'

'No, thank you.'

Paula explains that the trial has started. She expects that I'll be called, likely at some point this afternoon, and until then all I can do is wait. Tom can stay with me in the area I've been allocated. We follow her into a room, and she runs through a few things with me and then, after asking if I need anything, she leaves us to it. We sit, side by side, fiddling with our hands. The cereal and milk I forced down this morning curdles in my stomach, and I can't stop sweating. I can feel damp patches forming underneath my sticky armpits.

Stick to the plan.

The problem is, the right thing to do for one family is wrong for another. And I can't reconcile that. But my family must come first because their safety is paramount. And even though we're still planning to move as soon as possible if we can find somewhere to rent quickly, I'm not sure I'll feel safe, even miles away from here. I've gone past the point of no return and I know I'll always be looking over my shoulder, waiting for the next threat or worse. They found me at Tamsin's house and they can find me in Surrey too. It will never end.

That's why you have to stick to the plan.

Time drags. Tom tries to make conversation but eventually gives up. He goes to fetch us some coffees. He paces around then sits down again. At some point Paula comes in again and asks if we want any lunch. I shake my head. She tells me I should eat so I agree to a sandwich which I know I won't have. She says it shouldn't be too much longer. Tom asks her how the case is going so far but there's not much to report. I picture the people inside the courtroom, Samantha sitting in the public gallery, Amelia by her side. My hands begin to tremble and my mouth is dry. I look out of the window and wonder if I can climb out of it and run away, if I would survive the drop.

And then Paula's telling me it's time. My legs almost crumple beneath me as I stand up. Tom wishes me luck and then makes his way to the public gallery. I follow Paula into court and towards the witness stand. The courtroom is smaller than I imagined but it's still intimidating. Nerves are churning my stomach and I can feel everyone's eyes on me. I keep mine on the ground as I step into the witness stand and put my hand on the Bible. I vow to tell the truth, the whole truth and nothing but the truth. And then I instinctively look up into the packed gallery.

Samantha is sitting at the front. Her dad is on one side of her and Amelia is on the other. Behind them, just to the right, are Tom and Tamsin.

My eyes move between Tom and Samantha. I am in agony. I don't know what to do. My earlier, flimsy resolve has gone out of the window. My hastily hatched plan is falling apart. I thought I could do it but now I've seen Samantha, looking so brave and stoic, I don't think I can go through with it. I can't lie, even if it's to protect my family. Can I? I look at Tom, and think of Frankie and

Max, and the resolve returns. If I just say that I might have been wrong, that I can't be 100 per cent certain of what I saw, then all this goes away. The bad people will leave us alone.

Oh God, what do I do?

Lie.

Tell the truth.

I look at Samantha again and then it hits me, *really* hits me, that I can't do it. It's not just that I've sworn on the Bible, an action that has affected me more than I thought it would. I can't lie in court, in front of Samantha. In front of the bravest woman I know. The one whose friendship I have come to cherish these past months. She deserves the truth. Justice for Graham.

Oh God, what am I doing?

I lift my chin and face the jury, like Samantha and Paula have told me to. I refuse to look at Jason, sitting in the dock. I don't search the courtroom for the reporter who I suspect is there, scribbling hurried notes which will become printed words for all to read. I focus only on the twelve men and women sitting in front of me.

I take a deep breath and brace myself for questioning.

The prosecution barrister is first and I have been prepared for this. I answer her questions, telling her who I am and what I saw. I stick to my statement like glue. This isn't too bad, it's going well so far. The barrister is gentle, sympathetic. She's on my side. I relax a fraction, not too much, but I'm starting to ease into it.

After a while, I pause to take a sip of water. My eyes are dry, my throat scratchy. But I'm okay, I'm doing well. I glance at the jury and some look back at me kindly. Others simply stare. I realise that we are all just everyday human beings, here through duty not choice. The jurors are fulfilling their obligations, as I am mine.

I repeat what I said in my statement.

'The car in front of me slowed down and stopped at the junction. And the next thing I knew, the lorry had driven straight into it. It came from nowhere.'

I well up as I describe how I leaped from the car and went to the crash site. My voice wobbles as I explain how I guessed Graham was already dead. How the lorry driver cried out in anguish and it took me a few seconds to gather myself and call 999.

And then it's over. The prosecution barrister thanks me and sits down. I know that the hard bit comes next, because it's time for cross-examination. But I'm feeling more confident now, more certain of myself. I can do this. I'm halfway there and then I can walk out of this court. Only a couple more hours to go and then we'll move to Surrey as soon as possible and pray that no one finds us there. Or that they leave us alone.

Maybe, over time, I'll learn to stop looking over my shoulder.

'Mrs Appleby,' the defence barrister begins. He's a formidable man, in his fifties with a stern expression which suggests infinite experience and a voice that commands authority. I look him in the eye, remembering that I am not the accused here.

Do your worst. I'm ready for you.

'Why were you driving that evening?'

I'm thrown immediately by his opening question. What does that have to do with anything?

'Excuse me?' I splutter.

'It's a simple question, Mrs Appleby. Why were you driving that evening?'

'I was on my way home.'

'From where?'

The courtroom walls begin to close in on me as I try to recalibrate. Why is he asking me this? Is he just trying to throw me off? If he is, it's working.

'From work,' I say.

'Do you usually drive home from work?'

'I get the train to St Albans and drive home from the station.'

'And is that what you were doing that evening? Driving home from the station?'

My mouth is like sandpaper. I can feel every single person's eyes on me. 'I don't see what this has got to do with the accident,' I splutter, looking pleadingly at the prosecution barrister. Why is she not intervening? Surely this is irrelevant.

'Please answer the question, Mrs Appleby.'

The truth, the whole truth and nothing but the truth. Realisation comes crashing down around me as I understand what is happening. And there is no escape.

He knows.

'No.' My voice is small, uncertain.

'Can you speak up for the jury please, Mrs Appleby?'

'No,' I repeat, a little louder. 'I wasn't driving home from the station.'

'Where were you driving home from that evening?'

I'm going to be sick. My tongue feels huge in my mouth. I take another sip of water and some of it spills over my fingers. Slowly, I put the glass back down.

'Mrs Appleby?'

'I was driving home from meeting a friend.'

'And where had you met this friend?'

'At a hotel.'

The barrister raises his eyebrows theatrically. He holds the detonator to the bomb that will blow up my life, and he is planning to use it. I hate him. 'An odd place to meet a friend, isn't it?'

'Not really.'

'What were you and this friend doing at the hotel?'

'Objection!'

The prosecution barrister intervenes, arguing about relevance and the next thing I know, the judge has called a short adjournment and someone is guiding me out of the dock. I'm led to a room, this time without Tom to keep me company, and I pace agitatedly, trying to work out what's going on inside that courtroom. Why we've all been sent out. But deep down I already know the answer. The defence barrister has evidence, which he wants to use to destroy me for no good reason, and they are discussing whether it's admissible. I feel like a trapped animal, desperate to claw myself out of this room, this court. I'm angry at the injustice of it and I'm very, very afraid. But surely the judge won't permit the new evidence? It's not relevant to this trial, I'm sure of it. I cling to this hope but the longer I wait, the more of a state I work myself up into.

Finally, I'm called back in and I see the look on the prosecution barrister's face. She's angry. Furious. In contrast, the defence barrister looks satisfied. And my mind starts whirring at a thousand miles per hour because I can tell from his smug expression that the judge has permitted him to continue. And I am ensnared, acutely aware of what is about to happen next and completely unable to do anything about it.

The barrister repeats his question, one that I have no choice but to answer.

'Mrs Appleby, what were you and this friend doing at the hotel?'

Everyone is waiting. I swore on the Bible to tell the truth. I looked Samantha in the eye and made a solemn vow not to lie. All I've ever wanted was to do the right thing and now it's going to cost me everything.

'We were, um, you know, *together*.'

'Together? Can you explain what you mean by together?'

I can't believe he's going to make me say it. He's a cruel, nasty man.

I answer in a shaky voice. 'We were having sex.'

There is an audible gasp from the public gallery. I can't look up. My lip wobbles and tears begin to fall down my cheeks. But I still can't look up. I can't see the expression on Tom's face as he learns, along with a room full of dozens of strangers, what I've done. Who I am.

I'm a liar.

'Mrs Appleby,' the defence barrister continues. 'You said you were meeting a friend for sex. Was this man your husband?'

I want the ground to open up and swallow me. 'No.'

'Please speak up for the jury, Mrs Appleby.'

'No,' I almost shout, detesting this vile man with every inch of my being. Hating that Tom is here, listening to this. Most of all, hating myself.

'Who was this man?'

'Why is this relevant?' I cry. I can't even look at the jury any more.

'Please answer the question Mrs Appleby.'

Tears spill over my cheeks. It's done. There's nothing left to save.

I don't look at the jury as I mumble the answer. 'Graham Hunter.'

18

There is a commotion in the gallery. I hear a kerfuffle, a door opening and closing. Someone has stormed out. Is it Tom? Is it Samantha? I'm too afraid to check. I've let everyone down. I've hurt the people that I love and this is my punishment.

Because I didn't witness a stranger die. I witnessed the death of my lover. The man who had, just an hour earlier, been whispering into my ear that I turned him on.

The man who was on the way home to his wife with the scent of me still on him.

* * *

I met Graham Hunter on the train home from work one evening. He was sitting next to me reading a tatty paperback and I was scrolling on my phone. I barely noticed him until the train lurched to an abrupt halt and flung me against him.

'I'm sorry,' I said, righting myself.

He smiled, holding my gaze for a second longer than necessary. 'No problem.'

I looked away, thinking that the man sitting next to me had the kind of eyes you could get lost in. And I felt something stir inside me.

It was a welcome sensation that had come at a time in my life when I craved excitement. I was struggling with my mental health, feeling like I had no control over my life. Every day felt like an effort, my temper was on a short fuse and everything Tom did or said annoyed me. We were rarely intimate and I took his rejection personally, even though I was just as exhausted at the end of the day as he was. I was afraid of getting older and becoming invisible and my hormones were all over the place. I buried my head in the sand, refusing to seek medical help until the damage was done. These are not excuses because I have no excuse for what I did. But they are my reasons.

As I listened to the train driver apologising for the delay and reassuring us that we would be on the move again shortly, I peered at Graham's book and he noticed.

'Have you read it?' he asked, showing me the front cover. *Adam Bede* by George Eliot.

'No, is it any good?'

'It's a classic.'

'What's it about?'

'A horny squire who seduces a beautiful country girl.'

I blushed as I said, 'I prefer thrillers myself.'

We got chatting, about books, commuting and which stop we were getting off at. Graham was incredibly easy to talk to. He was fun, and charismatic. I was drawn to his eyes. They were glimmering pools that I wanted to bathe in and he was one of those people who, when they looked at you, made you feel like the only person in the world. The other passengers in the cramped carriage faded away so that it seemed like Graham and I were the only people who existed. In no time at all, the train had started moving again and a few minutes later we reached my stop. I didn't want to get up and leave this man; I could happily have kept talking to him until the end of the line and back again. But I stood up, said goodbye and walked off the train with a spring in my step. On the platform, I glanced in through the carriage window as I passed and my heart skipped a beat when I saw that he was watching me.

That evening, as I gazed at the television next to a snoozing Tom, I thought about Graham and the instant sexual attraction I'd felt. It was like I'd woken from the dead. I was alive again, invigorated, stifling giggles like a schoolgirl. I fell asleep with his face etched in my mind and when I woke up the next morning, my first thought was whether I'd see him again. I had a crush for the first time in nearly twenty years and I laughed at myself for how silly I was being. I was acting more like Frankie than a grown woman.

When I got on the train, I looked for him but he was not there. I stood in a vestibule, downcast and defeated. Then I gave myself a stern talking-to. I was being ridiculous and I needed to grow up and stop acting like a lovestruck teenager. So, I accepted that I'd probably never see my handsome stranger again and I got on with life.

A week later, I had just got on the train in London and secured a seat when I felt someone looming over me. I looked up and saw Graham smiling down at me. His eyes sparkled with mischief and, I thought, a hint of pleasure at seeing me.

'Is this seat taken?' he asked.

I scooted over to the window and he sat down beside me. Our legs touched briefly, and I was instantly turned on. We talked all the way home again, about our jobs, our lives, our hobbies. Occasionally, he touched my arm mid-conversation in a way that suggested the attraction was mutual. I had no idea where this was going, or even where I wanted it to go. I was married and I knew that he was too as he wore a gold band on his ring finger. I told myself that we were just enjoying a minor, harmless flirtation in the no-man's-land between work and home, and perhaps that was okay.

We were not doing anything wrong, only talking.

As we approached my stop, the disappointment was crushing.

'See you soon,' I said, standing up and gathering my things.

'I hope so,' he replied.

I lurched down the carriage towards the exit, grinning like an idiot at his final comment. I'd gone from zero to hero in seconds. My smile remained on my face all the way to the car park and on the drive home. Guilt crept in but I pushed it away. It was just a silly train crush and I wasn't going to act on it. I was married, not dead, and it was natural to feel attraction to other people, especially ones with eyes like Graham's. But I was going home to my husband and he was going home to his wife.

Later that night, as I lay in bed, I thought about Graham. I studied every inch of him in my mind. His dark, tousled hair, those damn eyes, the way his suit shirt fitted over his slender body, giving a hint of what lay underneath. As I listened to Tom grunting in his sleep, I drifted off, imagining that it was Graham beside me.

I started seeing Graham on the train more frequently after that. We learned each other's working patterns, what days we commuted into London. Soon we had an unspoken arrangement to meet in the same carriage. We saved seats for each other. And as the weeks went by, our conversations became flirtier. Knowing that I was going to see him became the highlight of my day, the thing that I lived for. I bounced out of bed in the morning and spent more time than usual getting ready because I was excited. I was teetering towards the danger zone, the area that I could definitely no longer justify as harmless fun, but I couldn't stop myself. I hurtled towards it willingly, blind to sense and reason. Graham had become an addiction and I was hooked.

I would never have made the first move. I was content to live in this world for as long as possible, flirting with a man who had put a spring in my step for the first time in ages, without ever acting on my urges. The fantasy was more than enough for me. But then one evening, Graham asked me if I wanted to get a drink instead of going straight home. I knew exactly what he was asking. This wasn't a drink. Warning bells echoed around my head. Danger, danger! An image of Tom flashed into my mind.

And then Graham leaned in and said quietly, 'You're the most beautiful woman I've ever met in my life, Ellie. I can't stop thinking about you. I'm obsessed.'

It was like he'd spoken the secret password to my heart. And before I knew it, I'd agreed.

I got off at St Albans as usual. Graham got off at Harpenden. But instead of going home I sent a message to Tom telling him I was going to be late and drove to a hotel that Graham had suggested because it had a decent bar. I turned off my thoughts on that drive to the hotel. Switched them off like a tap and it was frighteningly easy to do because I was just so excited. I was single-minded in my lust for Graham, my *need* to be near him. Nothing else mattered. Just one drink and never again, I told myself.

He was waiting for me in the car park and my heart lurched when I saw him, leaning up against his car, watching me with his head slightly cocked. I could scarcely believe that this was about to happen. We walked in together and headed to the bar where we ordered some drinks. Electricity was crackling between us as we sat down, side by side, in a booth and clinked our glasses together.

We never finished that drink. Halfway through, Graham suggested that we go upstairs and I nodded my agreement. Without saying a word, we headed straight for the reception desk where we booked a room for the night.

As soon as the lift doors closed, he was on me. He was all over me. Lips, hands, body. And I kissed him like it would be the last time I ever kissed a man. I could not get enough of him. And then, suddenly, I pulled away mortified.

'Graham, we can't do this,' I said. 'We're married.'

He looked contrite. 'I know. But you're not happy, and nor am I. We have something, you and I, a connection we can't deny.'

If I'd been rational, I would have seen right through his empty words. But I wasn't rational, I was a hot mess. And he was telling me exactly what I needed to hear. He was justifying what we were doing when I was unable to do it myself.

'I *see* you, Ellie. I see just how special you are.'

It was all I wanted, to be seen. To not be invisible. And so when he leaned in to kiss me again, I didn't push him away. We staggered to our room and the minute we were inside he pushed me up against the door, the weight of his body on me, his beautiful lips on mine. Somewhere between the door and the bed, our clothes were discarded and then we were in a tangle over the sheets and I was gazing into his eyes, wanting him more than I have ever wanted anyone or anything in my life.

How could it be wrong when it felt so right?

The spell was broken as soon as it ended. We lay side by side, our bodies slick with sweat and guilt overcame me, sending waves of panic through my entire body.

'We shouldn't have done that,' I said.

He turned on his side and propped his head up with his hand. 'I know.'

'Have you ever done anything like this before?'

'No, never, have you?'

'No.'

Graham's eyes moved greedily over me. 'We shouldn't have done it. But I wanted to. I really, really wanted to.'

'Me too.'

'You are so sexy, Ellie. I've wanted you since I first saw you, sitting on that train. I know it's wrong, but I've fantasised about the things I want to do to you.'

It was music to my ears. A symphony blasting through my brain and filling me with such immense pleasure that I didn't even care about the brutal comedown I knew I would suffer now that I had got my fix. I would take the eternity of guilt and self-loathing for just one more minute with this man. One *second*.

We went our separate ways soon after. We didn't arrange to meet again or make any promises that we couldn't keep. As I drove home, the comedown hit me and I was drowning in shame. I told myself that I would never do it again. It was a mistake, a one-off, an itch I had to scratch and now I had. I would focus on my marriage and my family and forget all about Graham Hunter. I would avoid what we now knew as 'our carriage', maybe even get a later train so that I could make sure I didn't bump into him again.

I went home and tried to act normal. To not wince when Tom touched me. To see my home in all its glory and my children in all theirs. But I just couldn't do it. Like any addiction, once I'd had a taste I needed more. I could never be sated.

A few days later I stood on the platform at St Pancras, knowing that Graham worked in the office on Fridays and would be on the train. And I also knew that no matter what my head told me, my heart was already in our carriage. And when I saw him walking down the platform towards me, heading towards the same doors, I knew that I was in this, hook, line and sinker, and so was he.

We swapped numbers after that. We didn't need to, because we could arrange all our encounters while on the train, but we enjoyed being in contact with each other. Sending secret messages, letting the anticipation build before we could meet up again. We started going to the hotel every couple of weeks and I counted down the days.

It was only sex. Maybe some infatuation, for a time, at least on my part. But I was not in love with Graham and he was not in love with me. There was never any doubt that this was anything more or that we would leave our partners. We knew what we both wanted and we gave it to each other, no questions asked. I tried to justify the unjustifiable. I wasn't hurting anybody, it was purely physical. I was lying to myself. But that's what addicts do. Because all that matters is the next fix, the next high. All that mattered was him.

I don't know how I did it. I'm not sure how I managed to go from ripping Graham's clothes off in a hotel room to asking Frankie if she had done her homework, or Tom if he fancied pasta for dinner. But I did do it, and my family were none the wiser. I became the master of deception, living two lives. Having my cake and eating it.

It took a few months for the high to wear off and, as my desire waned, I began to see our affair for what it was. Sordid. Two married people meeting at a nondescript hotel, lying to their families for their own pleasure. I'm sure that the staff on the reception desk knew exactly what was going on and I was ashamed. It began to sicken me.

Graham felt me beginning to withdraw. At first, he tried to

kiss my guilt away with an expertise that made me wonder if he'd lied about never having done this before. While I was grappling with my internal struggles, he didn't seem fazed by what we were doing. He didn't talk of remorse or guilt, only of how sexy I was and how much he wanted me. And slowly I began to see him in a different light. He was still charming, still handsome, but he became a man again, not the demigod I had made him out to be in my head. I humanised him, I saw his flaws. The way he interrupted me when I was talking or quickly lost interest in what I was saying. How he liked to show off about his successful career and his clever sons. His wife was a no-go area, as was Tom, but he mentioned her once in passing and when I heard her name on his lips, I froze. *Samantha*. The fantasy was beautiful, but the reality became ugly and as my remorse grew and my obsession with Graham withered; the glowing light of my attraction dimmed too.

On the evening of the accident, we had sex for what I decided was the last time. I didn't enjoy it and that was when I realised it was over. Graham wasn't surprised and he accepted it easily when I told him I was done. Too easily, I thought, as I was driving home from the hotel. I had done the right thing by ending it, but I still felt miserable. Graham, however, had simply nodded, wished me all the best and left me alone in the hotel room. I had hurried to my car and pulled out of the car park behind him, following his tail lights and growing in frustration. Had I meant nothing to him? Had all his pillow talk been a ruse?

I needed closure. I didn't want it to finish in the way that it had. I was being selfish, craving a romantic end to what had been the most exciting, nerve-wracking months of my life. I wanted him to tell me that he cared for me and he would miss me but that he understood and respected my decision. Frankly, I wanted a fairy tale, a perfect memory, because his reaction had made me feel seedy and used, and I didn't like it.

I used voice command to call him from my car and he answered after a few rings.

'Ellie?'

'Graham, I'm sorry to call, I just didn't like the way we left things.'

'What do you mean?'

'It felt very sudden and abrupt. And I don't want you to think that I don't care about you and what happened between us.'

He was quiet for a moment. This was when he was supposed to say that he cared for me too and that he was going to miss me. That he would always remember me.

'Graham, are you there?'

'What do you want me to say, Ellie?'

My heart started pounding as indignation bubbled inside me. Why was he being so dismissive? Was I being unreasonable to want to know that I meant something to him?

'I don't want you to say anything you don't want to say, Graham.'

I heard him sigh. 'I'm married, Ellie. You know that.'

I was exasperated as I stared at the back of his car, at his number plate which I had memorised months ago. 'Of course I know that. That's not what this is about. I'm married too, in case you forgot.'

'So, what do you want?'

My fuse blew. Perhaps my own guilt was making me defensive or perhaps I'm just so self-centred that I simply had to have this man's parting adoration.

'To know that I meant something!' I cried. 'To know that *we* meant something.'

'Look, Ellie, we had fun. I thought that was what you wanted.'

'It was what I wanted.'

'Good. Then what's the problem?'

'Graham, why are you being like this?'

His car slowed down as he reached a junction, and I looked through the windscreen at the back of his head. Saw him holding a phone up to his ear. He was not using hands-free like I was. And for some reason this infuriated me even more.

Arrogant prick.

'I'm not being like anything,' he said. 'I don't know what you want from me. You ended this, not me. You told me it was over. So, it's over. Why are you angry?'

His car stopped and I saw his eyes in the rear-view mirror as he glanced back. I stared at the man who, not too long ago, had been inside me. I was transfixed in his gaze.

And then a lorry appeared from nowhere and ploughed straight into him and the next time I saw Graham, he was dead.

I did not lie about the accident. My statement was a true and accurate account of what I witnessed.

But I lied about everything else. And I didn't tell the police that I knew Graham, because then my dirty secret would be out and I didn't see how it would help. It had nothing to do with what happened. The lorry would still have hit Graham, regardless of whether we were having an affair. Logic told me that I was not to blame. But the guilt and the grief were unbearable. I couldn't shake them off, no matter what I did. The nightmares plagued me, reminding me that I was the reason why Graham was on that road in the first place, why his wife no longer had a husband, and his sons had no father.

I felt wretched and disgusting and culpable. And that is what no one else understood. My friends and family thought I'd seen a stranger die and I couldn't tell them the truth. I couldn't explain that this man had been an important part of my life, the sole focus of my thoughts and desires for months. And I couldn't tell them that the crash probably wouldn't have happened if we'd never met. I pictured Graham's dead body every night, I obsessed over the accident, and I became overburdened with regret.

'*Help*.' I had to do something to make things right because I couldn't live with myself if I didn't. And the only thing I could think of was to help Graham's widow. To make amends for what I had done. I never expected to become friends with Samantha, only to support her in some small way. To make sure that she was okay.

I know it sounds irrational, but I was not rational after the accident. I wasn't even rational before the accident. A midlife crisis, Tamsin called it. Perhaps it was, but it felt more fundamental than that. It was all consuming, all I could think of. My need for excitement, to rebel against the mundanity of life, had ended in tragedy.

And now it was time for my penitence.

I thought if I just went to the funeral, I would have closure. I would see Samantha, pay my respects and move on. I also wanted to say goodbye to Graham properly too, to tell him how sorry I was. The ending I never got to have.

But then I met Samantha. I wasn't surprised that she was beautiful, because I had pictured her to be already, but I didn't feel any jealousy towards her, only acute guilt and remorse. And I was drawn to her in a way that I can't explain. It honestly wasn't about feeling closer to Graham, it was a mechanism to make me feel less guilty for what I'd done. Witnessing Samantha's healing was like cleansing my sins. As she began to grow stronger, so did I. I went to see a doctor and started taking antidepressants, wishing I'd done it earlier. I focused more on my marriage, knowing that I was just as much to blame as Tom for not making enough effort. I shared my feelings with Tamsin and realised that

I was not alone. And to know that I was part of Samantha's support network gave me respite from my inner demons. But it was more than that in the end because I grew to love Samantha. Over time, it became easy to be friends with her, until I almost forgot how I came to know her. I stopped seeing her as Graham's wife, and instead thought of her as my close friend. Someone I would never hurt.

At the same time, I realised how lucky I was to have what I did. How close I came to almost losing it because I gave in to my selfish needs and insecurities. I vowed that I would no longer take Tom for granted and I would never betray him again either.

I had done a terrible thing, and I would spend the rest of my life making up for it. I would seize the second chance I had been given, appreciate every moment with my family, show my love for Tom, and no one ever needed to know this sordid secret.

But now the entire world knows who I am. What I've done. 'Liar, liar, Ellie on fire.' They didn't need a flaming brick to decimate my life after all.

I did that myself.

19

The judge is warning people to calm down. He is reminding them that this is a court of law and if there are any more interruptions from the public gallery, they will be asked to leave. I slump in the witness stand, overcome with stunned humiliation. I may not be the defendant in this trial, but it feels like I am. And I am guilty as charged.

I can't believe this is how Tom and Samantha have found out about the affair. I will never be able to look either of them in the eye again. I will never forgive myself for what I have put them through. I'd rather be sent down to the cells than walk out of this courtroom and face the people I love. Will anyone have my back? Tamsin perhaps? I don't deserve it, but I crave her support anyway. Or will she leave with Tom, appalled by my behaviour and choosing to side with the innocent victim?

I won't get to find out just yet because my ordeal is far from over. The defence barrister isn't finished with me and I have no choice but to remain where I am, in view of the entire court, a hundred pairs of eyes fixed on me.

'Mrs Appleby, can you confirm for the court that the man you met with at the hotel is the same Graham Hunter who subsequently died in the accident?'

'Yes.'

'Were you having an affair with Graham Hunter?'

I hang my head, defeated. 'Yes.'

'How long had this affair been going on for?'

'Objection.' The prosecutor is on her feet again, arguing about relevance. But her intervention doesn't matter to me any more. It's too late for me, the objection is futile.

The defence barrister changes tack. 'To confirm for the court, on the night of the accident, were you driving home after having met Graham at the hotel to have sex?'

'Yes.'

'Why were you driving behind him?'

'We were both on the way home. At the junction, he was turning right and I was turning left.'

'Did you call Mr Hunter while you were driving?'

I'm still looking down at the floor, all pretence of speaking directly to the jury gone. But dread is crawling all over my skin like a swarm of insects because I know what he's getting at now. I finally understand why this horrible man has attacked me like this. It's not about the affair, that's collateral damage. No, it's about the phone call. But that call did not cause the accident. Graham was stationary when the lorry crashed into him. He had stopped at the junction. I know it. I *know* it.

And, even in defeat, a tiny spark of fight comes back to me.

'That has nothing to do with this,' I say, my voice rising.

'Please answer the question, Mrs Appleby.'

'Yes, I called him but—'

'Were you still on the phone to Graham Hunter when the accident occurred?'

'Yes, but—'

'And what were you discussing during this phone call?'

I didn't think it was possible to be more miserable, but it turns out I was wrong.

'We were arguing.'

'What were you arguing about?'

'We had finished things that evening and I didn't like the way it had ended.'

'You were upset?'

'Yes.'

'Was Mr Hunter upset?'

I give a small shrug. 'Not really.'

'Is it reasonable to say that you were distracted?'

'No!'

'And that Mr Hunter was also distracted?'

'No!'

'And was Mr Hunter having this phone call with you on a hands-free device?'

I picture the phone held up to his ear. His eyes on mine as he looked at me through the rear-view mirror. 'No.'

Another gasp from the public gallery. I still haven't looked in that direction, so I have no idea if Tom, Samantha or Tamsin are still there. If one or all of them haven't walked out.

'Can you please confirm to the jury that Mr Hunter was illegally using his mobile phone while driving?'

I'm in hell. The depths of hell. 'Yes.'

The barrister's smile is smug. Victorious. 'Mrs Appleby, I put it to you that when the accident happened, you were not paying attention to the road.'

I finally look up and stare down the defence barrister. 'I *was* on hands-free, and I was absolutely paying attention.'

'No, you were arguing with your lover, who was in the car in front of you. Graham Hunter. Who was, in turn, arguing with you. And as you continued to row, is it possible that Mr Hunter was also so distracted, while illegally using a phone without hands-free, that he began to pull out of the junction without checking for vehicles?'

Tears stream down my face and I don't even try to wipe them away. 'No.'

'And is it possible, Mrs Appleby, that you were so busy arguing with your lover that you didn't see exactly what happened in those few seconds before the crash?'

'No.'

It doesn't matter what I say or how much I deny it. The defence has made its case, and the jury has heard it. The seed of doubt has been planted.

The lorry driver is going to get off and it's all because of me.

Did I kill Graham Hunter?

No, I didn't. But the person who did, the individual who I am sure is responsible for the accident, and for tormenting me for months, is going to be acquitted. Graham will not get justice because of me. I have let him down. I have let my husband down, my children, my friends. Graham's family. Samantha. And all because of an affair that didn't end the way I wanted it to.

'I have no further questions.'

The defence barrister sits down and folds his robes over. He has done his job. He can go home to his family at the end of the day, enjoy a nice dinner and a glass of wine, and forget all about the witness he ripped to shreds that day. Perhaps he thinks I deserve it, or more likely he simply doesn't care. This win will be good for his career.

The prosecution barrister rises momentarily, shooting me a furious look. 'No further questions, Your Honour.'

I am dismissed from court, but I can't move. I don't want to go out there and face the world. A clerk approaches and tries to help me, but I wriggle out of their grasp. They try again, this time with a firmer grip and I force myself to stand because I realise that I can't stay here forever. I'm making a scene. My eyes are involuntary drawn to Jason, the accused, sitting in the dock. He is staring back at me, his face unreadable. There is emotion but I can't decipher it. Is it shock? Anger? Relief? Incredulity? Sympathy?

He probably won't go to prison now. As a free man, will he continue his vendetta against me? He got what he wanted, but he was put through hell to achieve it. I held critical information that could have prevented him from ever being charged so it's possible that he will be angrier than ever. And we can't relocate to Surrey now, not after what's happened. I don't know if Tom will ever forgive me, let alone move house for a new life together. I am stuck here, among these people who know what I did, for the rest of my life. And what will happen to our children? Our poor, innocent kids whose lives are also about to be blown apart? How many lives have I destroyed with my selfishness?

Maybe Graham will get his justice after all. Samantha too. Because what I did and who I hurt will hang over me forever, a life sentence. Someone *has* been punished for the accident and will continue paying the price for a long time to come. I deserve it.

As the clerk escorts me out of court, I force myself to look at the public gallery. I need to know who's there and who's not, what I'm dealing with when I go outside. I see Tamsin first, sitting next to the empty chair where Tom was. I wonder how much of it he heard before he left. She's watching me, her face pale, her mouth open. Then she looks away and this small gesture tells me everything I need to know.

My gaze moves towards the middle of the gallery and, inevitably, rests on Samantha. She has been crying, her beautiful face is red and blotchy. Her life was turned upside down when Graham died, and I've just sent it spinning again. She knows her husband betrayed her and that the woman she thought had become a close friend was the very person he was sleeping with. She does not deserve this and I am even more disgusted with myself. Samantha doesn't meet my gaze, but I can feel someone else's eyes burning into me. Amelia. There's no ambiguity in her expression. It's anger. Hatred. She knew all along that I was a bad egg and I've just proven her right.

I look away and hold my breath as the court doors open.

The first person I see is Paula, who comes rushing up to me.

'I had no idea,' she says hurriedly. 'It was late evidence and it should have been disclosed to us. The judge agreed to proceed anyway.'

At least one person in the world doesn't hate me. 'I'm sorry I didn't tell you,' I say, desperate to end this conversation so I can run away before Samantha and Amelia emerge. I look around anxiously for Tom but he's nowhere to be seen.

'You should have told us,' Paula says as her expression morphs from flustered to furious. 'Withholding information is a criminal offence.'

'I didn't think it was relevant.'

'Of course it was relevant, Ellie.'

'Will I be arrested?'

'It's possible.'

Let them arrest me. I don't care any more. I turn to leave but then I have a thought.

'Paula, where did this new evidence come from? Why was it so late?'

'I don't know yet but we're trying to find out.'

There were only three of us on the road that evening. One of them is me. The other one is dead. Which means that it must have been Jason. But how did he know? And why did he leave it so late to disclose it? Why did he spend months threatening me when he had the information that could acquit him anyway? I can't believe how foolish I've been not to see this coming. But I was convinced that only Graham and I knew about the affair, and that no one else would ever make the connection. Everyone was focused on the few seconds before the accident and I thought that I could do the right thing by giving a statement without it blowing up my life too.

I was naive because someone did make the connection, and I should have predicted it. I should have come clean when I got the chance because at least then I'd have been able to deal with the fallout in the privacy of my own home. I've got everything so wrong.

People begin to pile out of the courtroom and bile rises in my throat.

'I have to go,' I tell Paula.

I hurry to the stairs, gripping on to the handrail so I don't fall in my haste to escape. Then I see the defence barrister appear and I pause. He doesn't notice me as people start to surround him, shaking his hand. He smiles, his stance relaxed. I have never despised a person as much as I do this man. I look away and begin to descend the stairs but then I hear someone calling out and the familiar voice makes me freeze.

The barrister turns and nods at the person approaching him. And then I see Samantha. Her face is still blotchy but she's no longer crying. Is she smiling? Why is she smiling? I should go but now I can't move, I'm transfixed by the interaction playing out in front of me. My mind is frantic as I try to comprehend it. Why

Samantha is pleased that the person who killed her husband is likely to be acquitted.

She shakes the barrister's hand and then she turns, slowly, towards me as if she's known I was there all along. She tilts her head to the side, and I see it written all over her face. And in that moment, I know.

I know exactly who helped the defence team to obliterate me.

20

I'm too shocked to cry. Too distressed to stop and think about what to do next, where to go. I race down the stairs and hurry out of the courthouse on to the street. Outside, surrounded by strangers who, for now at least, don't know who I am and what I've done, I bend over double as though I've been punched in the gut.

It takes me a few seconds to realise I'm being watched and my skin tingles. I turn sharply to see who it is and my heart skips a beat. Tom is leaning up against a wall, his hands in his pockets. Is he waiting for me? Does he want to talk to me? I don't know but I can't just walk away from him. I stand up straight and approach him slowly, glancing over my shoulder to see if anyone from the courtroom has come outside. We need to talk, Tom and I, but I don't want to do it here. I want to go somewhere private.

By the time I reach him I still don't know what I should say to him. How to even begin to unravel this godawful mess. There are not enough apologies in the world to make up for what I've done to this lovely man.

But I have to start somewhere.

'Tom,' I say. 'Can we go somewhere and talk?'

He doesn't respond. He's no longer looking at me. He's staring straight ahead, across the street, at the pedestrians going about their day, unaware of the two shattered people standing outside court whose lives have been ripped apart.

'Please, Tom.' My voice, tinged with desperation, trembles.

'I don't want to talk to you.'

'Then why are you still here?'

'I don't know.'

'Look, let's just go home, I can explain everything.'

He finally meets my eye, but I barely recognise him. He has never looked at me like this before and his expression is devastating. Hurt. Anger. Disgust.

'I'm going home, Ellie. You are not.'

'Tom, we have to talk.'

'I have nothing to say to you.'

'I know you're angry and I know you're hurt. But please let me explain—'

'There's nothing you can say.' He pushes himself off the wall. 'There are no excuses for what you've done.'

My tears come now, thick and fast. 'I know. I know I don't deserve your forgiveness. I just want to talk to you, so you can understand what happened.'

Tom pushes his hands through his hair. 'What do you want to talk about? Having an affair? Lying to me for months? Lying to the *police*? Not mentioning this while we were being repeatedly threatened? Befriending the widow of the man you were sleeping with? Or letting me find out in front of a room full of strangers?'

I'm sobbing now, unable to catch my breath. 'I'm so sorry. I never wanted this to happen,' I manage between gasps.

'Well, it has happened, and we can't go back. Don't think for a minute that we can.'

'I know we can't go back. I just want to talk.'

I can feel people staring at us now but I don't care any more. Let them stare. Let them judge. The only person I care about right now is the one standing in front of me. The person I've hurt so deeply that I can feel his pain as if it were my own.

'It's over,' Tom says and his words, although not unexpected, are still agony.

'Tom, please.'

'I want a divorce.'

'You're angry and you're upset and you have every right to be but let's not make any rash decisions right now. Let's talk in a few days. I'll go and stay in a hotel.'

'I'm not going to change my mind, Ellie. Perhaps I could have forgiven an affair, in time. I don't know. But I can never forgive you for the months of lies and deceit. The way you let me find out about Graham and the way you tried to cover it up. You are not the person I thought you were. I really don't know who you are any more.'

My legs buckle and I almost fall to the ground as I continue to cry uncontrollably.

But Tom's eyes don't soften. He puts his hands back in his pockets. 'I'm leaving now.'

'What about the kids?'

'I don't know.'

'We have to tell them something.'

'Of course we bloody do,' he snaps. 'But I haven't worked out how to do it yet.'

Not *we*. I. He's already removed me from our family. Tom's a good man, he won't keep the children away from me, but he's made it perfectly clear that he wants nothing more to do with me and how do I even begin to convince him otherwise?

'Look,' he says and his tone, while not conciliatory, is a fraction less hostile. 'Give me a day or two and then we'll discuss the arrangements for the children. But until then, I don't want to see you and I don't want you in the house.'

'Tom, I need to see our kids.'

'I know. Just give me a couple of days, Ellie. It's not too much to ask.'

'Please don't make them hate me.'

'Of course I won't. But you need to be prepared. I saw someone taking notes in the courtroom and I think it might have been a journalist. I'm not going to let them find out what happened along with the rest of the public like I did.'

I hang my head in shame. 'I'll call you tomorrow. Please tell them I love them.'

Tom's expression is heartbreaking. But he doesn't relent. 'Goodbye, Ellie.'

And with that he walks away from me, and I know he's never coming back. The best I can hope for now is to salvage my relationship with Frankie and Max and to attempt to come to an amicable agreement over custody. I can't believe it has come to this. A few hours ago, my only fear was facing cross-examination in court. How can my life have been upended in such a short space of time? I've brought it upon myself, I know that, but it doesn't make it any less devastating.

I am alone now and Tom's absence makes me acutely aware that I've attracted an audience. I don't need to look behind me to know who's there. Samantha and Amelia probably. Maybe even Tamsin who, if she's there, has made no attempt to come to my aid. Tom drove us to court, so I have no transport. I have some belongings at the hotel, where we've been staying, but I assume Tom is headed there to pack up and then go and collect the children. He'll tell them they're going home and they'll ask where I am. And I have no idea what he'll say to them. Should I get to them first? Try to give my side of the story? But even as I consider it, I know I won't do it because it's not fair on Tom. I'm the one who has broken his heart and I have to live with the consequences.

I start walking, just to get away from the crowd, but I have no idea what direction I'm going in until I reach the long road that takes me out of the city centre towards where we live. The kids are still at school and Tom's probably packing at the hotel. Maybe I should go home now while the house is empty and gather some more of my things because I don't know when I'll be returning. I can't think of anything else to do so I keep walking, head down, and let my tears continue to fall. I cry for myself, for Graham, for Tom, Samantha and our children. I try to work through my options but my head is throbbing too much for me to think straight. I can only do things one step at a time. One, go home and grab some things before Tom gets back. Two, we'll see. Maybe go back to the hotel and stay there until Tom is ready to talk and I can see Frankie and Max.

I turn on to the smaller road that will take me home. I've walked down this road a thousand times and it hits me that this may be the last. My life will never be the same again. And I wish to God that I'd never met Graham on the train that day. That I hadn't given in to my own desires. That I hadn't lied or tried to befriend Samantha.

Samantha. It hits me again then. The memory of what I saw outside the courtroom. She knew. It was Samantha who passed on the incriminating information, I'm sure of it. She must have got hold of Graham's phone and discovered the texts between us, which explains the late evidence. I had assumed that Graham would be careful and would delete the messages as soon as he'd read them, just as I had. There was no trail on my phone, no evidence of the affair. Was he really stupid enough to keep those messages for anyone to read? But of course, he hadn't known that he was going to die. He had no reason to believe that his phone might end up in the hands of his wife.

If she found this out recently, it would explain why Samantha had distanced herself from me over the past few weeks, but she'd still been friendly, she'd even told me about Charlotte and who her biological father was. Why pretend to be nice to me if she knew the truth?

I wasn't the only liar, it seemed. But I still didn't understand her behaviour. How could she bear to be around me when she knew I'd had an affair with her husband?

'*Whatever happens.*' This was what she was talking about. When I was at her house drinking lemonade and she was telling me all about Charlotte, she already knew what she was planning to do. And she realised she shouldn't have told me because once I was ripped apart in court, I would no longer be loyal towards her. I might want revenge.

But why tell me at all? I can't wrap my head around it.

I should be angry with her but I'm not. I can't blame her for what she did. She probably looked at Graham's old messages seeking comfort and solace and instead found sordid messages between her husband and the woman she had welcomed into her life with open arms. No wonder she wanted to take me down.

Maybe if I hadn't met her, I could have prevented this from happening. She might have found the messages but not realised they were sent by the key witness. She would have been distraught, devastated, but not made the connection.

Or perhaps it was always going to end this way, because I deserve it.

What does it matter now? I'll never see Samantha again and, in any case, I need to focus on Tom and the children. Samantha has plenty of people in her life who will support her, and I need to salvage what's left of my shattered family. I must fight my urge to run and hide from this mess because Frankie and Max need me. But will they even talk to me when they find out what I did? The thought of their cold rejection makes me sob, my tears hot and wretched. I stagger, my vision blurred.

I hear a car behind me, but I ignore it, my thoughts focused on my family and whether I will ever be able to fix what is broken beyond repair. I lurch on, my body convulsing with grief. As the car gets closer, hope suddenly surges. Perhaps it's Tom! Maybe he's decided he wants to talk after all. We can go home, put the kettle on and I can try to explain it all to him. The whole story, warts and all. And although I'm sure he won't forgive me, we can make a plan for the children together.

I spin around to face the car speeding towards me. It happens so quickly that I don't have time to register what's going on. No time to move or even to scream. I feel the thud as the car ploughs straight into me.

And then I no longer feel anything at all.

PART II

21

The first time I met Ellie Appleby was at my husband's funeral. But I already knew exactly who the lying whore was.

Graham, my darling husband, was not as clever as he thought he was. Or as subtle. As soon as he started covertly checking his phone and then discreetly slipping it back into his pocket, I was on to him. I knew he was up to something, and I wanted to find out what I was dealing with this time around.

It was not the first time my husband had cheated on me. A year before, he'd been caught in flagrante with his personal assistant. They'd snuck into the stationery cupboard at the Christmas party and were discovered by some intoxicated colleagues who were looking for paper and pens for a drinking game they'd concocted. He'd come home to me, his face flushed with drink and remorse and immediately confessed. He said he couldn't live with himself if he didn't come clean at once.

I was angry and I was deeply hurt. I sent him to the spare bedroom, where he remained in purgatory for the next three months. But I didn't kick him out. I needed time to process his betrayal and see if there was a way forward for us, but I was reluctant to break up our family over one indiscretion. I was as determined as Graham to fix it, for the boys as much as for us. 'Once a cheater, always a cheater,' my friends warned, but I thought Graham was different. I reminded myself that we all make mistakes, that none of us are perfect. We had marriage counselling, we talked and got things off our chests and, slowly, we began to rebuild. At least he was honest with me, I told Amelia. At least he admitted it upfront rather than hide his dirty little secret.

It wasn't until later that I understood he'd only told me about it because he'd been caught. He didn't want to risk someone else getting to me first. This realisation finally sunk in when Graham failed to disclose his next infidelity, and this one was different because it wasn't a one-off, drunken pash, it was an affair. But, as hard as he tried, he couldn't hide it from me because I was already suspicious and paranoid, and no amount of marriage counselling could prevent me from checking his phone occasionally.

He had saved the woman in his contacts as Adam Bede, which he probably thought was genius, but it didn't take me long to work out that this was no *Adam*. This was a woman who, I read, was *very* horny for Graham (with added devil emoji for effect). Who would be wearing red lace underwear to their next rendezvous. Who couldn't wait to suck his *aubergine emoji*.

As I scrolled through dozens of illicit messages, dread spilling in through every one of my pores, I deduced that they had been sleeping together for weeks. They had met several times at the same venue, a hotel near the motorway that I'd driven past a hundred times. When I thought Graham was staying late in London or stuck on a delayed train, he was with his mistress ten miles away from his wife and sons. And then he was coming home, his arms open to embrace us, the doting family man.

It broke me. I sat on the floor with tears streaming down my face, as my whole world came crashing down. At first, I blamed myself. I wondered why I was so inadequate that my husband had to go chasing after someone else again. What I had done wrong in our marriage for his head to turn twice. In my career as a lawyer, I had been a force to be reckoned with, but years of being a stay-at-home mum had diluted my self-identity and chipped away at my confidence, and this revelation obliterated it. My only job was to be a housewife, and I couldn't even keep my husband satisfied. I was nothing.

I didn't confront him at first and this only added to my self-disgust. What was I waiting for? I didn't know. I think I was just afraid of losing my family. I felt vulnerable. And I was very, very sad. But it didn't take long for my self-loathing to become anger as I realised that I was pointing the blame in the wrong direction. I did not deserve this. I had given up my career to be a wife and mother and I had done an exemplary job. I had dedicated my life to looking after the boys, the house, Graham, myself. I didn't nag or give my husband a hard time. I forgave him when he cheated the first time. I accepted my responsibility when he talked about our waning sex life during marriage counselling and I made more effort in the bedroom. I even bought some sexy red lingerie. But it hadn't been enough because he had still found someone else to suck his *aubergine emoji*. I realised, with a painfully liberating clarity, that I was not the one who had messed up, Graham had. This was his fault and I wouldn't forgive him again.

Self-pity morphed into red hot anger. I was so enraged that I could hardly even be in the same room as him, but I still didn't have it out with him. I reverted to my comfort zone of solicitor mode. I decided to gather irrefutable evidence against Graham that I could present to him when I asked for a divorce. I wanted to make sure that Graham couldn't gaslight me like he had done the first time. But I think it was also driven by my need to regain some control in this horrific situation, to somehow have the upper hand. Hell hath no fury like a woman scorned. Well, I was twice scorned.

The only person I confided in was Amelia. It was a risk because she was close to Graham too, but I knew she would side with me on this. We had been friends forever and she would be furious with him for the way that he had treated me. I was right – my best friend was apoplectic.

'The bastard,' she had spat. 'How could he do this?'

'I will never forgive him,' I declared.

'And nor should you.'

Still, when I told her my plan, she advised caution. She thought I should have it out with him immediately. Kick him out of the house and be done with it. But I wanted more. I wanted to win. I know it sounds absurd, but it was my coping mechanism and I needed something to get me through these dark times. A purpose to my life, a reason to get out of bed when I knew that my marriage was over. A delay tactic, perhaps, but I was in survival mode and in extreme circumstances you do what you must. So, I smiled sweetly when Graham came home late, with a bunch of flowers or some wine. I thanked him for the thoughtful gesture. And as soon as his back was turned, I grabbed his phone and wrote down the number for 'Adam Bede'.

A quick internet search took me to the staff page of a health-care company and the profile of Ellie Appleby. It turns out that she wasn't that clever either, using her work mobile to send her dirty little messages to my husband. I scrutinised her profile photo, looking for similarities between us, but there were none.

She was as dark as I was blonde, as curvy as I was slim. Her lips were full and pouty. She was pretty, I thought grudgingly, but not Graham's type. Unless she *was* his type and I wasn't. I imagined her kissing my husband with those lips. I pictured them ripping each other's clothes off, him moaning and whispering her name, and I wondered if they talked about me as they lay together afterwards, limbs entwined in post-coital bliss. And I was so disgusted that I almost went to pack up Graham's things immediately.

But I picked myself back up and focused on my plan because it was the only way I could keep going. I learned through scouring Ellie's social media that she was also married with children. She lived on the outskirts of St Albans, only a few miles away, and I had a fleeting thought of tracking down her husband and telling him what our spouses were up to. But, in the end, I decided to keep out of her family business and concentrate on my own. I had enough to deal with.

A few days later, when Graham was asleep, I took his phone and read his messages to learn when his next rendezvous with Ellie would be, and then I paid a private detective to take photos. They were emailed to me the next day and as I looked at the grainy images of my husband kissing Ellie up against his car, his hand resting on her backside, I knew that it was time. I had my evidence and I couldn't put it off any longer. It was time to confront Graham, tell him that our marriage was over and make my demands. Of course I would never stop him from seeing the boys, but I wanted the house and I wanted reassurances that he would support me financially until I was earning enough money. After all, I gave up my career for our family while his own flourished.

I sent the boys to my dad's for the night, opened a bottle of wine and sat down at the kitchen table to wait for him. My fingers drummed anxiously on top of the brown envelope which contained the incriminating photos. My foot tapped impatiently as I awaited his arrival, nerves twisting my stomach and making me nauseous.

But the clock kept ticking and there was no sign of him. I wondered if he was with *her* again, and the thought made my blood boil. The night grew darker, the silence of the house increasingly oppressive until eventually I couldn't sit still any longer. I paced agitatedly, desperate to get this showdown over with. I couldn't go to bed because I was packed full of adrenaline and I had to have it out with Graham, no matter what time he eventually turned up. I would stay up all night if I needed to.

And then, finally, many hours later, there was a knock on the door. I raced towards it, assuming Graham had forgotten his keys, and pulled it open, ready to face my lying, cheating husband. But instead of Graham, it was two uniformed police officers.

I sensed immediately that something terrible had happened. I could tell from their sombre expressions and the way that one of them removed their hat as they introduced themselves. My heart started racing as scenarios flashed through my mind, but I think deep down, I already knew what they were going to tell me. I led them through to the living room and the short walk felt like both an eternity and a snip of time because I wasn't ready to hear what they had to say, and I wasn't sure I would ever be.

I sat on the sofa and listened as the officers told me that Graham had been in a car accident and had died at the scene. I stared at them blankly, struggling to process the reality. I didn't know whether to shout and tell them they'd made a mistake or accept that this was really happening. I was a pinball, oscillating between denial and horror. I couldn't face the pain that I knew was coming when the shock wore off.

All evening, I had been so angry with Graham that I had wanted to kill him myself. But I didn't mean it, I would never want anything bad to happen to him. I had always assumed that even when we separated, he would still be in my life and he would always be there for the boys. Somewhere deep inside me, I think I still harboured a faint hope that he would work through his issues and come back to me a new man. It's hard to let go of someone you've loved for so long, even when they've hurt you. But now that small glimmer of hope had been extinguished forever because Graham was dead.

Dead. Realisation hit me like a train and I broke down. I bent over and screamed, sobbing so uncontrollably that there seemed no way back. There was a flurry of activity, a phone call and the next thing I knew, Amelia was there, throwing her arms around me and telling me how sorry she was. Saying she was here for me.

I looked at her, tears running down my face, and asked, 'Is this my fault?'

And although she didn't understand what I meant, although I didn't really understand it either, she took my face in her hands and looked straight into my eyes as she answered firmly. 'No, Sam.'

The next couple of weeks were a blur. I tried to keep it together for the boys, to organise the funeral and field the flurry of calls. Amelia didn't leave my side, answering the phone, accompanying me to the funeral home, cooking and cleaning, looking after Jamie and Marcus. My dad came down and tried to help too. I barely remember it now.

I was functioning but I wasn't present. I was lost somewhere inside myself and I didn't know if I could ever be found again. I had prepared myself for life without Graham but not like this. No matter what he had done to me, he was still a wonderful dad to the boys and now they had lost their father and their lives would never be the same. Their anguish and grief pierced my heart and made it impossible to breathe. Guilt overcame me, trying to convince me that it was my fault. That my rage towards Graham had somehow caused this accident. Or that if I had confronted him sooner, I could have prevented it from happening in the first place. And I wished, over and over again, that I could go back in time and change the course of events that led to this tragedy.

I didn't think that I would wake from this hell. The idea of ever feeling alive again was as obscure as growing wings. When it finally happened, it was in the most unexpected of circumstances. Because the woman who gave me a reason to live, who brought me back to life with a gasping breath, was the last person in the world it should have been. And I was so relieved to finally *feel* something other than grief and despair that I didn't care about the dangerous path I was treading.

I knew there had been a witness to the accident. But what the police didn't tell me was who that person was. I discovered that for myself when Ellie turned up at my husband's funeral, her face a portrait of sympathy, and had the audacity to stand in front of me with tears pooling in her eyes and tell me how sorry she was for my loss. I recognised her instantly, but I didn't believe it. I stared at her, trying to work out if she really would be cruel enough to come to Graham's funeral. I even sent Amelia over to check who she was, convinced that grief had messed with my head and confused me into thinking this stranger was my husband's mistress. But when Amelia returned and told me that not only was it Ellie, but that she was also the witness, electricity surged through my body and jolted me back to life, like I'd been charged with a defibrillator.

And just like that, I went from numb to angry. *Perilously* angry.

And I knew exactly where to direct my rage.

Amelia told me to kick her out of the church. She was

outraged that 'the other woman' had turned up and spent much of the funeral glaring at Ellie, but I warned her not to say anything. Yes, I could have made a scene, screamed and shouted and humiliated her in front of everyone. But that almost seemed too easy. Because, as adrenaline flooded my body at the sight of this woman, dressed in black, her expression dripping with sympathy, sharing a few cross words with her didn't seem enough. Twisted with grief and fury, I found myself considering another option. I would get to know her. Find out exactly who it was that my husband had chosen to sleep with behind my back. I would gather every piece of evidence I could find against Ellie Appleby.

And then I would take her down.

So I forced myself to be polite to the woman who I was now certain was the villain of this piece, even inviting her to the wake. If she was the witness, then it meant that she and Graham had indeed been together that evening, because it was too much of a coincidence that they would be on the same road otherwise. And it also meant that I could finally absolve myself of the misplaced guilt that had burdened me. This was not my fault, it was *hers*. If they hadn't been having an affair, and if they hadn't met at the hotel that evening, then Graham would never have been in the accident. Deep down, I knew that of all the people to blame, she was not at the top of the list. There was the lorry driver who had allegedly caused the accident. Then there was my husband himself, of course. But they were not here, pretending to be sorry for my loss, *she* was. She had put herself in the centre of my world and, as a result, had unwittingly put herself at the centre of my blame too.

If she'd just kept out of my life, I'd have kept out of hers. I had no reason to find her, my focus was on rebuilding myself and protecting my boys. She should never have come to the funeral, but she did, and so she sealed her own fate. When I told her that I wanted justice for Graham, I truly meant it. But it wasn't the lorry driver who deserved to pay for what had happened to my husband. It was her.

Ellie Appleby.

22

Ellie became my obsession. Or maybe my distraction. Does it matter? The funeral was over, the people who had flocked around me were beginning to get on with their own lives and I was alone with my rage. I couldn't share it with anyone, so I kept it locked up inside, where it bubbled under the surface, ready to explode.

The boys weren't coping well and it devastated me that I couldn't fix it for them. They missed their dad, and so did I. In my grief-riddled mind, Graham had transformed from villain to martyr, his death erasing his sins, of which there had been many. Sadness came in waves, over and over, relentless in their brutality. I needed an anchor, something to stop me drifting away, and that anchor became the other woman.

I googled her every night, hungry for more information. I scoured social media but she rarely posted, and I needed more. I considered the different ways in which I could bump into her but, in the end, it was fate that helped me out.

I'd just left court after watching Jason Turner, head hung low, plead not guilty to death by dangerous driving. It had brought everything back again and I was tearful and overwhelmed as I stood on the pavement, trying to decide what to do with myself. Then I saw her striding along the pavement on the other side of the road. Ellie Appleby. She was dressed casually, in tracksuit bottoms and a raincoat, her thick, dark hair tied up in a messy bun.

It was surely a sign, I decided, as I began to follow her from a distance. I wasn't sure what I was doing, or whether I'd even approach her, but when she headed into M&S, I slipped through the doors a few moments later. She had no idea I was behind her. I watched her as she browsed the aisles, picking up a salad bowl and perusing the ingredients. And before I even knew what I was doing, I walked right up to her.

She looked startled when she realised it was me and it occurred to me that I had the upper hand. She had no idea that I knew who she really was, and I clung onto the feeling of control that it gave me. Everything else in life felt out of my grasp, like I was being swept along in a hurricane, unable to stop the devastation it had wreaked.

Because of Ellie.

I saw the terror on her face when I told her that Jason Turner had pleaded not guilty to killing Graham. She tried to mask it, but it was clear that she was worried about giving evidence in a trial and this gave me an idea. I could offer to give her some tips on how to cope in court and, at the same time, get to know this woman. I could get under her skin, until I was ready for a dramatic showdown.

I asked her if she wanted to get a coffee and she looked reluctant at first, her eyes scanning the crowds as if someone was going to magically appear and airlift her out of this awkward situation. It gave me a pang of bitter pleasure to see her obvious discomfort and I reminded myself that she had instigated this by coming to Graham's funeral. If she hadn't, I may not have even noticed her outside court. After all, she looked completely different without the full face of make-up and loose waves that she had on her company profile photograph. But weeks of research had emblazoned the image of Ellie in my mind and I could spot her a mile off now. I watched as she considered how to get out of my invitation, concluded that she couldn't, smiled and agreed. And the next thing I knew, I was sitting opposite my dead husband's lover, sipping coffee and crying about my loss. It was the most surreal experience of my life.

And the worst thing is that she had the audacity to comfort me as though we were friends. To tell me how sorry she was and to share her own experience of losing a parent, like that would make it all better. There were no words this woman could say to me to make me like her. No empathy she could express that would change who she was or what she did. The lorry driver may have caused the crash, but this woman was the reason why Graham was on the road in the first place. This woman was the one who had wrecked my marriage, long before the accident. Yet here she was, reaching out and grasping my arm, her own eyes pooling with tears of sympathy. It made me hate her even more than I ever thought possible and I was shocked that she could be so two-faced.

And yet I forced myself to smile and thank her. I think I even hugged her. What was I playing at? I'd started a game, but I didn't know the rules.

I made sure that we swapped numbers so that I had a way to contact her again. And I left it a few days before I messaged her so that I didn't seem too keen. In the meantime, I started hatching a plan. I could play on Ellie's insecurities about the trial and the obvious pressure she felt at being the only witness. I'd seen enough examples of witness intimidation in my career to know how unsettling it was for the people involved. Because wasn't it unfair that she got to go on living her life, scot-free, while my family was suffering? That she could go home to her husband and kids and pretend to be the perfect, innocent wife when I knew who she really was? No, it was not fair. It was not right. There was a reason why I had seen Ellie outside court that day, I was sure of it. So, when she replied to my message asking if I was free for lunch that day, I smiled for the first time in weeks. *Game on.*

* * *

I don't know how I did it. I can't comprehend how I continued to meet up with this woman, pretending to like her and forging a friendship built on false pretences. It sickened me. This was not who I was. I knew it was unhealthy and possibly dangerous, but I couldn't stop myself. I'd strapped myself into the roller coaster and there was no way off the wild ride. Each time I met her, I steeled myself beforehand and reminded myself why I was doing it. Justice for Graham. For my boys.

When Jamie became friendly with Frankie, I almost gave up. It sickened me that our children were spending time together and it muddied the waters too. I knew Jamie wasn't interested in Frankie romantically, because I'd suspected for some time that he was gay and I was waiting for the time when he felt comfortable enough to tell me. But their friendship served as a brutal reminder that innocent people were getting caught up in this mess and I did my best to warn Jamie off. I told him that Frankie had a crush on him and he would be leading her on if he continued to see her. It made me feel less guilty that it was probably true. He seemed to accept this and, mercifully, backed off.

But, actually, it did me a favour, because it gave me another reason to meet up with Ellie. She honestly thought we were growing close. What she hoped to gain from it, I couldn't begin to understand. Did it make her feel closer to Graham? Did she feel better by offering emotional support to me? Or was she just a twisted psycho who got off on hanging out with her lover's wife? Her intentions didn't matter. I would never like Ellie, no matter how sweet or innocent she pretended to be. Our grief was not shared, even if she dared to think that it was. I was doing this for one reason only – to ruin her life like she'd ruined mine. Because the closer I got to her, the easier it would be to destroy her. I was a Trojan horse, waiting for the right time to reveal myself.

I now had a front row seat to watch Ellie unravel and I began to think of ways that I could set the wheels in motion. My dad had told me that, after the funeral, he'd seen someone he recognised from the church walking down the street with her son. He had slowed down to see if she was okay after a difficult day, but said she'd looked startled, so he'd driven off. He told me this because he thought the woman was a friend of mine but when he described what she looked like and where he'd seen her, I realised he was talking about Ellie, and this gave me my first idea.

I told Dad that my car had broken down and Graham's had been written off after the crash. I asked if I could borrow his black SUV. He agreed of course, because he was desperate to help me in any way. Then I bought some false registration plates and used the car to start following Ellie.

It was easy to track her movements. That's the thing with mums, they have the same routine. Pick up from football practice on Tuesdays, work late on Wednesdays, and so on. I quickly found out where she lived and when she went out. The first time I followed her it gave me a thrill, especially when she turned to face me without knowing who was behind the darkened windows, and I saw the apprehension on her face. But the most memorable time was when I parked it at the pub where she was having dinner with her husband and then hid in the bushes, waiting for her to come out. When she finally did, she looked like she was going to have a heart attack. I saw her clutching onto her husband, almost shaking with fear. And I bathed in grim satisfaction.

But when I got home that evening, I knew it had to stop. Ellie's husband had seen the car too and they might have called the police. Although I'd used false plates, I couldn't risk the car being traced back to Dad. So, I changed the plates back, told my father that my car was back from the garage and returned the SUV to him. And then I went home and started thinking about phase two of my revenge plan.

Ellie deserved to be treated like the lying slut she was, and I was only too happy to oblige. I downloaded a couple of photos from her Facebook page and posted them on an app for people looking for casual hook-ups. I enjoyed writing her profile, detailing all the ways in which she was a dirty whore with no morals. And I made sure to connect with all the men in the immediate vicinity, young and old, ugly and handsome. It didn't take long for her to be approached in the supermarket, and when she came round to my house later that afternoon, clearly still traumatised, I could barely keep the smile from my face. But then Amelia somehow realised that I had something to do with it. That's the problem with best friends, they can read you like a book. She was supposed to go as soon as Ellie arrived but instead she hovered like a fly, looking at me suspiciously and it was taking the sheen off my cruel victory. And then she pretended to leave and hid in the house, waiting to warn Ellie off.

When I saw them, huddled in the kitchen, I was furious. After Ellie had left, Amelia and I had the biggest row we'd ever had. She'd already questioned me on why I was hanging out with Ellie and now she had her answer, she didn't like it.

'These incidents,' she'd fumed. 'Ellie being followed and approached by a man in the supermarket. It's something to do with you, isn't it?'

'It's only what she deserves.'

'Sam, what the hell are you playing at?'

'Stay out of it,' I snarled at her.

'You're losing the plot,' she hissed back. 'You're scaring me.'

'I can handle it.'

'No, you can't. You're going to get into trouble, Sam. It's dangerous.'

I stood, with my hands on my hips, facing down my dearest friend. 'She killed Graham! She ruined my life. My boys don't have a father because of her.'

'You were going to divorce him anyway!'

It was like a slap to the face. And even Amelia realised she had gone too far because she immediately backed down. 'Look, I'm sorry. Of course I understand why you hate her. But you have to stop what you're doing right now. That's why I warned her off, not to protect her, but to protect you. You shouldn't be spending time together, it's toxic.'

'So what, I have to just let her get on with her life?'

'Yes, Sam, that's exactly what you have to do.'

I shook my head. 'It's not fair.'

Amelia stepped closer, her expression conciliatory. 'None of this is fair and I'm so sorry it's happened to you. But the most important thing is that the right person pays for what happened to Graham.'

'Exactly,' I insisted. 'That's what I'm making sure of.'

'No.' Amelia shook her head. 'The right person is the lorry driver.'

I didn't want to hear it. Rational had no place in my warped mind.

Amelia put her hands on her hips. 'What if you get arrested and thrown in prison for stalking Ellie? Then the boys will have no one. Think of your children, Sam.'

She knew how to hit a nerve, she always had. For a moment the world came into focus again and I realised what I was doing, the madness I had descended into. Maybe I should stop now, for the sake of the boys. I had done enough damage to rattle Ellie. Amelia was looking at me with pleading eyes, and I reluctantly nodded.

'You're right,' I said. 'I'll stop.'

'Thank God.' Amelia finally embraced me. 'I'm sorry I went behind your back and spoke to Ellie, but I hope you know I did it because I love you.'

'I do,' I replied as I nestled into my friend's shoulder.

After Amelia left, I was lonely and agitated. The boys were studying in their rooms and I was restless. I couldn't resist logging on to the dating app and I found a message sent by a man to Ellie's fake profile. He lived locally and was keen to meet up. I went to delete it, but I hesitated as my anger returned to me. I pictured Ellie driving home to her family after having the gall to visit my home. Chatting with her husband and kids, thinking she'd got off scot-free. And then I started typing out a seedy reply to the man, telling him exactly what I was hoping to do to him when we met face to face.

I was spiralling, becoming a person I never thought I would be. But that's what grief and anger does to you. It twists you, contorts you into something else. Someone monstrous. I hated that I would have to lie to my best friend. I had isolated myself from everyone I loved in my need for vengeance, but I still couldn't let go.

Ellie wasn't done suffering yet. Not even close.

23

I can't pinpoint the exact moment when everything changed. I think it was so gradual that I barely noticed it and when I finally did, I struggled to acknowledge it.

It started with a reluctant acceptance. Anger was slowly leaking out of me, drip by drip. Getting out of bed became a little easier in the morning. Smiles came to me more naturally. At the same time, Jamie and Marcus were focusing on their exams and the distraction and routine was helping them too. Life was returning to some semblance of normality because it had to. We were all still grieving and I still had bad days, where something would send me plummeting without warning. Like hearing my phone ring and automatically thinking it was Graham or making dinner for one when the boys were out. But enough light was pushing through the bleak darkness that I could finally see clearly again. Firstly, I began to remember that I would have been alone anyway, even if Graham survived, because I had been planning to divorce him. I was reminded that he had cheated on me, not once but twice, and yet I was solely blaming Ellie. And finally, I realised what I had become since he died and it frightened me.

I'd always thought of myself as a good person. Not an angel, not perfect, but someone with morals. A loyal wife, mother and friend. I would never deliberately want to hurt anyone and yet that was exactly what I was doing and it was getting harder to justify my actions. The final straw was when I sent that degrading image to Ellie, the one I had created on the boys' computer because they used a VPN to watch American TV, which would make it difficult to trace it back to me. After I saw that the photo had been delivered, I had stared down at the burner phone in my hands and felt disgust, not pleasure. I imagined Ellie, a few miles away, receiving the message. I pictured her fearful reaction, her anguish, and a wave of guilt tumbled over me.

Somewhere, over the months I'd spent with Ellie, my perception of her had altered. Amelia had been right that it wasn't healthy for me to socialise with Ellie, but the outcome had been the opposite of what my friend had been worried about. Because, perversely, instead of becoming angrier, I had softened towards her. It was less of a psychological struggle to be in her company and I even found myself looking forward to seeing her. I refused to accept this at first, but the reality was that I had started to see Ellie as a human being rather than an evil villain, and I questioned if I'd got it wrong.

If, somehow, Ellie was a victim in all of this too.

Jamie had told me that Ellie was taking antidepressants. Frankie had found the medication in her mum's washbag and had told him about it during one of their deep and meaningfuls. Ellie had never discussed her mental health with me before then, but one afternoon, when we were out walking, the conversation naturally moved to our children and Ellie admitted that she had been struggling to connect with Frankie for too long.

'I just love her so much,' she'd said, her eyes wet with tears.

'Of course you do,' I'd replied, surprised at my sincerity.

'I'd do anything for her, but I just don't know how to communicate that to her. When she was little, I'd give her a big hug or hold her hand. Now she doesn't even want to talk to me, let alone touch me, and she rolls her eyes when I tell her I love her.'

'That's teenagers for you. Don't take it to heart.'

'I know I shouldn't. But I just feel so guilty. I've always felt guilty.'

I paused, intrigued. 'Why?'

Ellie paused. 'I had postnatal depression when Frankie was born. I wasn't in a good way and it took me a long time to get the help I needed. Then with Max, I was more on it with my mental health, having been through it once before. And I've always felt that I was a better mother to Max in the early years than I was to Frankie.'

Her words resonated. When the twins were born, I was a wreck. I'd considered myself a strong woman, a competent person who could tackle any challenge thrown my way. I'd very quickly discovered that I was wrong because I had no idea what I was doing with the boys. I felt completely out of my depth, like I was drowning. I couldn't sleep, I couldn't eat, I couldn't breast-feed, and I couldn't soothe my babies. Sometimes I thought they hated me. Most of the time I hated myself. And Graham had been no help at all. Busy with work, he had hurried back to the office after a week and offered to hire a nanny to help me. But I didn't want a nanny, I wanted to be a better mother, I just didn't know how to do it. This feeling had stayed with me for years and still sometimes haunted me now. I worried that my inability to parent my babies had caused long-term damage. I knew, deep down, that it wasn't true and that my boys had grown up with love from the moment they were born, but insecurities aren't always rational.

'I know how you feel,' I said quietly. 'I felt the same way when the boys were born.'

She looked at me earnestly. 'You did?'

'Yes. That mother's guilt you're talking about? I have it too.'

Ellie looked away. 'I sometimes wonder if that's where it all went wrong.'

'What do you mean?'

'I love my children and I am so grateful for them. But after I had them, my life changed beyond all recognition. My self-identity, my relationship with Tom. I'm not the same person I was and I think I've wasted too much time trying to be that person again. To be a version of myself that no longer exists. I've tortured myself and to what end? It hasn't helped me, and it certainly hasn't helped my family.'

It was like she could see into my soul. Every word was an echo of what I had thought myself. I'd tried to embrace my role as a housewife, and I'd given it my all, but sometimes I'd felt like I was pretending rather than being my true self. Trying to please Graham. Trying to stay young, to satisfy him, to keep him, without thinking about who I was and what I wanted. I was attempting a version of myself that wasn't authentic and look where it had got me. A widow, deeply grieving the man who had betrayed me.

'I went through a really difficult time a while ago,' Ellie continued. 'I was in a terrible state and I eventually went to the doctor for medication, although I know now that I left it too late. The damage had already been done.'

'What damage?'

'I don't know, my friend Tamsin thinks it was a midlife crisis and maybe she's right but it felt deeper than that. I questioned my marriage, my sanity, and myself. It was like I was outside of my own body, watching down with no control over what I was doing. And I buried my head in the sand and just ploughed on instead of pausing and realising that I needed some help to work through how I was feeling.'

This was the closest we'd ever come to discussing the affair, which I was certain was what she was referring to, and I held my breath, waiting to see what she'd say.

'I was selfish,' she said. 'I acted impulsively, fuelled by whatever crazy stuff was going on in my mind and my body. I put myself first, and my supposed needs before other people. I think I just wanted to feel *something* again, you know? I wanted to feel alive because I was so overwhelmed and numb.'

'What did you do?' I probed, morbidly fascinated to see if she'd confess.

But Ellie seemed to finally remember who she was talking to. 'It doesn't matter. All that matters is that I made a huge mistake and I hate myself for it. I will never forgive myself. But I'm going to spend the rest of my life trying to fix it. To be a better person.'

I looked her right in the eye and I felt her shame. I sensed she was trying to communicate with me, even though she had no idea that I already knew about her affair. She was confessing her sins and apologising in the only way that she could. And perhaps it should have enraged me, but it had the opposite effect. I finally *saw* her. I understood her struggles and her guilt. And in that moment, my cold heart began to thaw.

I remembered Ellie comforting me after Graham died, telling me the words that I needed to hear, words I assumed were false at the time but now believed were from the heart. And I relived all our interactions in a different hue, like someone had changed the light bulb in my mind. You can't fake that sincerity. She meant it. She felt wretched for what she'd done, and she was trying to make amends.

It hit me with painful brutality that what I was doing to her was far worse than what she had ever done to me. She had slept with my husband, and I rightfully resented her for it. But I was purposefully trying to ruin her. *I* was the villain.

When I got home, I sat on the sofa, trying to decipher how I was feeling. And the dominant emotion was regret. What I was doing was appalling and it had to stop. I was taken aback at how immensely relieved that decision made me feel. I could go back to grieving Graham, rebuilding my life and supporting my boys. My petty, vindictive game was over and I was finally seeing sense again.

I decided to pour myself a glass of wine, which quickly became two. I was still adjusting to being on my own and the boys were almost men, with their own lives to lead. I couldn't cling on to them because it wasn't fair. I knew alcohol wasn't the answer to loneliness but after the day I'd had, I felt I deserved it. By the third glass, I was feeling melancholy, my thoughts drifting back to the day Graham died and my shock when I had opened the door to two police officers, looking at me solemnly. I remembered the guilt I'd felt that it was somehow my fault, and then I remembered something else.

Somewhere between the accident and the funeral, the police had brought round some things they'd recovered from Graham's car. His phone, wallet, wedding ring. I'd been so distraught at the sight of these items that Amelia had squirrelled them away, putting them in a box in the spare room cupboard until I felt strong enough to face them. Was I ready now? I wasn't sure I'd ever be, but for some reason I suddenly yearned to look at them.

I stood up, swaying slightly, and made my way upstairs, opening the cupboard door and staring at the box on the top shelf. With trembling fingers, I stood on my tiptoes and took it down, sitting on the bed and summoning up the courage to open it. I lifted Graham's wallet out first, stroking the soft brown leather before placing it gently on the bed. Next, I picked up his wedding ring and twirled it around my finger, gazing at it. It brought back a tsunami of memories as I remembered our wedding day and how in love we had been. The many happy years that followed as we started our family. And then how it all ended.

Another wave of grief hit me as tears spilled down my cheeks and splashed over the duvet. No matter how much Graham had hurt me, I was still struggling to accept that he was gone. Perhaps we could have fixed our marriage if I'd confronted him sooner. More counselling and promises to try again. Or maybe it was beyond repair, but we could have found a way to co-parent our beautiful boys and, eventually, become friends. I hated that Graham was gone and our family was in tatters. Life was cruel and unfair, and it had created a gaping wound in my life that I didn't think would ever heal.

But I also knew now that it wasn't Ellie's fault.

I peered into the box again and saw Graham's mobile phone, its screen smashed, and fresh anger mingled with grief as I remembered the messages I'd read between Graham and Ellie. Then I thought about the things that Ellie had said to me earlier that day, the shame she felt and her determination to make amends. It was such a stark contrast to the sordid messages she'd sent Graham that I couldn't reconcile the two.

I needed to read them again. I had to analyse them to see if there was any evidence that Ellie felt guilty for what she was doing. If there was proof that Graham had somehow coerced her into the affair. For some reason, instead of wanting to see the best in my husband, I now wanted to see it in Ellie as it would validate the way I was beginning to feel about her. It would stop Graham being a martyr and that might help me to rise from the misery I was shrouded in and move on.

I picked up the phone and tried to turn it on. But the screen remained blank and as I looked at the shattered glass, I wondered if it was broken beyond repair and thought that maybe it was a good thing after all. Raking through the past wouldn't make me feel better, it would only aggravate my pain. But I couldn't resist plugging it into a charger anyway. Was I glutton for punishment? Perhaps. There was no benefit to reading those horrible messages again and yet, as I took another sip of wine, I couldn't stop myself.

After a couple of minutes, the screen lit up and I held my breath as I saw the family photo of us that Graham had as his wallpaper. A snapshot of another time, one that seemed a million years ago now, yet I yearned for again. When life was simple. When Graham and I loved each other. Before I knew about Ellie. When he was still alive.

I unlocked the phone using the passcode I'd known for years, the boys' date of birth, and went to his messages. The most recent thread was between Graham and Ellie and I'd already read most of it, but I went through it again anyway. It was like reliving it all over again and there was no denying that Ellie was as into the affair as Graham was. What was I doing, spending time with this woman? I had descended into madness. I remembered her words. *'It's like I was outside of my body.'* Maybe she was, but Graham was inside her body, and the image sickened me.

I scrolled right through to the end. There were a few messages, arranging their final meet. The last was from Ellie, saying that she was on her way. This message had none of the usual kisses and emojis. Was she already beginning to pull away from him? I closed the messages, hating the fact that I was putting myself through this.

I opened Facebook next. Graham rarely posted on social media and the most recent photograph was of the boys on their birthday, taken more than three years ago. I went through his list of friends, looking for Ellie, but they weren't connected. The only other platform that Graham bothered with was LinkedIn but there was nothing of interest on there. I needed to delete his profiles at some point, but it seemed too permanent, a public admission that Graham wasn't coming back, and I wasn't ready yet.

I was about to put the phone down when I decided to check his call log. I still don't know why I did it. My fingers were working without my brain giving them instructions. I looked at the last call Graham received and wasn't particularly surprised to see that it was from 'Adam Bede'. Then I looked at the time of the call and my heart stopped.

I knew the exact time of the accident because the police had told me. It had even been published in the local paper. And according to Graham's call history, he had still been on the phone to Ellie when it happened. But I was certain that the police didn't know this, because surely it was an important piece of evidence. It potentially changed everything. If Graham and Ellie were on the phone at the time of the accident, then it meant that they were both distracted.

Had Ellie lied to protect herself?

Had the lorry driver been charged with a crime he didn't commit?

I flung the phone down on the bed. And then I sat there until the sky went dark, running it over in my head and trying to work out what to do with this information. I ran back through every conversation I'd ever had with Ellie. She was adamant about what she saw, convinced that Graham's car had been stationary and the lorry had ploughed into him. If I gave this phone to the police, Jason Turner might be acquitted. But if he had caused the accident, then he deserved to be punished for it.

If I kept it to myself, then I was perverting the course of justice. And, I realised, with a sinking horror, that it came down to one critical thing.

There was only one witness, who was unwavering on what she saw.

But did I trust the woman who had slept with my husband?

24

I went back and forth for days. Hand in the phone. Don't hand in the phone. I was in a storm of indecision. I wanted to do the right thing, but I didn't know what that was. My heart was telling me that Ellie was telling the truth about what she witnessed but my head was warning me that I was committing a terrible crime by keeping the phone records to myself. I was pulling myself in every direction and it was exhausting.

I couldn't face it on my own any longer. It was time to call in reinforcements and there was only one person on my SOS list. Amelia arrived fifteen minutes later and I told her about my discovery. With each word I spoke, her eyebrows rose even higher, until I thought they might pop off the top of her head.

When I was finished, she blew out her cheeks.

'You have to hand that phone into the police.'

'But what if the lorry driver gets off as a result?'

'Maybe he should get off. This changes everything.'

'Not necessarily,' I argued. 'Ellie maintains that Jason crashed into Graham.'

'For God's sake, Sam, she's a liar! And she might have been

responsible for what happened to Graham. By calling him, she probably distracted him from the road.'

'No.' I shook my head. 'I don't think that's what happened.'

Amelia was looking at me like I'd lost my mind. 'It's like you're defending her.'

'Who?'

'Ellie!'

I looked away. 'I don't hate her.'

'Why the hell not? She had an affair with your husband and lied to the police. She's had the audacity to become friends with you. She's a psycho.'

'She's not a psycho. She's someone who made a mistake and is trying to make up for it.'

'Have you considered the fact that she's pretending to be friends with you so she can get into your house and seize the phone? Maybe she knows it incriminates her.'

In my frantic state, I hadn't thought of that. But I also didn't think it was true.

'She's only been here once and I invited her.'

Amelia shook her head. 'I don't know what's got into you.'

Anger rose inside me. 'I asked you over here for support, not a lecture.'

'Well quite frankly, you need a lecture. You're a mess, Sam. And the fact that you haven't handed in this phone already proves it.'

Was she right? Was I going about this all wrong? Was I on some subconscious level trying to protect Ellie because I had, against the odds, grown fond of her?

'I hated Ellie at first. Hated her with every bone in my body. But, you know what? She didn't force Graham to have an affair with her and she wasn't his first either. Who knows if there were others, Meli? You were right before when you said I was going to divorce him anyway. For too long, I've put him on a pedestal he doesn't deserve.'

'He didn't deserve to die, either.'

Her words stung. 'I know that!'

'So do the right thing, Sam. Hand in the goddamn phone. If you don't, I will.'

I nodded, defeated. 'You're right, I'll do it today.'

Amelia visibly exhaled. 'You're doing the right thing.'

We chatted after that, but things were tense between us. Amelia offered to accompany me to the police station, but I told her I had to do it on my own. She hovered, uncertain, and I knew what she was thinking. She was worried that I wouldn't do it.

'I'll go,' I assured her. 'I promise.'

'Call me as soon as you have.'

When Amelia left, I went and got the phone. I turned it over repeatedly in my hands. I stood up and sat back down again. And then I walked up the stairs and hid it in the box at the top of the spare room cupboard.

I would take it, I told myself. Just not today.

* * *

A few days later, I messaged Ellie for a chat. I wanted to test the waters, to bring up the accident and see just how certain she was about what she saw. I felt I knew her well enough now to tell if she was lying. But I didn't get the chance to probe because Ellie was upset. Someone had written the word 'liar' on her garage door in big, red letters. I was as shocked as she was but for different reasons. Because this time, it wasn't me who was messing with Ellie.

Which meant that someone else was out to get her too.

I'd been telling her for ages that the strange things happening to her were connected to Jason Turner, but I'd been deliberately misleading her. Now I wondered if it really was him this time. I couldn't think who else it might be.

As I tried to reassure her, I was also validating my decision not to hand the phone in. If Jason was trying to intimidate her then it meant he had something to hide. He knew he was guilty and so he had resorted to nasty tactics.

But wasn't it odd, that just as I stopped playing tricks on Ellie, someone else had taken over? And did that mean they also knew what I had been up to?

As soon as I hung up, I decided to go check on the phone. I opened the cupboard door and stood on my tiptoes, nearly losing my balance as I reached for the box and pulled it open. I had put the phone at the top of the pile, but it must have slipped underneath the rest of Graham's belongings because I couldn't see it. I placed the box on the bed and started rummaging around, feeling for the familiar soft, silicone phone case. But it wasn't there. Frantic, I tipped the box upside down, rummaging through Graham's things. After a few minutes I realised that my search was futile. The phone was gone.

After the initial panic subsided, I tried to calm down and think straight. I made a mental list of who could have taken the phone. Jamie and Marcus were the obvious suspects, given that they were the only other people who lived in the house. Then there was Amelia. Our house was like her second home and she knew exactly where the box was as she had put it there. She also knew what was on the phone.

And finally, there was Ellie.

My head was scrambled. But the more I thought about it, the more certain I was that it wasn't Ellie. She hadn't been to the house in the last few days and there had been no sign of a break-in. The CCTV hadn't picked up any movement. Ellie didn't have a key.

Amelia had a key. I had told her that I'd handed in the phone but maybe she'd known I was lying. She'd always been able to see right through me. Had she taken matters into her own hands? And did I have the nerve to confront her?

I decided to start with the boys. Perhaps one of them had taken it to look at old photos or feel closer to their dad. It was a far more palatable option. They were out with friends and I called Jamie first, but he didn't answer, which was typical. Next, I tried Marcus.

'Hi, Mum.'

'Hi, darling, sorry to bother you. Have you seen Dad's phone by any chance?'

'No. Is everything okay?'

'Yes, there's nothing to worry about, I was looking for it and I can't seem to find it.'

'Sorry, I haven't seen it since he—'

Marcus broke off and I immediately felt guilty for bringing it up.

'Never mind, forget I said anything. Enjoy your evening, darling.'

I hung up and tried Jamie again but he still didn't answer. I wondered if he was with Frankie and suppressed a shudder. But more likely he was playing a computer game with his friends, his phone on silent so he wasn't disturbed.

I should have just handed the damn thing in when I first found it. Now I didn't know what to do. Should I call the police and report it missing? They'd be interested if they knew that it held important evidence. But then I'd have to admit I knew about Ellie's call to Graham moments before he died, and I'd be incriminating myself.

How in the hell had I got myself into this mess? And how did I get out of it?

I was still agonising when Jamie got home, half an hour after his brother and seconds before his curfew, which he always pushed to the limit.

'Hi, Mum,' he said as he sat down on the sofa to take his shoes off.

'Did you have a good evening?'

'Yeah.'

'I tried to call you.'

'Sorry, my phone's on silent. Everything okay?'

'I just wondered if you'd seen Dad's phone.'

Jamie looked at me quizzically. 'Dad's phone?'

'Yes, it's not where I left it.'

'I haven't seen it.'

'You're absolutely sure?'

Jamie frowned. 'Yes, Mum.'

I visibly deflated. 'Okay, never mind.'

'Is everything okay?'

'Yes, darling, everything's fine.'

Jamie stood up. 'I'm going to bed. See you tomorrow.'

He sauntered back out of the room, and I stood up to go to bed too. It was too late to call Amelia now and I was exhausted and overwhelmed. I'd feel better tomorrow after a good night's sleep and then I'd be able to think straight again. I'd make a plan.

I brushed my teeth and slipped under the covers. I was still adjusting to sleeping on my own. Sometimes I heard a noise and thought it was Graham in the bathroom. My heart skipped a beat as I imagined him walking into the bedroom in his boxers and climbing into bed beside me. Picking up a tatty paperback from his bedside table and propping himself up to read it. And then I remembered that Graham was gone and I was alone. I had never felt it more acutely than I did right then.

I turned off the light and tried to sleep but I was too wired. I lay there, staring up at the ceiling, wondering again how I'd ended up in this situation. Who had taken Graham's phone and for what reason? Who had written that graffiti on Ellie's garage door?

And, most of all, how had the death of one person wreaked so much havoc?

25

The first thing I did when I woke up the next morning was to search for Graham's phone. The boys were still asleep and wouldn't be up for a couple of hours, so I had the house to myself. I looked in every cupboard, every drawer, but to no avail.

I tried to call it, hoping to hear the ring cut through the silence of the house but it went straight to voicemail. Had it run out of battery or had someone turned it off? Finally, I gave up, defeated, and slumped on the sofa to consider my options.

I was furious with myself for not handing it in straight away. I had let my feelings towards Ellie cloud my judgement. Amelia had warned me, in fact she'd threatened me. I sat bolt upright. Amelia must have known I was fibbing about giving the phone to the police and taken matters into her own hands. I was furious with her for going behind my back, but at least I had a plausible explanation for the missing phone.

I called her right away and when I told that her I needed to see her urgently, I had no doubt that she would drop everything to come over. That's what best friends do. But did best friends go behind each other's backs too, even if it was for the greater good?

What if the police questioned why I hadn't handed in the phone myself? Amelia could have got me into a whole lot of trouble and I was seething.

By the time Amelia arrived I'd hastily thrown on some clothes and was hovering by the door. She took one look at my unkempt appearance and said, 'What's wrong?'

'Graham's phone has gone missing.'

I scrutinised her face, looking for evidence of guilt, but saw none. She seemed as shocked as I was.

'I thought you'd handed it in to the police?'

'Not yet. I was going to but—'

'Sam! You said you'd taken it days ago!'

'I know, I'm sorry, I really was going to.'

Amelia stormed into the kitchen and put the kettle on, swivelling round to face me. 'I can't believe this.'

I braced myself as I addressed the elephant in the room. 'Did you take it?'

'What? No, of course not. I thought it was in the hands of the police.'

'You're the only one who knows what was on it.'

Amelia put her hands on her hips. 'That's not true. Ellie knew too.'

'It wasn't Ellie. She hasn't been here.'

Amelia frowned. 'Have you asked the boys? Maybe one of them took it.'

'I've asked them both and they say they haven't seen it.'

'Then it must be Ellie. There's no other explanation.'

'There's no explanation as to how it could be Ellie either. She doesn't have a key to the house, and the CCTV hasn't picked up on her being anywhere near the property.'

Amelia was silent as she made the tea, passing a steaming

mug to me. Then she said, 'Are you sure *you* haven't hidden it? To protect Ellie?'

'Amelia!' I was appalled. 'How could you even think that?'

'I'm sorry, Sam. I'm really sorry.' Amelia looked contrite. 'Forget I said it, I'm just stressed. What a mess. What an absolute, stinking mess. We need to find that phone.'

'But how are we going to do that? I've already called it and it went to voicemail.'

'What about Find My? You could try to trace it that way.'

'No, Graham turned it off a long time ago.' I laughed bitterly. 'Which I now realise was so that I wouldn't know when he was meeting his other women.'

'Women?'

'Come on, Meli, let's not be naive. There were probably more.'

'You don't know that.'

'No, and now I never will.'

'Look, I know he cheated and I'm as angry as you are, but let's not blow this out of proportion. Don't tarnish the memories you have of him.'

'It's too late for that. I've clung on to the image of Graham as the perfect husband for months. I've blamed everyone else for what happened to him. But now I see him for who he really was. Just look at the mess he's left behind.'

'But you said you wanted justice for him.'

'I do, of course I do. He cheated but, like you said, he didn't deserve to die.'

'And how can justice be served without this evidence?'

'Maybe it still can. Ellie's statement proves that—'

'Not this again. Come on, Samantha, what's happened to you? You used to be a solicitor. You know this is all wrong.'

'And what am I supposed to do about it now the phone is gone?' I demanded.

'Jeez.' Amelia sat down again, with her head in her hands. I could see how agitated she was, and I felt bad for putting this on her. It might have made me feel better to share my woes, but I had now burdened my friend and that was unfair. And if Amelia didn't have the phone, and neither did the boys, who on earth did?

Amelia looked up at me. 'Have you looked for it?'

'Of course I have.' I was exasperated. 'I've looked everywhere.'

'Why don't we text it?'

'Text what?'

'Graham's phone. Text it and ask who has it.'

It wasn't a terrible idea. 'Okay.'

I located my own phone and typed out a quick message. Tears threatened as I registered that I was sending a message to Graham's phone that he would never read. But I pushed them away and showed the screen to Amelia. She nodded her approval and with shaking hands, I pressed send.

'Done.'

'I'll wait with you to see if they reply.'

We sat there for an hour but the message didn't even deliver, which meant that the phone was still turned off. Eventually, Marcus appeared, bleary-eyed, followed by Jamie half an hour later and Amelia had to go to work.

'Call me if they text back,' she whispered in my ear before she left.

I tried to get on with my day as best I could. I did chores, I checked in on the boys and made them lunch and snacks as they revised. I went for a walk. I called the phone a couple of times, hope dipping every time it went to voicemail. I checked on the boys again, until they told me off for breaking their concentration. I tried to do some gardening. But I knew I wouldn't be able to rest until I got a reply to my message.

By the end of the day, I was forced to admit defeat.

I called Amelia. 'The message still hasn't delivered.'

'Keep calling it. Keep looking for it. Don't give up.'

'I will,' I promised.

'You should have handed it in when you had the chance.'

'I know.'

'I still think it's Ellie. And she's damn well got away with it. Maybe we should tell the police about it anyway. They might be able to trace it.'

'But then I'm incriminating myself by admitting that I withheld evidence.'

'Perhaps that's the lesser of two evils.'

'Look, we don't know if that phone call had any bearing on what happened.'

'Oh here we go again, the Ellie Appleby fan club.'

I didn't have the energy for another argument. 'Let's talk tomorrow.'

I hung up and put the phone down and when it beeped a few minutes later, I thought it was Amelia, apologising for the way things had ended. Although she had always been blunt, I knew she cared about me deeply. But it wasn't her, it was Ellie wanting to chat. She was feeling anxious after all the strange incidents and fearing what might happen next. She told me she was worried for her safety, and her family's, and I didn't have to pretend to be alarmed any more because my fear was real.

Someone was threatening Ellie. Could it be the same person who had the phone?

Were they finishing what I had started?

Although I had wanted to torment Ellie, I'd never had any intention of causing physical harm. I'd just wanted to mess with her head, the way she had messed with mine. But I wasn't sure the new perpetrator felt the same way. Was it Jason Turner simply trying to scare her as the trial approached or was someone else involved?

Graham's phone was key to it, of that I was certain. Whoever had stolen it had their own agenda, and I had no idea what it was. Or what they were planning next.

26

I looked for the phone every day, but it never turned up. Whenever I called it, it was switched off. I began to accept that it was gone forever.

But at the same time, things were getting worse for Ellie. The closer it got to the trial, the more threatening the incidents became. And the most puzzling thing about it was that none of it could be linked to Jason Turner.

I thought I had hated Ellie more than anyone else in the world, but maybe I was wrong. Someone else was out to get her and I had no idea who it was.

I was a wreck that summer. The boys had gone off to Cornwall with friends, Amelia was busy with preparations for her family holiday to California and I was all alone in a big, empty house, thinking increasingly dark thoughts. I withdrew from everyone, taking days to answer texts and politely declining offers to meet up with my friends. I couldn't eat and I lost weight I didn't need to lose, my clothes hanging limply off my skinny frame.

And I had too much time to think. To go over every detail of my life, my relationship with Graham, my friendships. I found myself thinking about Charlotte and how she had lost her biological father too, but she'd never know about it. I wondered if Amelia had thought about it too, when Graham died, and I remembered how much I'd had to convince Graham to help Amelia and Ed, how against it he'd been.

I think that's why I told Ellie about it. She came over, asking probing questions about Charlotte and it didn't take much for me to share the secret I'd vowed to take to my grave. I just needed to talk to someone, anyone, because I'd been spending so much time on my own, lost in my spiralling thoughts. To be honest, I think she welcomed the distraction too because she was so stressed about what was happening to her. Maybe we both needed to lose ourselves in another crazy story for a while.

But I regretted it very quickly. Amelia was like my sister and I had betrayed her. I had shared something we promised never to share, and with a woman she hated. And I panicked that Ellie would tell her she knew, or that she'd talk to Frankie who would, in turn, tell Jamie. Anxiety piled on top of anxiety as I made Ellie promise not to tell a soul. And after she left, I made a solemn vow to distance myself from Ellie once and for all.

I never should have struck up a friendship with her in the first place because it wasn't good for either of us. I no longer hated her, and I certainly didn't want to take revenge on her any more, but it was time for us both to move on with our lives. We could never be true friends when our relationship had been founded on deception.

I think she was a little hurt when I backed off, but it was the right thing to do for both of us. So I became a recluse, rattling around on my own, counting down the days to the trial and telling myself that once it was done and dusted, I would finally move on.

But I was haunted by guilt. Would Jason Turner get a fair trial without the phone evidence? Would anyone ever find out what I had done? I lived in constant fear of the police knocking on the door because they had traced Ellie's fake dating profile back to me or they'd discovered I didn't hand in the phone immediately. I could be arrested, disbarred from ever practising law again. I probably deserved it, but I knew how much it would hurt Jamie and Marcus and I couldn't bear the thought of causing them any more pain. And I was worried about Ellie too and all the terrible things that were happening to her. I couldn't help but think I had somehow caused them, that I'd set some sort of event in motion that was now beyond my control.

When Amelia returned from holiday, tanned and relaxed, she took one look at my gaunt face and sat me down for a heart to heart.

'You look dreadful,' she said, not beating around the bush.

'I'm not sleeping well.'

'You're not eating well either, by the looks of it.'

'I'm not hungry.'

Amelia stood up. 'I'm making you some lunch.'

'I said I'm not hungry.'

'I don't care. You're eating.'

I followed her to the kitchen and watched as she busied herself with rummaging around in the fridge. Amelia, my right-hand woman. Always there for me when I needed her. And I was riddled with guilt that I'd told Ellie about Charlotte. I was making mistake after mistake and I didn't know how to make amends any more.

Amelia made us both a salad and I forced myself to eat a few forkfuls to appease her. She watched me like a hawk, ensuring that I was eating.

'It'll be okay, Sam,' she said soothingly.

'Will it?'

'Yes. In a couple of weeks the trial will have started and, when it's finished, you can finally put all this behind you.'

'But, like you said, the lawyers are missing a critical piece of evidence. Evidence that I concealed.'

'I know. But there's nothing you can do about that now. And you said yourself, it might have had no bearing on what happened anyway. Speaking of which, have you spoken to Ellie?'

'No, I'm keeping my distance.'

'Is she still being threatened?'

'Yes.'

'And it's definitely not you who's doing it?'

I glared at her. 'No.'

Amelia's face softened. 'Well then, it must be Jason Turner, which means you were right all along about him knowing he's guilty and wanting to intimidate Ellie.'

'She told me she was thinking of changing her statement.'

'Do you think she will?'

'She then said she'd be sticking to it. She insists it's a true account of what happened.'

'There you go then.'

She was trying to cheer me up and I appreciated it. As the food hit my gnawing stomach, I began to feel a little better. Maybe Amelia was right. I just needed this trial to finish and then I could begin to pull myself together again. I was a strong woman, I reminded myself. A capable one. And I had to be a role model to my boys.

'Thank you,' I said to Amelia.

'For what?'

'Everything. I don't know what I would do without you.'

She leaned over and took my hand. 'It will all be over soon, Sam. Trust me.'

27

Walking into the courtroom as a spectator rather than a lawyer was surreal. And weeks of nerves, inactivity and barely eating had left me weak. Amelia propped me up, her hand gripping me firmly as we walked into the public gallery and found a seat.

I looked across the courtroom. My home for the next few days. I would come every day. I would listen to every statement, each piece of evidence. And at the end, I hoped, the jury would reach a verdict and I would walk away and get on with my life.

Ellie wasn't there yet. As the main witness, she would only enter the courtroom when it was her turn to give evidence. Although we hadn't seen each other for a while, she had texted me to say she was staying in a hotel after someone had targeted her at her friend's house. They must have followed her there after delivering a fake grenade, which she had been convinced was real. There was a time when I would have delighted in her misery but now all I felt was sorrow and fear for Ellie and her family. I had gone round in a circle and returned to the conclusion that Jason Turner was behind it all.

I saw him then, entering the dock, his head hung low. He was dressed in a smart but ill-fitting suit and his face looked haggard. And I didn't know what to think about him. What I wanted to happen to him. Whatever he had done, he deserved a fair trial and I berated myself again for not handing in the phone when I had the chance.

A few people entered the public gallery and I saw Jason look up and acknowledge them. It must be his friends and family. Being in such close proximity to them made me immensely nervous and Amelia must have sensed it because she took my hand and squeezed it tightly. But they sat down a few seats away and barely glanced my way. I exhaled, grateful that they weren't making me feel uncomfortable.

The jury was sworn in and I studied their faces, thinking about the burden on their shoulders. They were the people responsible for deciding who was at fault for the accident. I'd seen many jurors in my career, but this was different. This was personal.

'I don't know if I can do this,' I whispered to Amelia.

'You'll be okay, Sam. I won't leave your side.'

I nodded, wiping away a tear and wondering how many would fall over the next few days. Thank goodness the boys weren't here. Jamie and Marcus had asked to come but I'd told them no. I didn't want them to hear the evidence or see graphic images of the accident scene. I wanted to protect them as much as I could, especially now that they were starting to get on with their lives. But they would probably read about it online. I couldn't wrap them up in cotton wool and hide them from the world.

The opening statements began and I listened to every word as the prosecution barrister told the jury about the events leading up to Graham's death. I listened as the defence barrister opened his case, reminding the jury that guilty meant beyond any reasonable doubt and suggesting that there was much to doubt. I studied him, a man I'd met many times before. He was exceptionally good at his job and I'd seen him destroy more than one prosecution case. There was something about his stance, his expression, that I'd seen before. It was more than just the confidence of a barrister who knew what he was doing. He had something up his sleeve. And that's when it hit me.

I knew exactly what was going to happen.

And there was no way to warn Ellie.

She walked in, her face deathly pale. She looked so nervous. The door to the public gallery opened and a man walked in and sat down. Even though I hadn't met him, I knew it was Tom, Ellie's husband. I turned away quickly. I couldn't look at him, knowing what was about to happen. Finally understanding what had happened to the missing phone, I glanced at Amelia, searching her face for evidence of guilt, or triumph, but she was concentrating on the courtroom, her face composed.

Ellie's husband was about to find out about the affair in a public and humiliating way. And there was nothing I could to do stop it. I couldn't protect him, or Ellie, from what came next. Ellie had made her bed and now she had to lie in it, even if the punishment was harsh. But I was surprised at how sorry I felt for her. I did not want to see this woman destroyed in front of the people she loved and I felt a fresh surge of anger towards Graham, for leaving such a holy mess in his wake.

I stared at Ellie, as though I could silently communicate with her and warn her about what was about to happen. But other than briefly glancing my way, she kept her eyes averted. She looked so fragile, tormented by weeks of threats and harassment. I was about to watch a horror show unfold and it brought me no pleasure.

I fidgeted so much during the prosecution's questioning that

Amelia put a hand on my leg to steady me. It dragged on for ages, as these things normally do, the calm before the storm. And then finally the defence barrister stood up and I held my breath.

He went straight for the jugular. And I watched the woman I once hated, and then came to understand, get obliterated right in front of me. I heard the gasps from people around me as they discovered what I already knew. I saw Ellie's husband get up and leave. And I felt so desperately sorry for him. I knew how he felt but at least I'd discovered the affair privately, in my own home.

Somewhere along the way, this had stopped being about Jason Turner. It was as though he was a side actor, and I now had no doubt that he would be acquitted. Reasonable doubt was emanating from this entire room with each new question the barrister fired at an ever-shrinking Ellie. But worse than that, it had stopped being about Graham's death too. Because all anyone would talk about now was the affair.

I had to hand it to the barrister, he'd successfully broken the key witness. And I couldn't blame him for doing his job. I wondered, again, who had given him the phone and if I would ever find out. I feared that he would mention my name and accuse me of not disclosing the evidence. He'd taken Ellie down; was he going to do the same to me?

But he was wrapping up now, his brutal work over. Ellie was excused but she didn't move. I watched as a clerk tried to help her and Ellie shook him off before finally relenting. As she walked out of the courtroom she looked up, her broken face full of shame and defeat. And, equally miserable, I couldn't meet her eye.

Then she was gone and the judge was adjourning.

Amelia stood and reached out a hand. 'Come on.'

I took it and followed her shakily out of the courtroom. As

soon as we were outside, she blew out air and raised her eyebrows.

'I wasn't expecting that.'

'Me neither.'

'It was a good thing, I think. No more secrets. But who handed in the phone?'

'I don't know. I'm not sure we'll ever know.' I gripped Amelia's arm as I hissed, 'Do you think there'll be repercussions for me? For not giving it to the police myself?'

'I doubt it. I think it's over now. I have to say, I've never liked Ellie but I couldn't help but feel a little sorry for her in there. It was like a lamb to the slaughter.'

It was the kindest thing Amelia had ever said about Ellie Appleby.

'Jason Turner will be acquitted,' I said.

Amelia was downcast. 'I think you're right.'

'So, no justice for Graham after all.'

She looked me in the eye as she said, 'You know what? I think plenty of people have suffered enough already for what happened to him.'

Maybe she was right. I couldn't imagine how hard the past few months must have been for Jason Turner and his family. They'd been horrendous for me. And Ellie's marriage was probably over now too. I hoped that at least the threats would stop now that she had given her evidence. There was no reason to scare her any more because the damage was already done. In fact, the only person who hadn't suffered, I realised with shock, was Graham. He had died instantly and left the rest of us to fall apart. It was a sobering thought and one which made me feel wretched for even thinking.

As we reached the staircase, I saw the defence barrister surrounded by some of his legal team. He looked at me and fear coursed through my body. Did he know that I was in possession of the phone? I knew I couldn't get on with my life with the anxiety hanging over me, so I made a split-second decision. I walked right over to him and extended a hand. He smiled warmly, taking my hand and shaking it firmly.

'That was quite a show,' I told him.

'I'm so very sorry for your loss, Samantha.' His expression was open, sympathetic. 'And for what you just heard in court. I'm not sure how much of it you already knew.'

'How did you find out?' I tried to keep my voice steady.

'The phone was dropped off anonymously to the defendant's solicitor with a note containing the passcode. No one knew what it was at first, but apparently one of the assistants discovered the text messages and call log.'

'Do they know who handed it in?'

'No. To be honest, I thought it might have been you.'

I shook my head as I lied through my teeth. 'No. I haven't looked at Graham's phone since he died. I forgot I even had it.'

'Then you didn't know about the affair?'

I looked away to hide my deception. 'No.'

'I'm so very sorry, Samantha.'

He would never apologise for doing his job. He had represented the defendant admirably. His apology was a personal one to me, for making me listen to his revelations. But I also knew that I was in the clear. Whoever had handed in the phone had not incriminated me. It was finally over.

I shouldn't have been happy at how it had ended, but I still welcomed the relief that washed over me in that moment. This was a new beginning for me. I was going to sort myself out, stand on my own two feet. Maybe finally start applying for jobs. For the first time in weeks, a small smile played on my lips.

I felt someone's gaze on me and instinctively turned to see Ellie, hovering on the stairs, watching me. She looked awful, her eyes manic, her cheeks tear-stained. Before I could react, she hurtled down the stairs and dashed out of the courthouse.

Amelia appeared beside me. 'I have to go,' she said apologetically.

I nodded. 'Of course.'

'Will you be okay?'

'Yes, I'll be fine.'

'I'll call you later.'

I squeezed her hand. 'Thank you.'

I watched her leave and then I popped to the bathroom to freshen up. Washing my hands, I studied my pale, gaunt face in the mirror. I really did look awful. But I was done with that now. For the first time since Graham died, I accepted that he was gone and he wasn't coming back. There was no point in looking for someone to blame or punish. The only way forward was to let go of the last vestiges of my anger and finally say goodbye.

I gave my reflection one last glance and then headed outside, blinking in the bright afternoon sunshine. I heard a commotion to my left and turned to see Ellie arguing with her husband. I looked away quickly because it was rude to stare but then I couldn't resist glancing back. Her husband was walking away and Ellie was standing there alone, crying hysterically, while curious onlookers gawped at her.

I moved towards her instinctively, but she hurried away and I didn't follow her. Perhaps she just needed to be alone. I turned and headed towards my car, which was parked a few minutes' walk away. I sat in the driver's seat but I didn't start the engine. I couldn't stop thinking about the look on Ellie's face. Perhaps I should check on her, just to make sure she was okay. She must be feeling so alone and afraid, and I knew what that was like. I'd just go and see her once to check in. And then I'd leave her be for good. She'd supported me through my darkest times and I felt a strong urge to reciprocate.

As I drove towards Ellie's house, I decided to put some music on. It was months since I'd listened to any. After Graham had died, I just hadn't felt like it because almost every song brought back a memory. I turned on the radio and for a moment I was plunged back in time as Guns N' Roses blared out of the speakers. Graham loved rock music and listened to this station all the time. I would change it back to a pop station whenever I got in the car. And then he would change it back. It became a long-running feud between us, which had made us both roll our eyes and laugh. Now it had the opposite effect as it hit me for what must have been the hundredth time, but no less brutal, that Graham was gone. Not just the Graham at the end, who had cheated on me, but the Graham who I had loved for more than twenty years. Who had made me laugh until I snorted. Who had held my hand and told me I was amazing as I gave birth to our sons. Who had sat beside me, in this car, teasing me for my terrible taste in music.

I thought I was all cried out during the trial, but fresh tears sprung and blurred my vision as one of Graham's favourite songs blasted out. I had to change the station, and quickly, before I totally lost it. I took my eyes off the road as I frantically pressed buttons, desperate to turn the music off and make the deluge of beautifully painful memories go away. I couldn't cope with the raw, guttural agony.

Finally the music stopped and I shuddered with relief as my eyes returned to the road. I didn't even have enough time to scream before I jammed my foot on the brake with such force that I was propelled forward and then quickly backwards again as the seat belt jammed. And then, knowing that it was too late to stop what was about to happen, I closed my eyes and braced myself for the sickening thud.

28

On the same day that Jason Turner went on trial, accused of causing death by dangerous driving, I prepared myself to face the same charge.

Death by dangerous driving. That was all I could think of as I sat in a police interview room, telling the officers exactly what had happened. I didn't lie or try to defend myself and I ignored my solicitor's advice to answer with 'no comment'.

'It was my fault,' I told them repeatedly. 'I was distracted.'

No one would tell me if Ellie had survived. I'd seen her being rushed to hospital in the ambulance I'd called for, unconscious. I'd sat in the police station, waiting to be questioned, imagining medics trying to save her, looking at each other and shaking their heads. I'd pictured her husband's face, contorted with grief, knowing that his last ever conversation with his wife was an argument on the street, outside court.

Amelia had been my rock, as always. She'd gone straight to be with the boys while I was at the police station, comforting them when they learned about Graham's affair, which had been the top story on the local newspaper website. Clearly the journalist in court had wasted no time in filing his story. I felt wretched because I was the one who should be there with them. I should be hugging them and telling them that everything was going to be okay. Instead, I was sitting on a hard chair in a bleak room, answering question after question as honestly as I could and wondering how the hell I had ended up here. But most of all, praying with all the strength I had left inside me that Ellie would be okay. *Please don't let her die.*

When I was finally released pending investigation, I stood outside the police station and felt lost. I had not been charged, probably because the police were still waiting to see what happened to Ellie, but I knew that I would be. I should go home and be with the boys, but I was ashamed to face them and I needed a little time to compose myself. I wandered around aimlessly, ignoring the driving rain that soaked my hair and my clothes. I didn't know where I was going but when I ended up in front of the main entrance to the hospital, I wondered if this had been my subconscious plan all along. Because life was on hold until I knew what had happened to Ellie.

I knew how inappropriate it was for me to be there, but it didn't stop me. I steeled myself to walk inside and ask after Ellie at Reception. But of course they wouldn't tell me anything. After establishing that I was not a family member, the receptionist shook her head in apology before dismissing me and turning to someone else approaching the desk. I hovered for a minute, wondering if I could persuade her otherwise, until eventually I left, defeated and drowning in misery.

Was I a killer? Had I taken another person's life? It had been an accident, a terrible error of judgement on my part. Just as it had probably been when Graham died. Maybe Ellie had distracted him when she called, maybe the lorry driver had misjudged. Possibly it was a combination of both those things. It didn't seem to matter any more because, like Amelia had said, everyone had been punished enough and we'd all paid a price for the mistakes that we had made. But I did blame myself for what had happened to Ellie and I would never, ever forgive myself if she hadn't made it.

I left the hospital, looking up at the grey skies. The rain had stopped but my clothes were damp and uncomfortable. I was chilled to the bone. I hovered outside the entrance, psyching myself up to call a taxi to take me home, when I saw Tom emerge from the main entrance, pull out a vape and inhale deeply. I recognised him instantly and when he looked up and saw me staring, I knew he realised who I was too.

'You shouldn't be here,' he said.

'I just want to know if she's okay.'

'You shouldn't be here,' he repeated firmly.

'Please,' I begged him. 'Just tell me.'

He looked at me for a long time and I couldn't read his expression. He inhaled from his vape again and blew out a thick cloud of scented air. Finally, he said, 'She's broken her leg in several places and two ribs. She needs surgery. But she's going to be okay.'

A sob escaped and before I knew it, I was bent over, crying with relief. Tom didn't move, he just watched me from a short distance. Eventually, conscious that I was making a scene, I tried to pull myself back together.

'I'm so sorry,' I began.

'You need to leave,' he said.

I nodded. 'Please just tell her I'm sorry. I never meant for it to happen.'

As I began to turn, I saw tears in Tom's eyes.

'I was angry too,' he said quietly. 'When I heard about the affair.'

'It was an accident,' I said quickly. 'I never meant to hurt her.'

'So, you just happened to be driving down the road that led to our house?'

'I was on my way to see her, to make sure she was okay.'

'But why? I don't understand. You'd just found out she slept with your husband.'

I didn't really understand either. But I tried my best to put it into words because Tom deserved that at the very least. He was completely innocent in this mess.

'I knew about the affair already. I had done for a long time, actually before Graham died.'

Tom stared at me, dumbfounded, and I took a tentative step towards him.

'I was angry, of course,' I continued. 'I was planning to confront Graham on the night of the crash. But by then it was too late.'

'But you befriended Ellie. You were spending time with her. Why?'

'At first it was because I wanted to get to know her and then punish her for what she did. I blamed her for what had happened to Graham. But over time my feelings changed. Look, Ellie made a huge mistake. But we're all human and we all make them.' I looked away. 'I've learned that the hard way.'

Tom frowned as he tried to process what I was telling him. 'Did you ever talk to Ellie about the affair?'

'No, she had no idea that I already knew.'

'I just don't understand how you could do that. How you could pretend to like the person who was sleeping with your husband. What was your endgame?'

'Revenge,' I admitted. 'But then I changed my mind.'

'Hang on.' Tom took a step towards me and his expression

shifted to hostile. 'Was it you behind all those incidents? The vandalism and the graffiti?'

'No,' I answered truthfully. 'It was me in the SUV, but I have no idea who did that.'

Tom visibly deflated. 'So that must have been Jason after all then.'

At least he believed me about that, but I wondered if he still suspected me of deliberately hitting Ellie with my car. And I had to make sure that he didn't. It wasn't about me not being charged, it was because I hated the idea of anyone thinking that I would deliberately want to hurt another person.

'Tom, I promise you that the accident wasn't premeditated. I was distracted, trying to change the radio station, and I didn't see her in time to stop. I feel absolutely terrible.'

'It's strange, isn't it? Your husband died in a car accident and then his lover nearly did.'

I ignored his insinuation. 'Yes, it is. But they're not connected.'

He shrugged, looked down at his vape and then pocketed it. 'I haven't smoked for nearly fifteen years,' he said absent-mindedly. 'I stopped when Ellie was pregnant with Frankie.'

'You're under a lot of stress,' I told him gently.

'I hated her so much when I found out about the affair during the trial. I didn't think I could ever forgive her. And then when I thought I'd lost her I—'

'I know,' I said. 'I understand. I felt the same way when Graham died.'

'I don't know what to do now,' he said.

'Look, whatever happens between you and Ellie, you'll always be in each other's lives because of the children. And as furious as I was with Graham, I would give anything for him to still be alive right now.'

'I don't know if I can forgive her.'

'Maybe you can't, and that's okay. But as I said before, everyone makes mistakes. I got to know Ellie pretty well and I understood how much she regretted what happened between her and Graham. She was determined to make amends for it.'

'Would you have forgiven Graham, if he'd survived?'

'I did the first time.'

Tom looked at me, his eyebrows raised. 'The first time?'

'Yes. Graham had cheated on me before. But it was definitely Ellie's first time and I'm certain it will be her last. She knew what she risked losing.'

Tom started, realising who he was talking to, and took a step backwards.

'You shouldn't be here,' he said again.

'I know. I'm leaving now.'

I turned away from him and then hesitated. 'For what it's worth, I think Ellie is a good person. A better one than Graham, anyway. And I know how much she loves you.'

I didn't wait for his reply. I strode purposefully away from the hospital as the rain started to fall again and I thought about everything that had happened over the past year. How it started and how it would end. I thought about Graham, and the boys, who were waiting for me at home. And I thought about Ellie. Now that I knew she was okay, I could breathe again. I would take my punishment without a fight because I deserved it. With a criminal record, my law career was over before I'd even had a chance to restart it, but I deserved that too. I'd find other work. All that mattered now was being the best mum I could be to Jamie and Marcus. I hoped they would forgive me.

Seeing Tom was the wake-up call I had needed. I pulled my phone out and called a taxi. It was time to go home and face the music.

* * *

The boys were sitting in the living room with Amelia when I let myself into the house. I walked in, wary of the reception I was going to receive but prepared to own it.

Jamie stood up and rushed towards me, and I threw myself into his arms, fighting hard to keep my tears at bay. I was determined to stay strong for him.

'Are you okay, Mum?' he asked.

'I'm fine, darling. More importantly, how are you?'

He pulled away and I saw the pain in his eyes. 'Livid,' he admitted.

'At me?'

'No, at Dad. I can't believe he had an affair.'

I smiled sadly. 'Don't let it change your perception of Dad, sweetheart. He was still a good man who loved you so very much.'

Jamie scowled. He had experienced one of the worst possible things that a person could go through when his father died and now he had to deal with this too. He had idolised his father and that perfect image had been shattered.

I looked over his shoulder at Marcus. He was hunched over, refusing to meet my eye.

'Marcus?' I asked gently. 'Are you okay?'

I glanced at Amelia and she gave me an encouraging smile. A look that said, *You're doing great. You've got this.*

Marcus continued staring at the floor. I walked over to him, kneeling on the carpet and grasping both his hands. 'Sweetheart?'

'What's going to happen to you?' he asked.

'I'll be charged, probably for reckless or dangerous driving.

But Ellie is okay, I've just spoken to her husband. She's going to be fine.'

'Will you go to prison?'

'No,' I said, with more authority than I felt.

'What will happen to us if you do?'

'Marcus, I'm not going to prison. I've admitted responsibility. I'll probably get a driving ban and community service. Ellie is okay, she's going to make a full recovery.'

He looked at me then, his face more miserable than I've ever seen it. 'It's my fault.'

I thought back to the night I found out that Graham had died. How I had asked Amelia if it was my fault. My guilt had been misplaced then, just as Marcus's was now.

'Sweetheart, of course it's not your fault.'

'It is,' he insisted. 'It's all my fault.'

I frowned. What was he talking about? How could he possibly hold himself responsible for his father's affair, or me hitting Ellie with my car?

'I don't understand,' I said, squeezing his hands. 'What are you trying to say?'

I glanced at Amelia, but she looked as bewildered as I was. I turned to Jamie questioningly and he shrugged, his hands stuffed deep inside his pockets.

Marcus didn't speak. His expression was desperate, almost pleading. He was battling something, not with me but with himself. I knew how he felt but I hated seeing my own demons mirrored on the face of my beautiful son's. He'd got things all mixed up in his head, convinced himself he was a bad son and that's why all this had happened. I was certain that was the reason for his internal torture, and I was ready to reassure him.

'What happened to your dad was a terrible accident,' I said

gently. 'What happened to Ellie was an accident too. *None* of this is your fault. You've done nothing wrong.'

He started crying then. I hadn't seen him cry for years. He hadn't even shed a tear when his father died. It had worried me at the time, watching Jamie sob and Marcus sit there, dry-eyed. I knew he was in just as much pain as his brother but he couldn't let it out. I'd talked about it with my therapist and she'd helped me to understand that people process grief in different ways. That it would come out when he was ready. Had that long-awaited moment finally arrived, when Marcus let go of his grief?

I brushed away one of his tears with my fingertip. 'It's okay, darling.'

'I took Dad's phone.'

My hand froze mid-air. Everything stopped for a minute, no sound, no movement. I tried to understand what he was telling me. I attempted to find some words.

All I could muster was, 'Okay.'

'And I gave it to the prosecution team.'

My head snapped towards Amelia, who looked as stunned as I was.

I rested my hand on Marcus's. 'You're going to have to start from the beginning.'

It came out like a flood then as I realised how much he longed to tell the truth and finally release what must have been eating him up for months.

'I was looking for something in the spare room and I found the box of Dad's stuff. When I saw his phone, I decided to see if I could unlock it. I just wanted to feel closer to Dad, you know? To look at his photos and remember him. I guessed the passcode easily and then, after I'd been through his photos, I checked his messages.'

As I nodded encouragingly for him to continue, I was terrified of what I already knew he was going to say next.

'I found this thread between him and someone called Adam Bede and it was clear that they were having an affair. At first I thought Dad might be gay but then I googled the phone number and discovered that it belonged to a woman. The same woman I'd seen at Dad's funeral and in the garden, having a drink with you.'

My poor, poor boy. I knew from my own experience what a horrible way that was to find out, not that there ever was a good one. I wished that he'd talked to me about it but Marcus was a brooder. He'd kept his discovery to himself and it had festered inside him. No wonder he'd been even more withdrawn than usual. I had thought it was because of Graham's passing but now I realised there was more to it.

'I was so angry, Mum. At Dad for having the affair and at this horrible woman for pretending to be your friend when she'd been going behind your back with Dad. I thought she was such a bitch for doing that to you.'

I closed my eyes for a moment, letting his words wash over me. I knew what was coming next because the pieces were forming together in my head.

Jason Turner had nothing to do with the terrible things that happened to Ellie. I remember her telling me about the vandalism. '*Liar, liar, Ellie on fire.*' She'd said it seemed juvenile and that was because it was – it had been written by a teenager. I thought back to all of the times when Ellie had been victimised and realised that none of the incidents had happened in the two weeks when the boys were on holiday in Cornwall. Oh, God.

'You threatened Ellie, didn't you?'

'I just wanted her to know that someone knew what she'd

done. I wanted her to stop pretending to be your friend. To leave us alone. I wanted to protect you, Mum.'

I glanced behind me at Jamie, but he looked just as dumbfounded as I was. Marcus had kept this all to himself, not even sharing his burden with his twin brother.

'Did you send her that grenade? And smash her friend's window?'

Marcus nodded, sobbing. 'I persuaded a mate's older brother to drive me to her house and then we followed her to her friend's house. He didn't know what I was doing and when I smashed the window, he panicked, drove off and left me. I thought I was going to get caught by the police and I was so scared. After that I stopped.'

'When did you hand in the phone, Marcus?'

'I kept it hidden in my room, switched off, for ages. Then one day I turned it on again. I don't know why, I just wanted to see the messages again. But this time I checked the call log and saw that Ellie had called him just before the accident. And I realised that the police probably didn't know about it, so I decided to hand in the phone.'

'Marcus, why didn't you tell me all of this?'

'I didn't want to hurt you, Mum.'

'But you must have known it would all come out at the trial.'

Marcus looked away, shamefaced. 'I know. But at least it wouldn't be me telling you.'

'What the fuck, Marcus?' Jamie exclaimed, running his hands agitatedly through his hair. 'How could you have done this?'

I didn't chastise him for swearing. Curse words were, quite frankly, the least of our worries.

'Will I go to prison?' Marcus asked. He sounded like a six-year-old boy, rather than the sixteen-year-old he was. And I had a strong, motherly urge to protect him.

'No,' I said. 'No one knows it was you, and that's the way it's going to stay.'

'My friend's brother saw me smash the window.'

'We'll speak to him, make sure he doesn't say anything.'

'But I don't want anyone else to get into trouble for what I've done either.'

'They won't.'

'I'm so sorry, Mum.'

I took him in my arms and cradled him like I'd done when he was a little boy and had fallen and scraped his knees. I was shocked and appalled by what he'd done and the fear he'd inflicted but now was not the time to rant and rave and punish. Now, more than anything, Marcus needed to feel safe and loved. And anyway, I was hardly one to judge given my previous actions. The need for revenge, it seemed, ran in the family. But it ended now.

'We've all made mistakes, darling. But the most important thing is that we're honest with each other from now on. No more secrets.'

Amelia stood up then. 'I'm going to go home,' she said. 'Let you guys talk.'

I mouthed the words *thank you*, and she smiled at me before letting herself out. Then I turned to face my boys. Our family was broken but I was going to piece us back together. I was finally going to focus my energy on doing what I should have done all along. Mending my family and moving on from this tragedy.

I patted the sofa beside me. 'Sit down, Jamie. We all have a lot to talk about.'

29

It was no surprise that the jury found the lorry driver not guilty after the revelations about Ellie and her phone call to Graham moments before the crash. It had completely discredited her as a witness. Some people had been furious about the outcome. My dad said that a guilty man had got off scot-free on a technicality. Amelia maintained that it was Ellie's fault for lying in the first place. But after I hit Ellie on that quiet road, I saw everything differently. I understood how easily it could happen. A brief lapse of concentration or a momentary distraction and life is never the same again.

It could happen to anyone.

Two months later, Amelia and I met Ellie on a park bench overlooking the pond. Some ducks approached us hopefully, looking for food. We watched them silently, huddled together side by side, padded coats protecting us from the bitter autumn chill.

Ellie was finally back on her feet after six weeks in a cast. She was still wearing a special boot and would need more physiotherapy, but doctors expected her to make a full recovery. It was the first time I'd seen her since the accident, but we'd spoken on the phone. I'd told her everything and she had done the same. We had confessed all our sins and wiped the slate clean. There were no more secrets between us.

We both had plenty of reasons to be angry with the other. Two wrongs didn't make a right, we understood that. But we both needed to forgive and let go. We'd been holding on to hurt for far too long and it had led us down a treacherous path.

I had been charged with dangerous driving, which I planned to plead guilty to at the upcoming magistrates' court hearing. Ellie had given a statement to the police insisting that it was an accident. It didn't escape me that it was the second time she had been the only witness to a crash involving my family. Her statement hadn't prevented me from facing charges, but my solicitor had said that I would most likely be given a community order and banned from driving for twelve months. It was a small price to pay.

Ellie and Tom had separated, although he had stayed on in the house to help her while she recovered from surgery. She had told me, on the phone, that as the weeks had passed, they had found a way to be around each other. A middle ground that they could both live with. As hurt as he was, he had been there for her when she needed it and it proved just how much he cared for her. He had told her, one night, that he would always love her but he couldn't stay married to her. She had said she understood. They could never go back, but they would find a way forward, as a different kind of team. They would be in each other's lives, not just for the children but for themselves.

She was putting on a brave face to hide her heartbreak, but she had taken full responsibility for the role she had played in the marriage ending. I think that Graham had seduced her, realising that she was vulnerable. He had lured her with his charm and charisma, but Ellie hadn't tried to deny her involvement in the affair. She had willingly accepted Graham's advances and she was living with the consequences of that.

But, she told me, she was so relieved that there were no more secrets in her life. Everything was out in the open, for better and for worse, and now she was focusing all her efforts on supporting her children through this difficult time, just as I was.

I was taking things day by day. I was spending time with Marcus, helping him to work through his trauma. He had finally opened up to me and I hoped that he wouldn't shut down again. The boys were back at school now, settling into their A-level subjects and Jamie had struck up a friendship with a new lad who, I suspected, was on the fast track to becoming something more. He had a spring in his step, a lightness to him that I hadn't seen since before Graham died and it filled me with such joy that sometimes I thought I might burst. Jamie had been furious with Marcus after his confession but the wonderful thing about him is that he never dwells. After ranting and raving at his brother, he had let his anger go and concentrated on supporting Marcus too. Seeing my two boys being there for one another gave me the strength to face each day.

When I had asked Ellie if she would meet me at the park, we both knew it wasn't a social engagement. I had to know that she would keep Marcus out of all this. I had told her about what he did, along with what I had done, because I didn't want her to live in fear of further repercussions. If she was going to get on with her life, then she needed to know that there would be no more threats towards her or her family. After this, I doubted that we would see each other again. So maybe it was goodbye too.

Amelia had offered to come with me and I was grateful for her support. I'd seen a look of disapproval flash across Ellie's face when she saw the two of us approaching but Amelia had promised to be on her best behaviour. I trusted Ellie but given the charges I was facing and Marcus's crimes, it made sense to have a third party present.

'I know what you're going to say,' Ellie said, still looking at the ducks.

'You do?'

'Yes. You're going to ask me not to drag Marcus into all of this.'

'He's just a kid. A hurting kid. Take me down by all means, but please not Marcus.'

'I have no intention of taking either of you down.'

I looked sideways at her. 'Do you mean that?'

'I do. You shouldn't have done what you did, and nor should Marcus. It scared me half to death. The months of sleepless nights I had, the guilt when Tamsin's son got hurt...' Ellie shuddered. 'But I'm no angel, am I? I lied too.'

I had to ask, one last time. 'Did you lie about what you saw that afternoon?'

'No. I would never have done that. I'm sure Graham's car was stationary. But because of me, the lorry driver got away with it.'

'I don't think he did, not really. It must have been such an awful time for him, getting arrested and facing a trial. And after what I did to you, I'm acutely aware of how easily mistakes can happen on the road. I see things differently now.'

Ellie mulled this over. 'You're not angry?'

'No. I've had enough of being angry.'

'Me too. God, me too.'

'Have the police been in touch about the incidents?'

'No. To be honest, after the trial debacle, I think they've given up on me.'

'I wouldn't blame you if you told the police about what we did.'

Ellie turned and looked at me. 'I have children too. And I would do anything to protect them. Marcus needs to get on with his life. And he needs his mum.'

Tears sprang to my eyes. 'Thank you, Ellie.'

She smiled. 'Frankie says Jamie has a boyfriend.'

'It's looking that way.'

'I'm happy for him. He deserves it.'

'And Frankie and Max? How are they?'

'Well, they're talking to me, which is a start. Tom's been amazing and is making sure I'm not public enemy number one. And I guess it was hard for my family to be too angry with me when I was lying in a hospital bed, half dead.' Ellie gave a little half-smile. 'So at least I have you to thank for that.'

Amelia opened her mouth to interject, no doubt ready to stick up for me, but I nudged her in the ribs, and she remained silent.

'I'm so sorry, Ellie. For everything.'

She smiled sadly. 'I'm so sorry too.'

We were quiet then, lost in our own thoughts. The ducks had given up on us and had waddled away in the direction of a mother and her toddler. We watched the little girl, her face lighting up as she babbled and pointed at the ducks. I think we were all remembering those days, when our children were young and innocent and life was simple. Before one accident turned so many people's lives upside down.

Ellie took my hand and squeezed it. I smiled as our fingers intertwined. It felt like the natural end to what had been an unconventional friendship from the start.

Mirroring my thoughts, Ellie released my hand and stood up, wobbling slightly as she found her balance. 'I'd best go. I'm meeting Frankie for lunch in town.'

'Do you need a lift? Amelia drove me but she'd be happy to drop you home.'

'That's okay. It's only a short walk and I'm trying to get some strength back in my legs after weeks of inactivity.' Ellie glanced over at the entrance to the park. Then she turned back to me. 'It was so good to see you, Samantha.'

My smile was genuine. 'You too, Ellie.'

Ellie turned to Amelia, acknowledging her presence for the first time. My friend had stayed true to her word and had remained quiet throughout the conversation. I knew there was no love lost between Amelia and Ellie, but they didn't have to be friends, they just had to not snipe at each other. Mission accomplished.

'I'll always protect Samantha and her children,' Ellie said, still looking at Amelia. 'But I can't protect you.'

I frowned. What did that mean? Bewildered, I glanced at Amelia and saw something flash across her face. Terror. And dread trickled under my skin.

'What are you talking about?' I demanded.

Ellie's gaze remained fixed on Amelia. 'It took me a long time to work it all out, but I did in the end. I finally understood why you hated me so much.'

Ellie's ambush seemed to have stunned Amelia. Where was her outrage at this verbal attack? Her cutting words, telling Ellie that she was a psycho?

When Amelia finally found her voice, it was too late. Her silence had gone on too long. 'I have no idea what you're talking about. Come on, Samantha, let's go.'

Ellie blocked her exit and, even with an injured leg, her

stance was menacing. For the first time in the forty years I'd known Amelia, she looked intimidated.

'You loved him,' Ellie said. 'You always had. But by the time you realised it was more than friendship, it was too late because you'd set him up with Samantha.'

What did she mean? Amelia didn't love Graham, that was absurd. They were like brother and sister, always bickering and rolling their eyes at each other. Ellie had got this all wrong. But underneath my internal bluster, I was frightened. Because something was ringing true, something I had always told myself was ridiculous to even consider.

'You finally told him how you felt,' Ellie continued. 'You were upset after struggling to conceive for so long, angry at Ed for not being able to give you the thing you wanted more than anything in the world. At the same time, Samantha was going through a hard time. The boys were babies, she was battling with motherhood and this made you even more resentful of her. Of course, Graham was feeling neglected by his wife, second fiddle to his sons, and so your declaration of adoration came at the perfect time.'

Amelia opened and closed her mouth, but no words came out.

'You were probably his first affair. And Samantha, distracted with the boys, had no idea. But then you became pregnant and you told Graham you wanted to keep the baby. He begged you not to, but you were not going to give up the chance of finally becoming a mother, like you'd always dreamed of. You couldn't pretend it was Ed's because he knew he was firing blanks, so you concocted a new plan, to get Samantha drunk and coerce her into unwittingly offering Graham's sperm.'

This was ludicrous! If Amelia wasn't going to defend herself then I would do it for her. I began to interject but then I stopped. Because all I had to do was look at Amelia's face to see the guilt written all over it. She was too shocked to hide it. And it hit me that somehow Ellie had worked out what I had failed to see for fourteen years.

'You managed to make it seem like Samantha's idea. It's quite impressive, actually. Graham tried to talk her out of it at first. He thought if he could get her to say no, then you wouldn't keep the baby after all. But when he realised that neither of you were giving up and he'd been backed into a corner, he reluctantly agreed.'

She finally turned to me, her eyes sympathetic. 'Amelia was pregnant before she pretended to artificially inseminate herself with Graham's sperm. Charlotte wasn't induced early, Samantha, she was induced because she was late. They both lied to you.'

Amelia started crying, huge sobs that cut through the serenity of the tranquil pond. The mother feeding the ducks with her toddler looked up at us in alarm and quickly guided the little girl away. I didn't know what to do, what to say, where to start.

And Ellie wasn't done yet.

'When you found out that he'd had other affairs, you were outraged,' she told Amelia. 'You thought you'd meant something to him and learning that there were other women ate you up. You hated those women. You hated me. You hated Samantha too, sometimes, in your darkest moments. For getting to have Graham when you couldn't.'

I finally found my voice. 'How the hell do you know this, Ellie?'

'It was something Graham told me once. He said that a colleague from work had been having an affair with his wife's best friend and she'd got pregnant. She'd kept the baby and pretended it was artificially inseminated. He said the woman had got a little crazy, telling this man she'd always loved him. I didn't make the connection when you first explained about Charlotte but then I realised that he was talking about himself. I still don't know why he told me, if he was somehow bragging or just indirectly getting it off his chest. But the pieces started to come together. And I'd seen the way Amelia looked at you sometimes, a mixture of love and hate.'

I turned to Amelia. '*Do* you hate me, Amelia?'

'No!' she cried. 'I love you, Sam. I'm so sorry.'

'I think you must hate me, to do that to me. I think you must really hate me.'

'I don't hate you. I'm so sorry. I was feeling so vulnerable after the IVF. My hormones were all over the place. I didn't know what I was doing.'

'I think you did. I think you knew exactly what you were doing.'

'Sam, you mean to the world to me, you always have. Haven't I been here for you over the past year? I've been by your side the whole time.'

I considered this. She was right, she had been there for me, not just over the past year but for forty years. She had been my rock, my right-hand woman. But that was what made it even more hurtful. When Ellie had an affair with Graham, she was a stranger, a woman with no loyalty towards me. In contrast, Amelia had been like a sister. She had laughed and cried with me, all the while knowing that she had betrayed me in the worst possible way. Her deception winded me, forcing the air from my lungs.

'How could you do this to me?' I asked.

Amelia could barely speak through her sobs. 'I'm sorry. I'm so sorry.'

She hadn't even tried to deny it. Maybe it was because Ellie's accusations had taken her by surprise, or perhaps she was finally ready to confess. Did she think that, as I had forgiven Ellie, I would also forgive her?

'I'm so sorry, Samantha,' Ellie said. 'I went back and forth so many times about whether to tell you. I couldn't bear to hurt you after everything you've been through and I almost convinced myself that keeping quiet was the right thing to do. But we made a promise to each other. No more secrets and no more lies.'

I looked at Ellie. There was no triumph in her eyes, only trepidation and compassion. She was clearly upset that she'd told me and I knew that she hadn't done it out of revenge for the way Amelia had acted towards her, she'd done it because she thought I deserved to know the truth. She had seen Amelia for who she really was and had exposed her. Because it wasn't my friendship with Ellie that was toxic, I realised, it was my one with Amelia.

Now I knew what kind of a person Amelia really was. And Graham too. I was now aware of three woman he'd cheated on me with. And I pictured the countless others he had probably seduced over the years while I was raising our children and waiting patiently for him to come home.

I stood up. 'I know you care about me, Amelia, and I'm grateful for your support over the past year. I couldn't have got through it without you. But I can never forgive you for what you did. You must know that.'

Amelia reached out and tried to take my arm, but I brushed her off.

'You lied to me for years. You had a child with my husband. And you had the audacity to paint Ellie as the evil villain when what you did was far worse.'

'Sam, please!' she cried.

'I never want to see you again. Do not contact me.'

'You don't mean that.'

'Yes, I do.'

For a moment, I didn't know what to do with myself. I felt lost and acutely aware that now I was more alone than ever. I thought I had finally let go of the past, but it had returned to bite me, and I didn't know where to go from here.

Sensing my distress, Ellie came and stood by my side. 'Do you want to come to lunch? We can invite Jamie and Marcus too. Frankie would love to see them.'

It was the most ridiculous invitation I'd ever received. Ellie had just told me that my husband had cheated on me with my best friend. Had fathered a child with her and kept his dirty secret hidden until the day he died. I didn't want to go to bloody lunch, I wanted to scream and hit things. I wanted to curl up into a ball and cry for the next year. I wanted to drown in a pool of self-pity until there was nothing left of me.

But, most of all, I wanted a friend.

I nodded. 'Okay.'

'Sam, for God's sake!' Amelia begged but I ignored her as we walked away from her.

Ellie linked her arm through mine as she limped along the path towards the exit.

'It's going to be okay, Sam,' she said quietly. 'It's all going to be okay.'

'How can you be so sure?' I asked.

'Look at what we've been through over the past year, and we're still standing.'

I glanced at her injured leg. 'Barely.'

She laughed. 'We're strong, Samantha. We're survivors.'

'You know, I should hate you.'

'Well, I should hate you too.'

'You slept with my husband.'

'You ran me over.'

We smiled at each other and I marvelled at how the one person I had despised had become the only friend I could trust. The one I knew had my back. How easy it would have been for Ellie to walk away from me after the anguish my family had caused her. To forget all about us and focus on rebuilding her own, broken life. Or even to tell the police who was behind all those threats towards her. Instead, she had put herself on the line by telling me about Amelia and Graham and she had done it because she had made me a solemn promise. No more lies, no more deceit. And now she was by my side, offering me support despite everything going on in her own life. So maybe it wasn't goodbye after all. Maybe it was the start of something new, something we both needed.

Just before we went through the gates, I looked back and saw Amelia, slumped on the bench, with her head in her hands. I must have been in shock because for a moment, I swear I saw Graham sitting there next to her, looking as contrite as he had the night he told me about his shenanigans at the Christmas party. His false promises, his declaration of love and vows of devotion to his family, his years of lies and gaslighting.

They deserved each other, the pair of them. I'd spent years being the person they wanted me to be, the perfect wife, the perfect friend. I'd been naive and let other people take advantage of me, and it had taken Graham's death to finally revive me and make me stand on my own two feet. Because Ellie was right, I was still standing. *Barely.*

I wasn't going to fall again.

I took one last look at the bench. At Amelia and the empty spot where seconds earlier I'd seen Graham. And then, with my head held high, I walked away.

* * *

MORE FROM NATASHA BOYDELL

Another brilliantly gripping and unputdownable psychological thriller from Natasha Boydell is available to order now here: https://mybook.to/BoydellNewBackAd

ACKNOWLEDGEMENTS

As a journalist I spent many hours covering court cases, frantically scribbling in shorthand and hoping to God that I had got everything down. I remember thinking that I'd love to write a novel based around a trial, but it seemed an inconceivable pipe dream. Yet here I am, twenty years later, writing the acknowledgements for my ninth book, the one where I finally got to make that rookie reporter's dream come true. There are so many people who helped me along the way and I'm grateful to every single one of you.

To my teachers at the University of Sheffield who instilled a love of media law – any mistakes are obviously my deliberate attempt to see if you spot them. To my journo friends, who I've laughed, cried, complained and celebrated with after a long day, and who are still in my life two decades later. This one's for you.

To the incredible team at Boldwood Books, for your constant support, expertise, encouragement and belief. Special mention to my editor, Isobel Akenhead, for helping to make every manuscript the best version of itself. And to the production, marketing, copyediting and proofreading team – it is always such a joy to work with you.

As always, to my husband Jon and our girls, Rose and Alice, who are my biggest cheerleaders and only occasionally barge through the door when I'm writing to ask for a snack. And finally, to my readers. Thank you for coming on this journey with me.

ABOUT THE AUTHOR

Natasha Boydell is an internationally bestselling author of psychological fiction. She trained and worked as a journalist for many years, and decided to pursue her lifelong dream of writing a novel in 2019, when she was approaching her 40th birthday and realised it was time to stop procrastinating! Natasha lives in North London with her husband, two daughters and two rescue cats.

Download your exclusive bonus content from Natasha Boydell here:

Follow Natasha on social media:

facebook.com/natashaboydell

bookbub.com/authors/natasha-boydell

instagram.com/tashy_boydell

ALSO BY NATASHA BOYDELL

The Fortune Teller

The Perfect Home

The Doll's House

The Widow's Husband

The Last Witness

THE *Murder* LIST

**THE MURDER LIST IS A NEWSLETTER
DEDICATED TO SPINE-CHILLING
FICTION AND GRIPPING
PAGE-TURNERS!**

**SIGN UP TO MAKE SURE YOU'RE ON
OUR HIT LIST FOR EXCLUSIVE DEALS,
AUTHOR CONTENT, AND
COMPETITIONS.**

**SIGN UP TO OUR
NEWSLETTER**

BIT.LY/THEMURDERLISTNEWS

Boldwood

Boldwood Books is an award-winning fiction publishing company seeking out the best stories from around the world.

Find out more at www.boldwoodbooks.com

Join our reader community for brilliant books, competitions and offers!

Follow us
@BoldwoodBooks
@TheBoldBookClub

Sign up to our weekly deals newsletter

https://bit.ly/BoldwoodBNewsletter

www.ingramcontent.com/pod-product-compliance
Lightning Source LLC
Chambersburg PA
CBHW011643010726
47495CB00011B/2887